SUDDENLY, T
FOREST WA

He froze, his head tilting to listen as leaves rustled to the south.

(What?) Chyrie asked quickly.

(Perhaps only an animal,) he returned, reaching for his sword before he realized that in the safety of the altars they had left them beside their pallets. (Still, best be safe. I have not your thought-sense. What do you—)

His thought cut off abruptly as his body was suddenly torn away from her. A huge form filled Chyrie's vision, and for a moment her mind could make no sense of the impressions that bombarded her: a roar of fury; the scent of unwashed human flesh and poorly cured furs; the sound of Val hitting the earth; the fiery pain in his head that echoed in her own; a flurry of motion to her right as two more humans leaped from the bushes; and the welling terror in her own mind as a gigantic hand seized her throat. . . .

Praise for Anne Logston's SHADOW books:

"Entertaining . . . plenty of magic,
demons, and other dangers."
—*Science Fiction Chronicle*

"Thoroughly satisfying."
—*Dragon*

Ace Books by Anne Logston

SHADOW
SHADOW HUNT
SHADOW DANCE
GREENDAUGHTER

Greendaughter

ANNE LOGSTON

ACE BOOKS, NEW YORK

If you purchased this book without a cover, you should be aware that this book is stolen property. It was reported as "unsold and destroyed" to the publisher, and neither the author nor the publisher has received any payment for this "stripped book."

This book is an Ace original edition, and has never been previously published.

GREENDAUGHTER

An Ace Book/published by arrangement with the author

PRINTING HISTORY
Ace edition / July 1993

All rights reserved.
Copyright © 1993 by Anne Logston.
Cover art by Matt Zumbo.
This book may not be reproduced in whole or in part, by mimeograph or any other means, without permission.
For information address: The Berkley Publishing Group, 200 Madison Avenue, New York, New York 10016.

ISBN: 0-441-30273-4

Ace Books are published by The Berkley Publishing Group, 200 Madison Avenue, New York, New York 10016.
The name "ACE" and the "A" logo are trademarks belonging to Charter Communications, Inc.

PRINTED IN THE UNITED STATES OF AMERICA

10 9 8 7 6 5 4 3 2 1

To Mollie Fugett
1894–1992

Fair journey, Grandma

I

THEY SAT IN silence in the thicket, not particularly uncomfortable, watching the strangers' fire for several hours before Chyrie spoke silently to her companion.

(Not too close. What do you think?)

Valann knew better than to move, but his thoughts had the flavor of a shrug.

(They watch the territorial lines,) he said, (carefully staying just beyond the Wilding markers. I think they mean not to intrude. Still, they bear watching.)

(What does not?) Chyrie teased half seriously, her fingertips moving soundlessly over his thigh. (Must we wait here all night? They are Silvertip, and Silvertip never walk at night. Their nighteyes are blind as an owl by day.) No Wilding would have made such a camp, so open, fire so large and visible. Even Silvertip would be more cautious if they cared to avoid detection. There was nothing to learn here.

Valann's pointed ear-tips twitched briefly in body-language amusement.

(Does my she-fox-in-heat mate grow impatient? Then we will go—quietly if you can!)

Chyrie wrinkled her nose. (You speak so to me, you who rustle the leaves like a stumble-footed human in your passing? And to think I would wish to couple with your overly furred body—)

(Ah, peace, my own spirit.) Valann's hand crept to touch

1

her cheek. (You are silent as moonlight and as lovely. Come, I have dreamed a new pattern for you tonight.)

The Silvertip elves were laughing and drinking now, less alert than when they had made camp, and Chyrie and Valann slipped unnoticed from the thicket.

It was only a few minutes run to their latest home—a woven bower in a huge willow tree overlooking a small creek-fed forest pool; like most Wildings, Val and Chyrie preferred the safety of the trees. It was complete even to the baked-clay firepot that would allow a tiny, careful fire to be built for light or cooking, while the camouflaging woven-switch walls would prevent the light from being seen by anyone passing by.

They dined on cold roasted rabbit, and Valann carefully selected pots of dye from his collection nestled securely in a nook. By the flickering light from the firepot, he painstakingly pricked the new design into the skin of Chyrie's slender forearm, carefully adding a dew-sparkling goldenflower to the green vine twining its way down from her shoulder.

"It is beautiful," Chyrie admitted, critically examining his work. A purple, blue, and green butterfly perched on the flower's lip, so real that the fragile wings seemed ready to flutter.

"As is she who wears it," Val said, smiling, running his healing touch over the design so that the last itching soreness faded away. "Tomorrow I will begin a new tendril."

Chyrie chuckled, flashing teeth startlingly white against her amber skin.

"You are vain of your work," she teased. "It will be said of you that you find my form unsightly and would hide it beneath the beauty of your art."

"The trees of the Mother Forest, with leaves of silver and flowers of ruby, are beyond compare," Val said, tracing with his finger the path of the vine crossing Chyrie's collarbone and disappearing down the front of her tunic. "Yet she adorns them with ivy. Will I let my mate, most perfect among elves, want for such finery? No, she must have all that is most beautiful of the world for her own."

"Hah!" Chyrie captured his hand before it could dip under the neck of her tunic. "My own soul, you seek to win by flattery what is already yours by right. Well do I know that you work your art so freely upon my skin only because none could see the pictures upon your hairy hide." Playfully, she tugged at the wiry black curls on his chin. "If you would grow so unelflike a pelt, none wonders why you work your vanity upon the person of another."

A too sharp tug at his beard brought a yelp from Valann, and he gave Chyrie's short golden-brown curls a yank.

"If my fur displeases you, you need not pluck it out by the roots," Valann growled with mock anger. "Else I will take my vengeance by pulling these unseemly shorn locks out to their proper length."

Chyrie gave an exaggerated sigh.

"If you have no better way to pass your time than to curse my cut hair," she said with dignity, "then I will take my leave of you."

Before Valann could react, she ducked out the side of the bower, paused only briefly to pull her tunic over her head, and dove from the branch into the moon-dappled pond.

Valann, stripped of his own tunic, was only a breath behind her, but Chyrie was ready for him. As soon as his head emerged from the water, he found a handful of mud slapped abruptly into his face. By the time he had rinsed the dirt out of his eyes, Chyrie had vanished.

Chyrie peered out from the mossy platform behind the waterfall as Val glanced about him, watching the water for telltale ripples or bubbles. When he saw nothing, he frowned and climbed out of the pool, searching the mossy banks for tracks, unaware that his mate was silently stalking him.

Chyrie caught him only half by surprise, for as she leaped, some stray noise or thought caused Val to half turn, so that he carried her with him into the water. For a moment they sputtered and grappled under the water; then, as if by a signal, the frantic contact of their slippery skin took on a different quality. Their eyes met for a moment; then they scrambled from the water to fall, dripping wet, on the moss.

They coupled fiercely in the moonlight, then lay resting on the moss, sharing wine and idle caresses.

"My time of ripeness will soon be upon me," Chyrie said

in the darkness, rubbing her cheek over the springy hairs on Valann's chest. "It is only a day or two away, no more."

Val was silent for a moment.

"I thought as much," he said. "Your scent has begun to change. Do you wish for a child? You are less than nine decades, young for bearing."

"This is my second ripening," Chyrie said.

Val propped himself up on one elbow to look at her.

"You never said you had ripened before," he said curiously.

Chyrie shrugged. "I had less than three decades and had not taken the rites of adulthood. Nor did I have you."

Val traced the line of her jaw with his fingertip.

"If you wish to bear, we should return to the clan," he said. "Many men have no life in their seed. You should return to dance the High Circle in case I am one such."

Chyrie hesitated. It was seldom that a Wilding female ripened, and the celebration would draw in every member of their small clan, even those solitude-loving folk, such as Val and Chyrie, who chose to live apart. But still . . .

Chyrie shook her head at last. "Let it be your offspring or none. I am still young, and there will be other ripenings if I fail to bear this time. I would like a child of your seed."

Valann's black eyebrows raised, pride and concern warring in his dark eyes.

"I am honored," he said, "but it would rest uneasily on my spirit if you were to miss your chance to bear because of such sentiments."

Chyrie smiled. "It is said that women who couple at the forest altars during their ripeness will surely conceive."

Val stood, pulling Chyrie to her feet.

"Then tomorrow we leave for the altars, as soon as we have seen the Silvertip safely past our boundaries," he said. "Come, we need rest."

Snuggled in soft furs in their bower, however, they did not sleep.

"A child of my seed and yours," Val said dreamily. "Perhaps a girl-child with your amber eyes."

"Have you sired before?" Chyrie murmured into his hair.

Val shrugged.

"The Mother Forest knows," he said. "When one of the women danced the High Circle, I tried with the rest. Until now, my heart, I never cared whose seed bore fruit."

"A rutting stag such as you can only have potent seed," Chyrie teased. "In a decade or two we shall yet see some of the clan's men-children sprout your furry chin."

"Would that we had such proof," Val sighed. "Ah, well, the Mother Forest knows best where her saplings should grow. Sleep now."

Chyrie smiled, kissed his shoulder, and closed her eyes.

"I do not understand," Chyrie said, kneeling beside the dead fire. "It is barely light, yet they have been gone so long that the fire is cold. Silvertip do not travel by night, yet these did. They seemed not alarmed last night, laughing and drinking their wine; yet this has the look of flight."

"Could something have come upon them in the night?" Valann asked puzzledly. "Yet there is no sign of violence, nor did they abandon any of their belongings. Their tracks do not show the spacing of flight, but they turn upon themselves and hastily return from whence they came."

Chyrie knelt beside a small footprint, sniffing.

"There is no smell of fear, nor of blood," she said. "Need we return to the clan and tell this to the Eldest?"

Valann grimaced and shook his head.

"If misfortune befell Silvertip, it is no affair of ours," he said. "Perhaps one of them fell ill and they returned home to seek out their healer. Surely there would be a beast-speaker among a wide patrol; perhaps they received a message to return. At any rate, their trail leads away from Wilding boundaries."

Chyrie nodded, shouldering her light pack.

"Then we need not follow?"

Valann shrugged. "As long as they respect our boundaries, it matters not what they do. Still, if they are returning home, their track will cross the common road to the Forest Altars. If we should come within sight of them, we shall see; if not, then not."

Chyrie nodded again, sniffing the air as she cast out with scent and thought.

"There are deer at a pond south-southwest," she said. "A stag and three does, and a fawn."

"I still have some of the sap-sugar to tempt them," Valann said, grinning. "Will they bear us?"

"They will not refuse *me,*" Chyrie said pointedly, taking the sugar from him. "But stay hidden until it is agreed, lest they think a bear has happened upon them."

"Continue to taunt me, little one," Valann threatened, "and when we reach the altars you will think a bear has happened upon *you.*"

Chyrie chuckled.

"You have far to go to equal a bear's size and might," she teased. "But you will do as you are."

Valann growled and reached for her, but she had already disappeared down the trail ahead of him, her laughter floating back to him on the morning breeze. When he caught up, she had already reached the pond and was feeding the sap-sugar to the deer there. The deer startled at his sudden appearance, but Chyrie soothed them back to calm.

"They will bear us to the altars." Chyrie smiled, scratching the stag around the base of his spiraling, ebony horns. "They were moving south already, for there have been human poachers seen in North Heart."

"That is near Silvertip territory, only a little to the northeast," Valann said, frowning. "I like it not. That might have been the cause of the Silvertips' hurried return."

"Humans, far enough into the forest to threaten Silvertip territories?" Chyrie returned. "They prowl only at the outskirts, afraid to match their clumsiness against our swords and bows. Still, if humans infringe on Silvertip lands, at least the Silvertip will be too busy to trespass on ours. If it pleases you, I will dispatch a message to the Eldest."

"Best be safe," Val agreed. "Then we need not hasten to return."

Chyrie's questing thought coaxed a squirrel from its play, and after accepting a bit of dried fruit as its reward, it scampered northwest toward the Wilding village.

"Let us hurry," she said, climbing awkwardly onto a doe's back. "I feel my body ripening."

Valann chuckled and, with less difficulty because of his greater height, mounted the stag.

"Do not fear," he said gently. "You will remain ripe for some days. There is time aplenty."

Chyrie was silent, running her fingers nervously through the doe's thin late spring coat. Many women, she knew, remained ripe for half-moons at a time, but there was an unreasonable feeling of urgency in her that had nothing to do with her body. She was relieved when Val set a quick pace south.

It was four days ride to the altars, but they took time to note disturbing signs about the forest. Although the Silvertip trail crossed the common road leading to the altars, the Silvertip had been traveling fast and the tracks were old. The animals of the wood seemed agitated, although to Chyrie's questing they could give no reason.

By the time they arrived at their destination, Chyrie's uneasiness had grown so great that she half feared to find the Forest Altars vanished as mysteriously as the Silvertip. To her vast relief, however, the holy place had not changed much since the journey she had made during her trials of adulthood decades before.

The altars, ornately carven slabs of stone, were scattered widely apart over an area of the forest carefully tended by the local clans, but set apart from any clan's territory by specially inscribed markers. Within the markers, which also bordered the common road, lay the only land held in common by every elf in the forest, and campsites free to any who would use them.

Chyrie and Valann selected a camp near one of the most remote altars and ate the preserved food they had brought, as custom forbade either hunting or fire within the sacred place, and Valann could not hunt in the other elvan territories surrounding it. As tradition demanded, Chyrie tied a green cord, denoting a ripe female, around her arm, but she did not so mark the camp; if she had, the marker would have obliged any visiting males to offer their services in a High Circle, and Chyrie and Valann had no wish to be disturbed.

When the moon rose, Chyrie carefully moved the few offerings from the chosen altar.

"This altar is little used." Val grinned. "Well enough. I have no mind to be interrupted while at such important business."

Chyrie glanced around. "Nor I, my mate, but I feel as if there are eyes upon me."

"Then let them watch," Val murmured into her ear, lifting her onto the cleared altar. "Perhaps they will learn something from us."

Val was of a mind to be especially pleasing, and Chyrie was glad of the peace-laws of the Forest Altars, for otherwise surely her cries would have brought enemies upon them. It was some time before they rested, panting and slick with sweat, on the passion-warmed stone.

"I was wrong," Chyrie whispered, nuzzling Valann's beard. "I fear even a bear might find cause for jealousy of my much-furred mate."

(Well enough,) Valann told her silently, not wasting breath to speak, (for I have little mind to seek a bear for you now. You will have to be satisfied with my attentions.)

Chyrie moved a little to kiss him.

(Of those I am more than pleased—but not yet satisfied. It will be many days before I know whether your seed has put life in my womb.)

Val's hands moved over her with renewed passion.

"Then we must take every opportunity to assure it," he murmured against her mouth.

Suddenly he froze, his head tilting to listen as leaves rustled to the south.

(What?) Chyrie asked quickly.

(Perhaps only an animal,) he returned, reaching for his sword before he realized that in the safety of the altars they had left them beside their pallets. (Still, best be safe. I have not your thought-sense. What do you—)

His thought cut off abruptly as his body was suddenly torn away from her. A huge form filled Chyrie's vision, and for a moment her mind could make no sense of the impressions that bombarded her: a roar of fury; the scent of unwashed human flesh and poorly cured furs; the sound of Val hitting the earth, the fiery pain in his head that echoed in her own; a flurry of motion to her right as two more humans leaped from the bushes; and the welling terror in her own mind as a gigantic hand seized her throat.

There was no time to react. Chyrie struggled for breath, her nails clawing at the fingers encircling her neck; her feet sought for purchase as she simultaneously sent a silent scream for help to anyone or anything who might receive it. The human's face, grizzled and huge, was only handspans from her own; his breath was foul, and his eyes held a gleam Chyrie instantly understood.

She had no breath to scream, but still she fought with the blind instinct of a fox caught in a trap. Blindly she lashed out with feet and hands, eliciting a yelp of pain from her captor. His free hand came up, and there was an explosion of pain in her head—

—then nothing.

II

SLOWLY, WITH DIFFICULTY, Chyrie fought her way up from the darkness. The pain in her body—head, throat, chest, and loins—gave mute testimony of the violence done to her. Grimly she used the pain to anchor her to a world that floated and reeled drunkenly under her.

For a moment she could not sense Val, and the panic brought her to consciousness. Immediately she found his thoughts— he was nearby—and simultaneously a voice spoke in clumsy, heavily accented Olvenic.

"Be still. You're safe."

Chyrie's eyes flew open. Looming above her was a human face framed in yellow hair—a human face! Suddenly came the awareness that her hands were bound in front of her, not tightly, but securely. Panic replaced thought—she struggled wildly, and would have screamed if her tortured throat had allowed anything more than a hoarse, painful croak.

"I said be still." Strong hands came down on her shoulders, easily overcoming her weakened movements. The human was now recognizable as female, clad in leather, her blue eyes grim. "No harm will come to you. We bound you because you were—" Her huge brow furrowed. "You were lost in dreams, and we thought you would hurt yourself. Lie still and I'll free you."

Chyrie set her jaw and obeyed, and the human's hands moved to the bindings at Chyrie's wrists. Another human appeared beside her, a similarly colored male, saying something in a guttural language Chyrie could not understand. The woman nodded and replied in the same tongue.

Chyrie slithered free of the last of the thongs and bolted upright, ignoring the human's protest and the red-hot streaks of agony that the motion brought.

(Valann!)

(Chyrie!) Immediately he was at her side. There was a large bruise covering half his face and disappearing into his black hair, but he was alive. (Be still, love. You are much hurt.)

Chyrie clutched desperately at him. (Val—the humans—)

Val held her carefully. (I do not know what they want of us. They came quickly and killed those who hurt you. They tended my head with magic and the female, a sort of healer, tended you. They bound me at first, but released me after I swore I would not flee. I feared for your life.)

The female human, now joined by two males and another female, had been watching them curiously; now she took up a wooden cup and extended it slowly.

"Drink this," she said to Chyrie, speaking slowly. "It will ease your throat. You can see we offer you no danger."

Chyrie sniffed the cup distrustfully. It contained only herbs she knew well, so she acquiesced when Val held the cup to her lips. The potion was bitter, but some of the pain in her throat eased as she drank.

When she had swallowed the last of the medicine, she pushed Val's hand away and looked about her. They were at their own campsite; the deer were gone, but the packs lay where they had been left. Near the altar lay the bodies of three human males dressed in crude skins, their own hides black with blood. There was more blood splashed on the altar.

Now that she had a chance to look more closely at the humans who had captured them, Chyrie saw to her surprise that they did not all look alike, as she had expected. The female who had first spoken to her was smaller and slighter than the other three, with amazingly light yellow hair, blue eyes, and fair skin. Her features were almost delicate for a human, and although it was difficult to guess ages in humans, she seemed young.

The second human male she had seen was also yellow-haired, although the yellow of his hair was darker than that of the female, as was his skin. His features were stronger, and his dark gray eyes were keen.

The other male and female maintained their distance, so it was more difficult to see them. They were both dark brown of hair and dark of skin, more sturdily built and heavily muscled than the fair humans, and taller in stature. The woman had laughing brown eyes. The male had a beard as Valann did, and more—hair grew between his nose and upper lip, too, and over his cheeks. When he saw Chyrie looking at him, he glared back.

Besides the four humans, there were six horses—Chyrie had heard them described but had never before seen one—heavily laden with leather bags and tethered with ropes to the trees.

Chyrie coughed and spat apprehensively, but although her throat was painful her spittle was clear. She clutched Val's hand and faced the human woman squarely.

"What do you want of us?" she rasped fearfully.

"For now only your safety," the woman said, her eyes meeting Chyrie's without flinching. "Later we'll talk. I'm sorry for what happened to you. Those men were—I don't know your word. Not of our own folk, meaning violence against us."

"Out-kin," Val said.

The woman nodded.

"They and others attacked us and killed four of ours six days ago," she continued. "We killed five, and these three fled. We've been tracking them since then, hoping to capture them and force them to explain their presence here. I'm Rivkah. My friends are Romuel, Sharl, and Ria—Doria." She pointed to the two males and the other female in turn. "Will you tell us your names?"

Val glanced at Chyrie and shrugged.

"I am Valann, my mate is Chyrie. We are Wilding. If you mean us no harm, let us go."

"Your woman can't travel yet," Rivkah said. "I've exhausted my healing magic until I rest. And it's not for me to decide. Sharl is our leader." She nodded in the direction of the younger, fair-haired man.

"He is not *our* leader," Chyrie said hoarsely. "He has no voice over us. Why does he not speak himself?"

"Rivkah best speaks your language," the man Sharl said in even more accented Olvenic. "She was taught by an elvan mage. My guards speak very little of your tongue." He glanced at her curiously. "We saved your lives. Does that mean nothing to you?"

"You are not Wilding," Val retorted. "We owe you nothing."

Rivkah frowned, then spoke to Sharl in his language. For some moments they spoke back and forth, and at last Rivkah turned back to them.

"Sharl says that you should be grateful that we helped you, when we had no need to do so," Rivkah said. "He also says that you should remember that you gave your word you wouldn't leave."

"He dreams, to think my word binds me until his whim gives me back my freedom," Val growled. "Gratitude he might have, were it all I thought he would ask. And my mate gave no word at all. Let her at least go free."

"I tell you, she can't be moved," Rivkah said wearily. "Tomorrow I can use my magic again. Wait until then, at least."

"She needs no human magic," Valann growled, placing one hand on Chyrie's aching head and the other on her abdomen.

Chyrie ground her teeth but made no sound as liquid fire shot through her body. She was accustomed to Val's healing touch, but he had not had to use such power on her since she took an arrow in the shoulder during a Silvertip raid nearly three decades ago. At last the sensation faded, and with it most of her pain, although a lingering ache remained in her ribs when she breathed.

(Forgive me, love,) Valann thought wearily, panting as he rested his head on her shoulder. (I did not mean to hurt you. And my healing is not strong enough to mend cracks in bone.)

She stroked his hair.

(It makes no difference. Our Gifted One can treat me, and in the meantime, a tight wrapping will suffice. I can travel; how long need we linger here?)

(Let us stay the night,) Valann told her after a moment's thought. (We should learn why these humans are here in the forest, where they are bound, and whether there may be others. The Eldest must know of it.)

"Is your husband a healer?" Rivkah asked, oblivious to the unspoken conversation.

Chyrie raised one eyebrow, but said, "My mate is a fine healer, second only to our Gifted One."

"Your—mate?" Rivkah asked, stumbling over the Olvenic word. "I don't know that word. What's that?"

"We were mated, our spirits joined as one, when Chyrie finished her training and passed her trials of adulthood," Valann said with a frown. "What is this word 'husband'?"

Rivkah again exchanged words with the others, then turned back to Val.

"A husband is a woman's permanent companion, bound by oaths between them that they'll remain faithful to each other throughout their lifetimes, taking no other lovers until one of them dies," she said. "Romuel is Doria's husband. I don't know the word for it in your language."

"Because there is none," Val said impatiently. "We take no such oaths, else those who are of barren seed would fare poorly indeed. Mating is a matter of spirits. What has that to do with coupling?"

Rivkah shook her head dubiously. "It's different with our kind."

(That gives me cheer,) Val thought sourly. (It would ill suit us to behave so foolishly.)

"Is Sharl your—'husband'?" Chyrie asked curiously.

"No." Rivkah flushed darkly, glancing briefly at him and as quickly away. "Why do you ask?"

"His scent is strong upon you." Chyrie shrugged, amused when Rivkah blushed again.

"What do you want of us?" Val asked aloud, his eyes warning Chyrie against pursuing an apparently offensive line of questioning that might incite the humans to violence.

"Stay at least for the night," Sharl urged. "Share our supper and speak with us, that's all."

Val shrugged.

"For this night, then, but no more. Then nothing binds us, agreed?"

Rivkah spoke to the fair-haired Sharl, and he answered in a manner that seemed to trouble the healer. For several moments they appeared to argue; then Rivkah sighed and nodded resignedly.

"Agreed," she said, but she sounded unhappy.

"Agreed," Sharl repeated more firmly.

The dark-haired male and female, Rom and Doria, unloaded parcels from the horses and spread out sleeping pallets, building a fire and preparing food. Sharl paced the area nervously, peering often into the forest.

"Be at peace," Chyrie said irritably to Sharl. "There is no one about."

"He fears that other elves might attack us," Rivkah explained, brewing tea. "We're so few now."

"None would touch him here," Chyrie told her. "This is a place of peace. Or was," she added, glancing at the human corpses befouling the altar. "You were ill-advised to come here."

"This is some sort of . . . sanctuary?" Sharl asked.

"In a manner of speaking," Val said warily. "It is a place of worship. But not for you. No peace bond will keep the other clans from driving you forth should you remain here long, especially as you and your kind have dared shed blood here."

"What are those markers?" Sharl asked, gesturing at something beyond the perimeter of the camp. Val helped Chyrie to her feet and they went to look, leaving Rivkah preparing the food.

"It is but a symbol to mark the boundaries of the Moon Lake clan," Val said, shrugging. "There are none about now."

When they returned to the fire, a haunch of plainsbeast was roasting, and Rivkah had poured mugs of wine.

"We brought our own food and drink," Valann said, looking warily at the mug Rivkah gave him.

"You think we'd poison you?" Rivkah asked, shocked. "Why would we do that, after saving you? We're offering you our hospitality and friendship."

Val scowled dubiously, but the elvan custom of food and fire made it inexcusable to refuse and he sipped gingerly, although he omitted the customary reply. To Rivkah's consternation, however, Chyrie refused her cup and took Val's.

"Mates share a cup," Chyrie growled at the human's expression. "It is our way." The wine was an odd-tasting brew, less pleasant than their own, but, like Val, Chyrie could not quite bring herself to the rudeness of refusing food and fire.

Rivkah watched, troubled, as they shared the wine, and glanced once uneasily at Sharl, who shrugged.

As the meat cooked, they cut away slabs of it. For the most part, Valann and Chyrie sat like stone, half listening as the humans conversed in their guttural language. At last Val spoke.

"You wished to pass words with us," he said dryly at last. "Do so or we will retire for the rest of the night, and at dawn we take our own path."

Rivkah looked at the ground for a moment, then spoke quietly to Sharl. He spoke back at some length, but this time Chyrie watched the healer's expression.

(Something is amiss,) she told Valann. (I sense deceit here. Be ready, if there is trouble.)

Valann's slightly bored expression never changed, but his thoughts were edged with cold anger.

(Ah, these humans,) his thoughts fairly growled. (Had I not tongue-tried the wine I would indeed believe it poisoned. I am ready.)

"We hoped that the wine and food would loosen your tongues," Sharl said. "We wanted to learn your business here, out of your clan's territory."

Valann scowled. "Whatever our business, it is our own to pursue and no concern of yours. Be warned that you will not loosen our tongues either by wine or by fair words cloaking deceit. Say what you will and be done."

A frown of annoyance troubled the human's face, quickly concealed.

"This, then," he said at last. "We are traveling through your forest to join in the building of a great city to the south and west. It is of great importance that we reach it without delay; there is no time to pass around the forest's border. It is my wish to hire your services to guide us through the elvan places, lest the elves attack or capture us."

Chyrie laughed. "Even were we willing to agree, human, we would be no use to you. We are Wilding, and you pass not through Wilding lands, and other clans care nothing for us, nor we for them. They would as gladly strike us down as you. And even did you pass through Wilding land, we have no special voice there to shield you from the wrath of others. That you slew other humans to my benefit would not buy you passage through our territory, and to other elves you have not even that poor excuse for favor."

"Is there no agreement of safe conduct between the elves?" Rivkah asked. "You mentioned that this place was safe to all."

"Safe to all *elves,*" Valann corrected. "And to you perhaps for a short time, not long, and only because it is forbidden to shed blood here."

"How long are we safe here?" Sharl asked worriedly.

Val shrugged.

"I know not," he said. "Until the neighboring clans tire of your presence and decide to kill you. They would not wait until you moved of your own accord, for already you have spilled blood against our law in this place."

"You would have killed the men, if you had the chance," Sharl countered. "What then would have happened to you?"

"We would have wounded them if we could, and bound them," Chyrie said lightly, "and left them outside the markers to the justice of the clans who keep the altars. It would be no quick death they would earn so. Humans found trespassing in elvan lands are—" She stopped abruptly.

"Are what?" Rivkah pressed.

Chyrie shrugged.

"I cannot say," she said. "In Wilding lands they would be stripped of skin inch by inch while acid sap is applied. What Moon Lake or Redoak clans would do, I cannot say."

"But you have traveled safely," Sharl argued, "through other territories."

"We used the common road," Valann said patiently. "Those bound for this place or returning from it may do so." He gestured at the green cord around Chyrie's arm. "We are doubly safe while she wears the mark of fertility."

"Then could we not take this common road through the forest?" Sharl asked.

"I say again, you are not elf," Val snarled. "That you trespass in our sacred places and upon our common road is a greater transgression, not less. Any elf would slay you for such presumption."

"Need we fear even your knife at our throats?" Rivkah asked softly.

Val glanced at Chyrie before answering.

"You need not," he said at last. "You trespass here, but it is not our duty to punish that, and you aided my mate when you need not have done so, even though you acted in your own cause. For ourselves we will not harm you if you do us no other discourtesy. That should serve as our . . . gratitude."

"But if we traveled on the common road in the company of elves?" Sharl pressed. "Would other elves then attack us?"

Chyrie exchanged looks with Val, then shrugged.

"I know not," she said. "Never has such a thing been done. But no elves would travel with humans, not through their own territory and with their Eldest's blessing, much less through the lands of other clans."

"We would pay well," Sharl said persuasively, drawing forth a small leather sack from his waist. He poured its contents onto the ground in front of Chyrie and Valann.

Val picked up one of the golden coins and examined it closely, smelling it and passing it to Chyrie.

"What is the use of this?" Chyrie asked, hefting the coin in her hand. "It is wrongly shaped for a sling and too small for other uses. We use flat rocks for ten-stone; is this then a playing piece?"

"It's a gold coin," Rivkah explained. "We use them to buy other things we desire."

"I had heard rumors that humans traded in bits of metal but had never seen such," Valann said curiously, sticking out his tongue to taste the coin. "It is like the stuff we pick from some streams to pound out for jewelry, but in not so pleasing a form. See?" He brushed back Chyrie's short, curling hair to show the small rings in her ears.

"None of our kind would take this in trade," Chyrie said scornfully. "It is of no use."

"It's made of gold!" Sharl protested. "Gold is valuable to you, isn't it, if you use it for jewelry?"

"I have not the skill of pounding out jewelry"—Chyrie shrugged—"nor has my mate. It is too soft for the making of weapons. Are humans so poor that they have nothing better to trade?"

"It matters not," Valann said firmly. "Even if they had all the riches of the Mother Forest they could not buy us. Is it not so?"

"Indeed," Chyrie agreed hastily. "It is not a matter of payment. We cannot help you."

"Cannot or will not?" Rivkah probed.

"We cannot, nor would we," Val said coldly. "My mate needs the attentions of our Gifted One, and we have other business of import to us if not to you."

"Perhaps we could help you in your endeavors in exchange for your services," Sharl suggested, "if you will tell us what you need."

Chyrie exchanged flabbergasted looks with Valann, and they both burst out laughing.

"Have we said something offensive?" Rivkah asked worriedly.

"Nay, only amusing," Chyrie choked. "We have come that my mate may plant seed in my womb. I doubt you could offer any assistance in that matter."

All four humans reddened darkly, and Rivkah mustered a weak chuckle.

"In that case I'm afraid you're right," Rivkah said ruefully. "But, Chyrie, are you certain you can bear after—well—what happened?"

Chyrie shrugged.

"Valann is a fine healer," she said. "How great the harm was done me I cannot say until we couple next. Still it would be wise that I consult with our Gifted One when we return home, and he can say truly if Valann's seed has taken root."

"And we must go about assuring that," Val said gently, his eyes sparkling at Chyrie. "It is in my mind that a slow death should befall they who next interrupt our . . . endeavors."

"Sharl," Rivkah said pleadingly, "don't you think—"

"No," Sharl said regretfully, but firmly. "We may never have this chance again. The risk is too great. Valann, I'll ask once more: Will you guide us on this common road? We'll pay you well, I promise. If you don't want the gold, we will find some other way to compensate you."

"And yet again I say we will not," Valann snapped. "You can say nothing to change our course."

Sharl looked old suddenly, and tired. "I'm afraid I can, Valann."

Instantly Val's sword was in his hand, and Chyrie's was equally ready.

"Think not to threaten us, human," he snarled. "My gratitude has its limits, and you fast exceed them."

"It's no threat," Rivkah said unhappily. "Valann, I'm sorry. I didn't want to do it, but . . . I've cast a geas upon you. It was in the wine. I'm sorry that Chyrie drank. I didn't mean for her to be included in the geas."

"You lie," Chyrie hissed. "Valann tested the wine, as did I. There was no potion therein."

"It's not a potion, but a spell," Rivkah said. "I added nothing to the wine but a few words to seal the binding."

"I wanted to avoid this," Sharl said. "If you had agreed to lead us freely I would have had Rivkah lift the binding. We will still pay you well, I swear it, in gold or trade goods, whatever you like. What is she doing?" he added as Chyrie dropped her sword, crouching on the ground, eyes tight shut.

Chyrie sank deep within herself, seeking around her until she ran into a barrier, thick and hard. With mind and spirit she battered it, feeling no yielding. Refusing to waste her energy, she ceased her assault and explored the barrier within herself.

(Tell me,) Valann told her.

Chyrie shook her head bleakly.

(It is truth, beloved,) she thought, showing him the barrier. (We are bound until the man Sharl grants us release, or until the woman Rivkah lifts the spell. Nor may we lift hand to do them harm while we are so bound.)

(Is there no way to break this binding?)

(Not now.) Chyrie was silent for a long moment. (I pledge I will see those humans suffer long for this.)

(We will suffer with them if we accompany them on this fool's journey,) Valann thought wryly. (Still an arrow loosed cannot be recalled. What are the limits upon our freedom?)

(Perhaps a hundred paces or so, no more,) Chyrie told him.

"Release at least my mate," Valann said aloud. "I alone will suffice for your purposes."

"I will not leave you!" Chyrie said hotly.

"You must go to our Gifted One," Valann said aloud, but inwardly he spoke differently.

(You can follow behind,) he thought. (Freed from the binding you can slay the humans and free me, fleet one.)

"No child is worth your life!" she argued. (A fine plan, beloved,) she added silently. (They will not go far.)

"I'm sorry," Rivkah said. "But since you drank the wine, Chyrie, I can't release you without releasing Valann."

"Then do so," Valann said with dignity, "and I will freely guide you. That was your offer, was it not?"

Sharl chuckled. "I'm sorry, but somehow I don't think we can trust you now, Valann."

Valann spat on the ground.

"How lightly you apologize, as if your words alone will make amends for any crime. Yet you will make amend in full measure, I swear it, and you will pay in blood and in sorrow." He folded his arms around Chyrie. "And should my mate take harm because you have bound her, may your treacherous spirits never return to the earth to find peace."

Chyrie touched his arm.

"This bickering profits us none," she said gently. "Come, quiet your anger. Let us spread our furs and take comfort together and see what the dawn brings." (Beloved, do not give them warning. It is the silent blade that finds its mark. There will come a time, and a way.)

"Yes, sleep and mend," Rivkah urged. "You'll feel better in the morning."

"I do so, but not at your bidding," Valann said icily. He helped Chyrie to her feet and led her to their bundles, which they arranged at another campsite. Valann returned to the humans' fire only to take one of the buckets of water, which he carried mutely back to their pallets. He scrutinized the fur in which Rivkah had wrapped Chyrie, then cast it aside scornfully.

"Soiled with the smell of humans and their tame beasts, and they know not how to tan a hide to softness," he said contemptuously. Taking a soft, absorbent leather from his pack, he wet it and began gently cleaning the dirt from Chyrie's skin.

"Curse me for a poor healer," he said, frowning. "There are still many bruises under the soil and blood. Do you feel much pain?"

Chyrie shook her head. "Only on deep breathing. In the morning we must bind my ribs tightly. I am ill-inclined to let the human woman work her touch on me again, even if she could heal my bones." She lay back, sighing contentedly as he continued his ministrations.

"Neither she nor any other human will lay hand on you again as long as I live to stop it," Valann said tenderly. He drew from his pouch a handful of leaves, which he crumbled into the water before he continued.

"This may sting," he warned, "but the Mother Forest alone knows what diseases those stinking human males carry. Do I hurt you?" he added as Chyrie gasped.

"No, love," she said with a chuckle. "But if you continue such attentions we must soon try the extent of your healing."

Valann's smile carried more than a little relief.

"I am glad to see you are not spirit-wounded by their violence," he said gently. "But my hungry-bodied mate must wait until tomorrow at least."

"How much longer will I remain ripe?" she wondered worriedly.

"If my seed did not take root, another hand of nights," Valann guessed. "Plenty of time, love, and there is every hope we have already succeeded."

Chyrie's smile faded, and when she spoke, her voice was small.

"Valann . . . is there any chance that a human's seed could grow in me?"

Valann froze, then forced a semblance of composure as he wrung out the leather.

"I think not," he said. "Should a wolf mate with a fox, or a fox with a weasel, there would be no get of them. The Mother Forest breeds only like with like."

"But a wolf will not couple with a fox, nor a fox with a weasel," Chyrie murmured. "The Mother Forest has seen that one kind does not desire another. Yet the humans desired me. Have you ever known a human and an elf to couple, that we can say this or that is so? It frightens me, love."

Valann stretched out beside Chyrie, gently running his finger-tips over her skin.

"I wish you could return to the Gifted One," he said. "Who knows how long these humans may expect to keep us? But surely it cannot be more than a few days, and that will be plenty of time. The Gifted One can see for certain if and what you bear, and if anything is amiss there are magicks and potions to cleanse you without harm."

"Oh, Valann," she wailed. "It may be another half century before I ripen again."

"Hush. You are still young," Valann said firmly. "There will be many times of ripeness left to us both."

"Not if we are killed," Chyrie said.

"If so, then it matters little what you bear within you," Valann told her practically. "Come, do not torment yourself with fear. The Mother Forest is wise and our Gifted One is great, and you can trust in them both."

"You left out my mate, who is perfect beyond the lot of elvankind," Chyrie said drowsily. "And I trust in him most of all."

Valann smiled silently, pulled a bear pelt over them both, and followed Chyrie down into sleep.

III

ROM SAT POKING restlessly at the fire, glancing occasionally into the darkness around the camp and yawning. It was nearly two hours till dawn, and he had not slept nearly long enough to suit him.

Abruptly he yelped as a small foot nudged his ribs. Valann had materialized at his side as silently as moonlight.

"We must go," Val said. "There is no more safety here."

Sharl struggled up onto one elbow.

"What is it?"

"Others watch with hostile eyes," Val said. "Chyrie feels it. We must go, and soon. Is there one of your oversize riding beasts for Chyrie and myself?"

"Plenty, since our comrades were slain," Rivkah said, crawling out of her sleeping furs. "Did you and Chyrie walk all the way here?"

"Our mounts would not travel in the company of the likes of you," Valann said sourly, "and unlike us, they have that choice open to them."

He returned to Chyrie, who was tying up their packs.

(Why did you bid me warn them?) he asked silently. (Let the Moon Lakes slay them and we are freed.)

(If I were certain of that I might agree,) Chyrie thought unhappily. (But I know not their human magic. Perhaps only the woman or the man can lift it by speaking the words. If they should die, then we might be chained to their dead flesh.

I had hoped they might free me, so that the woman Rivkah might be captured and the others slain. Our clan could force her to remove the spell. But bound as we both are, we cannot act against them, and I fear what might happen if both the man Sharl and the woman Rivkah should die. Besides, we cannot escape while they live, and the Moon Lakes might well slay us with them.)

(Mother Forest blight the loins of all humans,) Val thought bitterly. (Well, there is nothing for it. They are giving us one of their leather-strapped riding beasts.)

Chyrie was appalled.

"One of those living mountains?" she asked. "How shall we ascend to its back?"

"We will find a way," Val said grimly. "I will not be lifted to its back like a child by one of those humans, I vow. Give me the packs. You must not carry until your ribs heal. Is the binding tight enough?"

Chyrie took an experimental deep breath and winced.

"As well as can be expected," she sighed. "I can ride."

"Well enough." He drew a leather thong from the pack, tying it into a complex series of knots, and tied it around Chyrie's arm below the green cord.

(Wear this openly,) he told her. (The humans will not know what it means.) He tied an identical thong for himself.

Chyrie examined the thong with some surprise. The knot-language was old but well known. This was a hostage-knot, showing that the elf who wore it was captive, but that her clan would pay ransom for her. An even heavier ransom could be charged for the return of an elf known to be fertile.

(A clever idea, love,) she thought admiringly. (Perhaps even if we are set upon, we will be spared for a ransom.)

(Any elf seeing would know that we could only be captives of the humans,) Val mused, (but our lack of visible bonds might confuse them. None will care to help us, but at least this may spare us harm. Will you send word to the Wilding camp?)

(I have already sent two birds and a squirrel.)

Val barely smiled. (Do you think there is any chance they will come to our aid?)

(I think not,) Chyrie thought sadly. (It would mean sending a hunting party out of our territory, and they would be many days behind us, even so. But perhaps they can send us information of use to us, or send offers of ransom to other clans.)

"Are you ready?" Sharl called. "It was you who wanted haste."

The humans waited impatiently while Chyrie, standing on a stump, stroked and murmured to the horse and Valann removed the saddle and bridle.

"I would think," Sharl said sarcastically, "that the two of you will have trouble enough staying on a horse."

"He does not like them," Chyrie said simply. Valann made a cup of his hands and lifted her to the horse's back, then used one of the altars to mount.

"Well, you will have to put the bridle back on him when we camp," Rivkah said practically, "or he would just wander away in the night. And he *is* Lord Sharl's horse, not yours."

Val looked impatiently at Sharl.

"You promised us payment," he said icily, "for our slavery to you. Therefore give us this horse and two females, that we may breed them for our clan."

Sharl looked startled, then chuckled. "The horses are yours, Valann, but the one you ride will be no use for breeding; he has been gelded."

"Gelded? What is that?" Chyrie asked.

"It means that the horse's gonads have been cut away," Rivkah explained. "It is often done to male horses, to make them more docile, but it also renders them unable to breed."

Valann echoed Chyrie's horrified expression.

"You mean," he said slowly, stunned, "that you would deprive one of the gift of reproduction? Simply so that he is more docile for your enslavement?"

"It is a simple process." Sharl shrugged. "The horse suffers little."

"Are you a beast-speaker that you know this?" Chyrie snarled. "Or is it that you yourself have been so treated?"

Sharl scowled furiously.

"I would think," he said coldly, "that in your position you would find it safer to keep a civil tongue."

Val shrugged.

"What threat will you make to us now?" he said indifferently. "You can but kill us, and you will not do that. You are, I see now, no better than those other humans you call out-kin. You simply take what you want and do what you please to bend it to your will, be it elf or—or horse, regardless of the harm you do it thereby."

"It's not the same," Rivkah protested. "The horses are only animals. You kill animals for meat."

"That is the natural order," Chyrie maintained. "We hunt, as does wolf or cat or fox, and we kill what we need. Never did the Mother Forest make one creature to be bound to the will of another."

Sharl scowled as Val languidly gestured to show the road they must take. "Do you see no difference between people—elves and humans—and animals?"

"I see much difference between elves and humans," Val said quietly. "But what matter how we believe? I see that your kind sees no difference between elf and animal, since my mate and I are enslaved even as your horses, albeit our bridles are of magic rather than leather."

Rivkah flushed miserably.

"You judge us harshly," she said. "I'm not proud of what I did, but it's a case of great need. Lord Sharl is a kind man and wants allies, not prisoners. Under other circumstances he would never—"

Val spat derisively. *"That* for your lord's kindness. If his need was great, he made no mention of it. A kind man does not deceive and enslave others under pretext of friendship. Wildings would not so treat even our enemies. Let him seek his allies among his own kind, such as those who forced my mate. He shall have nothing from me that I can deny him."

Chyrie rode in silence, her mind far from the argument, trying to ignore the persistent stabbing pain of spurs gouging at the horses' sides. The pain was not as great as that in her ribs, but it was distracting, and she dared give no sign of it;

the secret of her ability as a beast-speaker was one of the few advantages she and Val still retained. To escape the pains from without and within, she cast out her thoughts at random, seeking whatever she might find.

All around her she could feel the myriad small minds of the forest, bird and beast, as well as minds filled with intelligent thought, watching them as they passed. The hostility was not as great as she would have expected; rather, she felt resentment, then realization and a horrified pity as watching elves realized the implication of what they saw.

(Valann, love.)

(What is it?) Val reached to touch his bow. (Is there danger?)

(No, I am only surprised. Moon Lakes watch us, yet in them there is hatred only for the humans. I almost think they would trouble themselves to aid us.)

(What?) Valann was as surprised as she. (How can that be? We are Wilding, not Moon Lake.)

Chyrie probed further, careful to make her touches light lest they be felt.

(They feel differently toward strangers than we,) she thought at last. (Perhaps it is because they tend the altars and are more accustomed to the sight of out-kin. They see us not as Wilding, but as elf. They are furious that humans could capture us and would kill these humans lest it happen again, but they are frightened of the woman who could cast such magic.)

(Dare you speak to them?)

Chyrie pondered a moment. (I fear they might see it as trespass. I have heard that many clans have lost the silent speech, and I sense no beast-speakers among them. If I offend, we lose all chance of aid.)

(Then let us send a token. They can take no offense at that.).

Chyrie nodded almost imperceptibly. (You are behind me and less visible to the humans. Tie a cord with the promise-of-reward sign and the Wilding knot, and drop it on the trail behind us.) Unobtrusively she slipped the gold rings from her ears and passed them back to him. (Tie these into the cord.

If humans so value this soft metal, perhaps other clans do, as well.)

To their consternation, Rivkah rode back to them.

"You're very quiet," she said. "Is something wrong?"

"I have nothing to say to you or any of your kind," Chyrie said with dignity. "And my body pains me."

"I will try a strong healing spell when we stop at midday," she said. "Bone is hard to mend, but ribs are less difficult than other, thicker bones."

Chyrie locked her amber eyes with those of the human, and her voice was hard as stone.

"Never," she said quietly, "will you lay hand to me again. Nor will crumb of your food, nor drop of your wine, pass my lips or those of my mate, though we were dying for want of them. Before I suffer your foul magic to touch me again I will turn my dagger and open my body to spill my entrails upon the earth."

Rivkah's eyes dropped.

"Why must you hate me?" she murmured. "I did only what my lord required. I tried to persuade him."

"You have heart and mind of your own," Val said sourly. He surreptitiously dropped the knotted cord behind the horse. "If you seek forgiveness of us, you seek in vain. You care nothing for the harm you do my mate by keeping her from our Gifted One. If she does not take my seed, it is many decades before she may ripen again, and who knows what harm those you pursued have done her? What should have been a joyful time for us has become a horror. You give our kin anxiety by taking us from them, and you endanger our lives by forcing us among those who would gladly see us dead. You earn only our enmity."

Rivkah sighed.

"I can see why you feel so, but you're wrong. We all care what we have done to you. Sharl is deeply pained. I would have spared Chyrie if I could. I would heal her if she would permit it. If there was anything else to be done, I would do it. But there's nothing else I can do."

"Free my mate," Val said stonily. "Tie me if you must, or chain me, or strike me senseless, and then lay your spell

upon me again as you like, but let at least Chyrie return to
our people. There is no need that she and the child she may
bear die with me."

"I'll speak to Sharl again," Rivkah said unhappily. "Perhaps
he will give in." She gloomily kicked her horse to a trot.

(I am not sure I approve of your plan now,) Chyrie thought
slowly. (Even freed, if I did not kill all the humans and they
turned on you, you could not lift hand to defend yourself, and
if their death did not release you, I do not know what we
could do.)

Val shrugged. (You can approach the Moon Lakes. If they
are for some reason sympathetic to our cause, perhaps they
will aid you.)

(And perhaps not, and perhaps they will slay the humans
and you with them,) Chyrie protested. (And even if they kill
the humans and leave you alive, as I have said—)

Val clasped his arms around her waist. (If that should happen
we will take their dead flesh back to the Gifted One and let him
do what he can. But the Moon Lakes will not want them all
dead. At least one, likely the lord, must be kept and made to
tell why these humans have come here, and how many more
there may be. This has grown beyond you and me, love; now
it is for the welfare of our clan as well. If humans who can
enslave us to their will wander freely through our territory, no
Wilding is safe. The Moon Lakes will see this also if you tell
them all. I would risk much to see these humans in torment
for what they have done.)

(Then we must persuade the humans to camp before we
leave Moon Lake territory,) Chyrie thought. (The elves of the
Inner Heart clan may not be so sympathetic, and also the sight
of humans camping on their land may incite the Moon Lakes
further.)

(Leave that to me.)

Valann nudged the horse with his heels, bringing it forward
to ride beside Sharl.

"We must strike an early camp," he said. "Soon we will
enter the territory of the Inner Heart clan, and their territory
is even larger than Moon Lake, and their temper fierce. Only
with an early start and a quick pace can we hope to pass their

lands in one day, and we dare not camp there. Therefore we must camp within Moon Lake lands, and far enough within the boundaries that no Inner Hearts will know of our presence."

Sharl glanced up at the sun, barely visible through the leaves. "How much farther?"

"At the pace of these horses, we will reach the bounds of Moon Lake lands in perhaps six hours. I would advise to stop in no more than five."

Sharl thought a moment, then shook his head.

"The delay is too great," he said. "It would cost us almost half a day's ride. No, we continue until dark. According to what you say, every elf in the woods would have my blood anyway, so it matters little which clan we risk."

"You enslave us to give you safety, yet disregard wise counsel," Val said sourly. "As well you had not brought us."

Sharl shook his head regretfully. "I'm sorry, Valann, but as long as your presence improves our chance we cannot spare you. Unfortunately, I'm not sure I can trust your counsel under the circumstances. You have my word that you will be freed as soon as we reach the edge of the forest."

Val snorted. "My concern for you would not dwarf the least grain of soil, but I do not hold my life and that of my mate in equal contempt. Therefore you may rest assured that I do not lead you into hazard, for Inner Heart knives will drink our blood as readily as yours."

They fell back.

(What can we do now?) Chyrie wondered. (If they will not stop, we may pass from Moon Lake territory before the Moon Lakes will have a chance to help us, if indeed they might do so.)

Val sighed.

(They could not but hear our speech,) he thought encouragingly. (And we will stop at midday for food. The dark would give advantage against these night-blind humans, but still there may be hope. An attack by bows would be most effective—the humans have only swords. The Moon Lakes must see this also.)

He ran his hands over Chyrie's body, healing the remaining bruises.

(Would that my poor skill could deal with cracked bone,) he thought regretfully. (I can feel the pain of your ribs. That will serve you ill should there be violence and the need for quick action. Perhaps you should relent and let Rivkah heal you.)

(Never!) The thought came so powerfully that Val winced slightly. (Love, there are weaknesses in their binding. While we cannot ourselves raise hand to harm these humans, we can allow or even aid others to do so. We can plot and send messages as we will. What if one of these humans has already realized as much? If the woman lays her magic upon me again, how know we what bindings or ills she might lay upon me in the guise of healing?)

They rode in tense silence while the sun climbed higher in the sky, and higher. At last Sharl called back to them.

"Time for a rest," he said after speaking to his companions. "We can stop at the next clearing."

An old roadside campsite was located only a few minutes later, and Val helped Chyrie down from the horse's back.

(Keep the humans' attention,) Chyrie thought to him. (There is something in the bushes.)

"Do these humans never stop to make water?" she grumbled aloud, hobbling to the bushes. "I am bursting."

"We are no more than a short ride from Inner Heart territory," Val said, wandering over to where the humans were tying the horses. "Have you made a plan for passing through their lands whole-skinned?"

"We have been safe enough so far," Sharl said, shrugging. "We haven't seen another elf since we left the camp. They seem to be avoiding us."

"Sharl, surely we can let Chyrie go," Rivkah said persuasively. "I can see she's in pain. Valann offered to let us tie him, or even knock him unconscious, if we lift the geas to let her leave, and then lay another on him. I can mix a sleeping potion for him to drink, if you like."

"What makes you think she's any better off alone and injured in hostile lands?" Sharl said, eyeing Valann suspiciously. "At least with us there are five other swords between her and death."

"Each step takes us farther from Wilding lands," Val argued.

"Even should we reach the forest's edge and live to be freed, we two must then travel alone back to our own place. Having violated the territories of other clans, think you that they will be willing to let us pass again unmolested? If you care nothing for my life, allow at least my mate and the child she may bear to have some slender hope of reaching our people."

"Sharl, listen to him," Rivkah pleaded. "You'll still have Valann as a hostage."

Sharl was silent for a moment, then shook his head.

"I can't allow it," he said. "Chyrie's presence insures that Valann won't lead us into danger deliberately, and he said himself that they were safer from attack because Chyrie is fertile. Rivkah, I can't let you waste your magic. If you hadn't pressed yourself so hard healing Valann and casting the geas, you would have power available to conceal and protect us, and an additional geas would tax you even more. Chyrie will just have to go with us. If necessary, I'll send guards to escort them home around the forest when we—after we're out of the forest."

Rivkah looked sharply at Sharl, but was silent. Valann scowled and walked back to Chyrie, who had emerged from the bushes.

(Sharl refused, as I knew he would,) he thought sourly. (What did you find?)

(This.) She showed him a knotted cord, her earrings tied at the bottom. (It is puzzling indeed. Here is the sign promising aid, but they have returned my rings. And I know not the clan sign at the bottom. Are they raiders, here to prey on the Moon Lakes, or have the Moon Lakes been conquered and their territory taken?)

(It matters not, if they offer help,) Val thought grimly. (I would ally with the very Silvertips who raided our lands last summer against these humans. But when will they strike? Soon we will leave Moon Lake lands, yet they give us no instruction to delay departure. What should we do?)

Troubled, Chyrie probed the forest.

(There are watchers nearby,) she thought. (Doubtless they have understood the humans' plans and know that we soon leave. They will act in their own time. Let us take a good meal and rest. We may well need all our strength.)

Valann untied their packs, ignoring the supplies and wine Rivkah offered, and drew out their own dried meat, berries, and wine. They ate quickly, half expecting elves to leap from the brush, but the meal was uneventful.

(I know not what to think,) Val confessed as they rode away from the clearing. (Wildings would have attacked while the humans ate and their hands were occupied without weapons. Now there is little time before we cross the Inner Heart boundary, and the humans are alert.)

The Moon Lake markers came into sight, the signs glowing gently from stones beside the road. Val and Chyrie were still, listening intently although their expressions showed only composure. The group came closer to the markers, and closer—

—and then they were past.

Behind Val's calm face, his thoughts were leaden with despair.

(Their offer of aid was a deception,) he thought disgustedly. (Why would even out-kin do such a thing, promise falsely and return your rings? What did it profit them?)

(Perhaps the offer was made in good faith, but some plan went awry,) Chyrie thought sadly. (Perhaps fear of the mage Rivkah's powers held them back. Why should they risk themselves for out-kin?)

(True,) Valann admitted. (We should have expected no more. Certainly there is no reason to expect aid from Inner Heart, either. We must hope that the humans will honor their word to free us.)

Acute disappointment made the ride long and weary, although Sharl's composure grew with each hour's progress. By the time the sunlight began to fail, he was positively cheerful.

"My idea has worked," he told Val. "It seems even these elves, fierce as you say they are, won't attack us. Your fears for your safety are needless. You see we're safe as long as—"

His words were interrupted as a shrill cry sounded above them. With amazing suddenness, a large and heavy net dropped, entangling elf, human, and horse alike in coils that seemed to constrict more tightly at each movement. Immediately, nearly a dozen elves dropped from the branches, swords and spears leaping to hand, and more materialized from the bushes at the sides of the road, bows at the ready.

"Drop your weapons if you wish to live!" an elf shouted.

IV

CHYRIE AND VALANN exchanged glances, then dropped their swords and bows. For a moment Sharl hacked at the net, clutching his sword despite the hopeless odds. Then, resignedly, he sighed and dropped the weapon. Rivkah, Romuel, and Doria quickly followed suit.

A slender female elf, nearly half again as tall as Chyrie, black hair coiled high at the top of her head and a hawk on her shoulder, stepped forward.

"I am Rowan," she said, "Eldest of the clan of Inner Heart. For violating the boundaries of our lands, you are now our prisoners."

Rowan waited until the elves had collected all of the weapons, then nodded. One of the elves stepped forward to slit the net open in front of Chyrie and Valann, and Rowan nodded to each as they stepped out.

"Welcome, kinsfolk," she said, extending a hand to touch Chyrie's cheek, then Valann's. "My word assures your safety and fair treatment among us."

She turned to the elves guarding the still-netted humans.

"The fair-haired female is as one Gifted," she said. "Bind them all well, and cover their eyes, but gag her as well, also, lest she bespell us as she has our kin."

She smiled at a stunned Valann and Chyrie.

"Reclaim your weapons, friends," she said gently. "Did you not receive promise of aid?"

"That was in Moon Lake lands," Val murmured. "But are you not Inner Heart?"

"I am," she said. "Those elves there"—she gestured—"are Moon Lake, and those Redoak, and that one Owl clan. Our clans have joined our lands two years past, four clans and yet one. You are Wilding, are you not? Your people have been but legend to us, of a clan known but never seen by any."

"Our ransom will be full paid," Chyrie said quickly. "Our Eldest will send furs in trade, or rare herbs—"

"And a rich ransom indeed could I claim"—Rowan smiled—"for an elf who may be bearing child. I will decide what I may ask in return for your release when I have questioned all of you. For now there is food and fire awaiting in our village, and our Gifted One to tend your hurts, and many, many kinsfolk awaiting my slightest word to begin a festival to welcome you. Which word is now given," Rowan said, raising her voice slightly. One or two of the elves laughed and disappeared into the undergrowth.

"But I see you are in pain, kinswoman," Rowan continued, gesturing at the leather wrapping Chyrie's chest. "If we assist you to remount your riding beast, can you reach our village, or need I summon our Gifted One to tend you here?"

"I am not much pained," Chyrie lied. In actuality when she fell from the unaccustomed height of her mount, she had landed badly, further battering her wounded ribs. Rowan looked at her dubiously, but glanced at the hawk on her shoulder. It launched itself airborne and disappeared into the trees.

Chyrie walked slowly back to where the elves were freeing the frightened horses, concealing her pain as best she could, more worried about the beasts than herself. The elves had obviously never seen such creatures before and did not know how to safely free them, and the horses were half-panicked, the whites of their rolling eyes showing, their hooves tangling in the netting. Chyrie soothed them silently and they quieted, but she let Val help the other elves handle the heavy nets and lead the now-calm horses away from the trap. While she was with the horses, she quickly removed the three carved-bone bracelets and the bear-claw necklace she and Valann had planned to leave as an offering at the altars.

It took some time and difficulty for the elves to assist Chyrie back onto the horse's back, and Val protectively behind her, and by the time they were done, the humans had been searched, bound, and blindfolded. Rivkah had been gagged as well, but the others muttered to each other in their own guttural tongue until a sharp warning poke from a spear silenced them.

(It makes no sense,) Chyrie thought puzzledly. (We are no kin of theirs, yet we are treated as such. The humans are bound, but we, equally trespassers, are left free and our weapons returned to us. And four clans joined to become one? If Moon Lake or Inner Heart had captured Redoak or Owl clan, yes—the latter are but small clans. But this is clearly no such simple taking of territories.)

(Perhaps it is some trick,) Valann suggested. (Perhaps the clans fear human or Wilding invasion and wish us to believe their numbers larger to make them appear a more formidable foe.)

That made sense, Wilding sense, and Chyrie was, as always, impressed by Valann's wisdom. She leaned back against his chest comfortably. Despite the pain in her ribs, the humans' geas still upon them, and now their capture by an enemy, she felt safer than she had since they had arrived at the altars.

As would be the case with any sensibly cautious clan, there was no visible trail to mark the way to the Inner Heart village, and the horses were plainly not made for travel through the tangled growth of the forest. Their journey, already slowed by the painful pace of human and horse and punctuated by yelps and what Chyrie presumed to be curses by the blindfolded and stumbling humans, was further delayed while the elves at the rear of the group concealed the traces of their passage. Just as Chyrie thought wryly that she would have made better time, injured as she was, on foot, they emerged into a clearing and Inner Heart was abruptly before them.

Chyrie gasped, and Valann involuntarily tightened his arms around her, drawing a second gasp, of pain this time. The village was easily five times the size of the Wilding camp—and unlike the Wilding camp, which changed with the season, the amount of game available, and the supply of forage, this was obviously a permanent village. Some round huts had been built cradled between the branches of the trees as the Wilding clan did, but others were of a kind Chyrie and Valann had never seen—built on the ground in a sort of thick cone shape, point up to shed rain.

The elves who had run ahead had had plenty of time to alert the village, and apparently had done so, for it seemed to Valann and Chyrie that every elf in the forest must have been gathered in the clearing. Some of them were hastily stoking firepits or preparing food, and others were carrying wine, nuts, and vegetables out from storage, but most simply stood and stared.

Valann slid off the horse, instinctively reaching for his sword before he remembered they were fairly Rowan's prisoners. Rowan stepped up, laying one long hand on his shoulder soothingly.

"These are our kinsfolk and guests, Valann and Chyrie of the Wilding clan," she said. "They have brought us four human prisoners and tidings from the north. Valann and Chyrie, share our food and fire, and be made welcome among us."

"We are honored to share your food and fire," Valann answered. "May joy and friendship be our contribution."

"We bring gifts for the Eldest, in thanks for the honor of our welcome," Chyrie added, producing the bracelets and the necklace, which she held out to Rowan.

"I accept your gifts," Rowan said, sliding the bracelets onto her wrist and tying the necklace around her neck.

A murmur ran through the elves, but they relaxed somewhat, some dispersing to help with the preparation of food, others coming forward to help lead humans or horses to some unknown destination.

"While my kinsfolk prepare the food, come to my speaking hut," Rowan said, guiding them away from the central clearing. "Our Gifted One can tend your hurts, Chyrie, and there are questions to be answered."

"Speaking hut?" Chyrie asked.

"When our clans joined, we built it for private meetings of more elves than one person's hut would hold," Rowan said, gesturing to a large cone-shaped hut, from which a few small wisps of smoke drifted from a small hole at the tip of the cone.

Private meetings? Chyrie wondered, although she said nothing. Wilding clan meetings were held around the central fire with all kin, as was proper. Who could be excluded from any business of the clan?

"You have not named the price of our release," Valann reminded her.

"I will consider it," Rowan said, "when all the truths are told."

(All the truths?) Chyrie thought to Valann. (Truth is truth, and lies are lies.)

(Not at all,) Valann thought back, squeezing her hand reassuringly. (If I kill a doe, I say that is good, because we will eat well for many days, and that is true. But the stag would not agree, for his mate is gone, and that would be true, too.)

Two elves were standing guard outside the door of the hut, conversing with a third. The third elf was obviously no guard; judging from the ornate dyed patterns and beaded decorations of his tunic and the various feathers braided into his black hair, this elf was obviously someone of importance.

"Valann and Chyrie, I make known to you Dusk, our Gifted One," Rowan said. "Dusk, Valann and Chyrie are our Wilding kin, brought here by the human prisoners. Has the hut been readied?"

When the Gifted One spoke, his voice was as warm as his rich brown skin.

"The speaking spell has been cast, and food and wine laid ready." He glanced at Chyrie, his large eyes sparkling green. "So this is the beast-speaker. A thousand small minds have whispered your name to me. Come into the hut and I will tend your hurts, although I understand that your mate is a healer himself. Doubtless there is little enough damage left to mend."

When they stepped into the hut, it was surprisingly bright, although the cone had no windows. A small fire had been built at the center in a pit lined with stones, and furs were strewn around it for seating. Small clay fat-lamps hung from the walls as well, explaining the hut's surprising brightness. Platters of meat and fruit, and skins of wine, were laid by the fire.

The humans were seated around the fire. Their blindfolds had been removed, as had Rivkah's gag, but their hands were still bound. They watched the approaching elves—Sharl indignantly, Rivkah anxiously, Romuel and Doria warily.

Rowan faced Sharl squarely.

"As I said before, I am Rowan, Eldest of this clan. What is your name, and do you speak for these others?"

Sharl struggled to his feet, awkward because of his bound hands. "I am Sharl, son of Loran of Cielman and High Lord of Allanmere. My companions are the Lady Rivkah, a mage in my employ, and Doria and Romuel, my guards, and yes, I speak on their behalf, although Rivkah is more fluent in your language than I."

"Do you understand that you and your people are fairly our prisoners, captured trespassing upon our territory?" Rowan asked him.

"I understand, but I must explain that—" Sharl began.

"No." Rowan cut him off sharply. "There will be a time for explanations. Answer me simply. Do you understand that it was our right to take you prisoner, and that we have fairly done so?"

Sharl sighed.

"Yes, I understand that."

"Then if you, as leader over these three others, give your word that none of you will attempt violence or escape, nor will your mage cast any magic, we will free your hands and treat you with the courtesy due those who share food and fire until my judgment has been rendered," Rowan said. "Will you give such word?"

"Do I have a choice?" Sharl asked wryly.

"Of course you do," Rowan said evenly. "You can choose to remain bound and treated as an enemy, if that is what you prefer."

Sharl sighed again.

"I give you my word as High Lord of Allanmere, on behalf of myself and my companions," he said.

Rowan nodded, and Dusk drew a knife and cut the thongs binding the humans' wrists.

"You are welcome to share our food and fire," Dusk said, sheathing his knife, and Chyrie and Valann glanced at each other. His phrasing was of the lesser offer of food and fire, given to prisoners, rather than the full welcome given to guests and kin that had been made to Val and Chyrie. The subtle distinction, however, was apparently wasted on the humans, for Sharl and Rivkah glanced puzzledly at each other even as they rubbed the circulation back into their hands.

Val and Chyrie sat down, the jar making Chyrie gasp and press a hand to her ribs. Immediately Dusk turned back to her.

"Forgive me," he said. "You should not have had to wait."

"It is possible she is with child," Val told him. "She ripened only days ago, and there has not been time for her scent to change again. Is it too soon to know?"

"I will see." Dusk flattened one hand against Chyrie's belly. Chyrie was impressed; Dusk had obviously honed his power much more finely than Val, for she felt nothing but a slight tingling warmth from his touch. He sat back and eyed her puzzledly.

"You say you ripened only days ago?" he said slowly.

"No more than five days." Chyrie nodded. "I am certain of that." She hesitated. "Is something awry? The truth is that I was assaulted by humans, and Val and I feared—"

"And when was this?" Dusk interrupted.

"But two nights past," Val said.

Dusk touched Chyrie's belly again, frowning, then turned to Val.

"Was she injured in her childbearing parts such that you used healing magic upon or near them?" Dusk asked.

"It was the greatest healing I have ever attempted," Val admitted.

"Then that is the explanation," Dusk mused to himself. He turned back to Chyrie.

"You are indeed with child," he said. "I was puzzled twofold. First, the life within you is too strong for a seed planted but five days before. It is as if the seed were planted months past, which was not possible if you only just ripened. But I have seen it happen that when very strong healing magic was used upon recently impregnated females, both animal and elf, that the seed of life was hastened toward fruition. We try to avoid such hastening because little is known of the consequences. You may expect to feel movement very soon, and birth in perhaps six to seven moons, not twelve."

"You said you were puzzled twofold," Val said quickly. "Is something amiss with the child?"

"Naught but the fact that there are two sparks of life, not one," Dusk said, shrugging.

There was a moment of complete silence.

"Two?" Rowan asked in a very, very quiet voice. "She is carrying two?"

"Another Gifted One can confirm it, but I am certain," Dusk said, shrugging again. "Both are healthy and strong, as far as can be told now. I have never seen the like. It is surely a gift from the Mother Forest."

"Surely you have been sent to us for a great purpose," Rowan murmured.

"We were not sent for any purpose of yours or of the humans," Val said adamantly. "Surely you must see that Chyrie must be returned to our people for protection. She and the lives she bears are too precious for any other course."

"Certainly nothing must endanger seed touched by the Mother Forest," Rowan agreed absently. "I will consider this. Be assured, Valann, that no harm will come to you or your mate so long as one of us stands to defend you. Dusk, finish tending her, and then there must be talk."

Again Chyrie was impressed at Dusk's skill, for she felt nothing more than the easing of her pain as her ribs healed under his touch. When he had finished, he stepped to the side of the hut and touched one of the curving wooden supports. A line of pale light shot up the wood and spread to the other supports, flowering out until the entire interior of the hut glowed softly. Dusk returned to the furs beside the fire and sat down next to Rowan.

"This hut contains us within a spell of true speaking," Rowan said. "No lies may be spoken within it by any of us. Take food and drink as you will, and I will hear Valann and Chyrie speak first."

"There is little to tell," Val said, shrugging. "But a few days ago we were on wide patrol for the Wildings, and saw Silvertip camping on the edge of our boundaries." He quickly told of Chyrie's impending ripening, their decision to travel to the altars, the attack by the humans, and the rescue by Sharl and his companions. "I can think of nothing else of any significance, unless you wish the details of our coupling."

"Any coupling that could produce two lives at once might well be worth learning"—Dusk laughed—"but we will spare the privacy of your memory. Let us hear the humans speak now."

Sharl was silent for a long time. At last he poured himself a goblet of wine and spoke.

"I am the youngest son of five of the House of Loran," he said. "It became plain to me that I could remain in my father's house as a hanger-on, living on my title and the inheritances of my brothers, or I could start anew and build a House of my own. I did not think it would be difficult. There were many rich lands to the southeast, and many peasants who would be more than happy to migrate to them in exchange for plots of land and the expectation of a profitable and thriving trade city. I chose the land and my settlers with equal care, traveling often to other holdings to seek out the restless, the discontented, those living in places where all the good land was already taken and the trade roads overburdened. The Brightwater River, I said, would be our trade road and our protection, and water for our crops. Quickly the settlers came to claim the lands they would hold under me, and the beginnings of a city began to rise above the land.

"But there were other difficulties," Sharl continued. "Farmers were mine for the asking, as were some craftsmen who would come on a venture, but that was all. I lacked merchants, more craftsmen, troops—and more than that, I needed money and materials. Nobility were harder to entice away from their comfortable homes. The forest surrounding our new home was tenanted by elves who harried and hunted any who entered the forest for wood or game. Those elves showed no interest in treating or even speaking with us—they were far more interested in peppering our hides with arrows.

"I decided to return to my family holding and seek assistance from my brothers in the form of money, boats, troops to protect my people, and mages for hire," Sharl said. "I received"—

he paused briefly—"promises of such aid. I was returning to Allanmere with my guard, when north of the forest we were attacked by a large group of fur-clad barbarians with crude weaponry. In the battle we lost most of my guard— you see before you what remains—and only three of our attackers survived. We pursued them into the forest, hoping to question them, but when we found them they were near to killing Valann and Chyrie, and we killed them instead."

When he was silent, Rowan scowled.

"That is but the beginning of the tale," she said. "Continue."

"We nursed the elves," Sharl said slowly. "We realized that we were already deep in the forest and were likely to be set upon. We attempted to persuade Valann and Chyrie to guide us through the forest, believing that in their company, other elves would be less likely to kill us. They refused. We tried several times to persuade them, and still they refused. I at last told my mage, Rivkah, to lay a geas on them to restrain them to our company, and she did so. She did it most reluctantly and entirely under my instruction; I wish that known. I alone am entirely responsible for the actions of my people, and I think that—"

"What you think is of no importance," Rowan said. Her gaze at Sharl was as hard as steel. "What *I* think is that you have told me nothing."

"You said yourself that your spell assured the truth," Sharl protested.

"What you have told me is worthless," Rowan said coldly. "You do not endear yourself to me with half-truths, and you do not spare yourself punishment by hiding behind silence.

"That these fur-clad men ambushed you I believe," Rowan said slowly. "But that you found them important enough to follow into the forest when you already knew, as you said, you would receive no kindly welcome there, that I question. That having already incurred elvan wrath by trespassing on their lands, you decided to further enrage them by bespelling two elves and display them through the territories of numerous other clans, that I question. Those acts have the sound of desperation."

Sharl said nothing.

"The humans who attacked you fled into the forest," Rowan mused. "Perhaps they did not know the danger in that course. But *you* knew. You knew they would not come out the way they went in, because you were there. You knew that they might be killed in the forest, or they might emerge to the southwest, where your new city is, and where they would be captured. And while they wandered in the forest, walking in circles or being killed, you could quickly and easily take the road around the forest and reach your city in safety. No. You came into the forest for a specific purpose. Tell me that purpose."

Sharl was silent.

"Your offenses are many already," Rowan warned. "If I judge you upon what facts we have already observed your death is certain. If you would have a chance for life, speak now."

"You would let them live?" Valann demanded angrily. "They have captured and enspelled us, risked our lives, and worst of all interfered with our endeavors to conceive a child. How can you even consider sparing them?"

"I did not say I would spare them," Rowan said calmly. "I said only I would hear them and consider their words, and I shall do so. Well? Will you speak, or will you die?"

Sharl was silent again for some moments. At last he sighed.

"Very well," he said. "I have nothing more to lose.

"What I told you of my past is true," he said, "and complete enough. However, my true reason for returning to Cielman, for the reasons I gave, was further prompted by a summons sent by messenger bird from my father and brothers. When I returned they said that there were rumors of war in the north, of displaced peasants fleeing southward ahead of a massive army of barbarians moving slowly but steadily south and west and leaving a trail of utter destruction behind them. Small groups, possibly scouts for such an army, had apparently bypassed many of the larger cities and towns and fared even farther south."

"These rumors made it even more vital that I obtain troops," Sharl continued. "My father dared send none with me, for such an army would reach Cielman first if they traveled westward enough, but mercenary soldiers and mages for hire were arriving from the west, and we arranged messages for several companies to travel directly to Allanmere. They are likely arriving even as we speak. However, the defenses of Allanmere are hardly begun, and I hurried homeward to speed their construction. At the same time I worried about the hostility between the city and our elvan neighbors, because the enmity of the elves, and our inability to obtain game and timber from the forest, would be a serious hindrance. A wagon of trade goods would follow from Cielman, but I had to find some way to make the elves listen to us."

"You chose a strange manner in which to make friendly overtures," Valann growled.

"Hush," Rowan said, refilling Val's goblet. "Let him speak. Do you see it as a certainty that this barbarian army will not pass us by?"

"Some part of the force certainly will," Sharl answered. "But it is inevitable that others will come. There are no other cities within many days travel of Allanmere, and certainly some part of the army must follow the trade roads to Allanmere in search of supplies. Even if they were farther east, the river is deeper and swifter there, much harder to cross, and they must either change their course radically or fare farther west looking for a ford, which will, in turn, lead them back toward Allanmere."

"Continue your story," Rivkah commanded, nodding her understanding.

"When we were attacked by a small party of the barbarians as I told you," Sharl said reluctantly, "I at first had no thought to pursue them into the forest. Then I realized that pursuing these men made a likely excuse to enter the forest and perhaps earn a little goodwill with the elves. At least if we killed those who might endanger them, elves might be disposed to listen rather than slay us immediately. And a little time could be gained, as well, if we could travel directly through the forest instead of around it.

"I wish we could have caught up with the three before they happened upon Valann and Chyrie," Sharl continued earnestly. "I swear to you that I have never wished them the slightest harm. We were delayed, however, fleeing an elvan patrol roused by the barbarians, and forced from our intended road for some time before Rivkah's magic allowed us to find our way back to their trail unseen. Her magic concealed us while we followed, although it was a heavy drain on her. We found Valann and Chyrie at the place of the altars as I said.

"Valann and Chyrie's reaction, even in the face of our rescue of them, convinced me that my plan to gain the elves' gratitude would never work," Sharl said. "I would be lucky even to leave the forest alive to warn my people. I told Rivkah to cast the geas upon Valann, hoping that his presence would at least get us through the elvan lands safely. We had no idea that Chyrie would share the bespelled wine and become similarly bound."

"To free Chyrie would have meant lifting the spell from Valann as well," Rivkah interrupted. "I might have risked it, but—well, Sharl felt that Valann couldn't be trusted, and in any event, by that time it was almost as far back to their own territory as it was to the edge of the forest. Sharl was right that it was safer for Chyrie to return around the woods with Valann than to travel back through it by herself."

"And you would have freed them at the edge of the woods?" Rowan asked, turning to Sharl.

Sharl was silent.

"I thought not," Rowan said. "No, when their presence seemed to grant you safety, you had another thought: They could be used as hostages to force the elves to listen, to deal with you, and a female ripe with child would be doubly valuable."

"That I did *not* know," Sharl countered. "Your folk are far different from the other elves we have met to the north. We had no way of even knowing that Chyrie was with child. She herself only now knows."

"That is true," Rowan agreed. "But you would have held them as hostages nonetheless, is that not true?"

Sharl glanced briefly at Rivkah, then lowered his eyes.

"Yes," he said. "I hoped to force them to act as go-betweens with the elves, and as hostages against a favorable trade treaty."

"Did you never consider warning Valann and Chyrie of the approaching army?" Dusk asked, scowling. "Or us, when you were captured? Did you not hope that such warning would buy your freedom?"

"Our freedom wasn't enough," Sharl answered slowly. "I had learned from Valann and Chyrie how little unity there was among the elves. I knew that if they were free, they would simply return to warn their own clan and likely no others, and there would be no chance of a treaty. I thought the same of your folk, Rowan—that even if you warned the other elvan clans, that you would become involved in your own protections and have no reason to grant us anything."

"So you would have held us ransom against a favorable bargain with the elves while they yet had no knowledge of the approaching army," Valann said quietly, "and warned us and our folk when it was advantageous to you to do so—time enough for us to arm ourselves and provide a buffer between you and the advancing forces, but not so soon that we would turn our resources to our own preparation before you had all that you needed from us. That at least I can understand—the first action you have taken worthy of a Wilding."

"Thank you," Sharl said sourly.

"And what manner of trade goods were you intending to offer us?" Rowan asked, ignoring the exchange.

"We had no way of knowing what elves might need," Sharl said. "So we brought what we wanted them to have—metal and weapons."

Weapons! Chyrie and Valann exchanged glances. Chyrie's dagger was over six centuries old, thin and worn, and Valann's not much newer. Their short swords were just as old but in somewhat better condition, due to less use.

"You offered us no such weapons," Valann said suspiciously. "Only the useless soft metal disks."

"As I said, the wagon of trade goods was to follow," Sharl said. "I had no extra weapons to offer."

"Is there anything further you wish to tell me?" Rowan asked.

Sharl thought for a moment, then shook his head wearily.

"No," he said. "Only that these other three acted completely on my orders. Any offense they might have committed against your people is entirely my responsibility. I ask that you not punish them for following my orders, as your people would follow yours."

"And you have concealed nothing more from us?" Rowan asked.

Sharl looked her directly in the eyes. "Nothing."

Rowan turned to Rivkah.

"And you, do you concur with what he has said?"

"Well, I—" Rivkah paused. "What happened, yes. I honestly believed that Valann and Chyrie would be released when we reached the edge of the forest. Sharl never told me the rest of his plan. But yes, he told you everything that happened. I—I am ashamed that I cast that spell."

"Then lift it now," Rowan said quietly.

"It is already done," Rivkah said tiredly. "I lifted the spell when the nets fell upon us, so that if we were killed, Valann and Chyrie at least would be free to escape if they could."

Sharl gaped openly at the mage, and Chyrie, as surprised as he, searched her mind for the invisible barrier and found it was gone. She nodded at Rowan's questioning glance.

"That speaks in your favor," Rowan said. "I will consider it in rendering my judgment."

"What *will* you do with us?" Sharl demanded.

"I have not yet decided." Rowan turned to Dusk. "It has come, then, sooner than I supposed. All the other clans must be warned. First, tell me this: How far is this army, and when might we expect it to reach us?"

Sharl shrugged.

"They have only the horses they have captured on their way," he said. "They move with great speed for foot soldiers, but parts of the army stop to attack and loot wherever they can for supplies. At the rate they have traveled so far—and this is only hearsay and rumor—the first wave should reach us in a month and a half or less—possibly much less, since as I said, there's little to delay them north of Allanmere. The main body will come less than a week afterward, although I can only hope part of the main force will pass us by. How many there are, no one knows."

"Then there is no time to be lost," Rowan said, nodding to Dusk.

Dusk stepped to the back of the hut and returned with a rolled skin, which he unfolded near the fire. To Val's and Chyrie's wonder, the skin held a map of the entire forest, with clan symbols marked in places.

"There are still many clans we have not located," he said. "It would take many days to question bird and beast to find them. Wilding is one we have not located."

Rowan turned to Val and Chyrie.

"When the humans began to settle near the forest, we feared a day would come when our many clans would face a common threat," she said. "I thought it would be the humans of the city. I joined the clans of Inner Heart, Moon Lake, Redoak, and Owl against such a time. It has been difficult, but four clans together are stronger than four clans apart. Do you understand?"

"I understand that you must send us back to our people," Chyrie demanded. "They are on the northeast side of the forest and must be warned. Our lands will be among the first attacked."

"It would take you many days to return," Dusk said patiently. "A message sent by magic would reach your people in moments. But I must know where to send it. And not only Wilding, but every clan must be warned. Every hand must hold a sword, every eye watch for intruders, every ear listen for signs."

"You propose that Wilding work for the defense of Inner Heart?" Chyrie asked incredulously. "You ask that we spend our lives to save out-kin?"

"I propose that we form an alliance, many strong against many," Rowan said firmly. "I propose that Inner Heart and Wilding stand together, back to back, to defend the forest in which we all live. At the very least each clan must be warned; can you not agree with that?"

Chyrie was silent, but Valann bent over the map.

"Silvertip is here," he said, touching the skin. "Lightfoot here, Riverside here"—he glanced at Chyrie, and she gazed back, troubled—"and Wilding here."

Dusk silently penned in the symbols at the indicated locations.

"I can only hope that other clans will help," Rowan said. "Dusk, warn what clans we can, and we will send messages as others respond. And add to the warning to the Wilding clan the message that Valann and Chyrie are safe and well."

"And us?" Chyrie asked. "What are we to do now?"

"For now, go and enjoy an evening with my people," Rowan said kindly. "They see your arrival as a sign from the Mother Forest, and I am inclined to believe it is true. I promise you justice for the wrongs done to you, and I promise you safety among my people."

"Thank you, Grandmother," Valann said, dipping his head.

"Thank you, Grandmother," Chyrie repeated. She let Val help her up. "And what of the humans?"

Rowan looked sternly at each of the humans in turn.

"Very well," she said at last. "You may also go. Remember that your word is given, and there will be eyes watching you."

Sharl rose and bowed again.

"Thank you—Grandmother."

Valann and Chyrie glanced at each other and grimaced, but Rowan let the presumptuous claim of kinship pass.

"Go, all of you," she said. "I have much thinking to do."

V

"HOW WILL YOU send messages more quickly than a beast could carry them?" Valann asked Dusk as they left the hut and walked toward the bustle of elves at the central clearing.

"There are other Gifted among us," Dusk said. "We will combine our strength to raise the very forest spirits from the roots of the Mother Forest to bear our words. They travel faster than thought, and sending the messages thus will assure the clans of our sincerity."

"We have experimented with mages combining their power, and achieved wonderful results," Rivkah said, her eyes lighting with interest.

"You do ample damage alone," Valann said sourly. "The Mother Forest protect us if more like you should come."

Rivkah winced as if struck, and was silent.

The excited murmur of the busy elves swelled into a confused babble of excited greetings and questions as Valann and Chyrie approached. Edging warily around the humans, the elves pulled Valann and Chyrie here and there, some embracing them, others just wanting to touch these oddly dressed strangers. At least twenty different elves tried to press goblets, pipes, bowls of fruit and nuts, or joints of meat into their hands; as many more draped gifts of bead, bone, or tooth-and-claw necklaces or bright garlands of flowers over their heads. Valann and Chyrie, having never received so energetic a welcome even from their own clan, were more dismayed than pleased by the excitement and were glad to retreat to a quiet corner to eat and watch Rowan's clan celebrate. A little more hesitantly, the elves offered the humans food and wine.

"I have never seen the like," Chyrie murmured to Valann, watching a handful of elves dance to the enthusiastic if not well-matched talent of nearly twice as many musicians. "Look—Redoak and Owl clan dancing together, and over there, Moon Lake and Inner Heart sharing cup. Do you think—can they be mates?"

"Indeed they are," a stick-slender female elf said, sitting down beside Chyrie. She was apparently Redoak, judging by her pale skin and the fiery red braid hanging down her back. "Welcome, kinsfolk. I am Brena. There are many mates between the clans now. It is one of the reasons our clan accepted Rowan's offer to join the clans. Many of us are barren. There had been no children born to Redoak for nearly two decades."

"But you have hopes," Chyrie observed, gesturing at the green band wrapping the elf's arm.

"I have hopes." Brena paused. "Is it true that you have two seeds growing in your womb?"

"Dusk says it is true," Chyrie said. "I have no reason to doubt him, but I can scarce believe it."

"I would ask—" Brena fell silent again, glancing at Valann. "We know nothing of Wilding customs, but those of us who wear the green cord tonight will dance the High Circle, and I would ask—"

Valann laughed.

"I am honored, of course, kinswoman," he said. "Why would you hesitate to ask?"

"Customs differ between clans." A tall male, bearing a striking resemblance to Brena, joined them, bearing a joint of roasted fowl. "We have heard it said that some clans couple only with their mates, like—" He glanced at the humans. "I am Suan, and Brena is my mate. It would be a great kindness if the mate of one touched by the Mother Forest would serve at her High Circle."

Val turned to Chyrie.

"You will be all right alone?" he asked tenderly.

"Hardly alone." Chyrie smiled. "Go and welcome. May you sow the seeds of many strong young ones tonight."

"There is not one in this village who would not honor your mate," Suan told Val. "She will lack for nothing we can provide her."

"Then, as I said, I am honored. But be warned, for my insatiable vixen of a mate will exhaust every man in your village if she is let." Val grinned. He kissed Chyrie before he stood. "You should dance for them, my own spirit." He took Brena's hand and let her lead him out of the firelit clearing.

"Is it true that you are a beast-speaker as well?" another elf asked Chyrie. "Gifted, and bearing child—two children? Are you an emissary of the Mother Forest?"

"It is true that I am a beast-speaker," Chyrie said patiently. "That much I know. The turn of the seasons will prove or disprove the rest. I would be well content with but one healthy child. If the Mother Forest has chosen to bless me with two, I will find it as much a marvel as do you."

"And look here," Suan murmured, taking her hand and tracing the vine design on her arm. "I had heard that some clans make art on their very bodies, but I had never seen such. Is there more than this?"

In answer, Chyrie stretched out her legs in the firelight and pulled up the edge of her leggings, showing how the vines had twined up the smooth amber skin.

"Val has been working his art upon me for five decades," Chyrie said, chuckling. "What he will do when I have no more undecorated skin, I do not know. Already my back is full covered. He tried to teach me the art, but I have no skill or patience for even the simplest of designs."

"Did Val say you danced?" Rivkah asked eagerly. "Like that?" She gestured to the hard-packed ground, where the elves—now hard-pressed for breath—were still dancing.

"Not like that," Chyrie admitted. "Wildings dance alone. I dance a sword dance."

"Sword dance?" Sharl asked, finally breaking his brooding silence.

"How many swords?" Suan asked.

"Eleven," Chyrie said. "Sometimes I can dance twelve, but I am only confident with eleven."

"Eleven," Suan repeated, impressed. "We have no sword dancers in the village now, and the last I saw could dance only eight. Would you possibly consent to dance for us? If you feel fit, of course, after your ordeal."

"What is a sword dance?" Sharl repeated.

"I will show you," Chyrie said, "if I may have the loan of ten swords."

She could have had thirty if she wanted them, as every elf near her thrust scabbards at her. While the elves in the clearing finished their dance, Chyrie selected ten blades. When the clearing was empty, Chyrie took the blades out of the scabbards and placed them carefully at angles, one sharp edge hammered firmly into the earth with a wooden mallet, the other edge gleaming upright. When all eleven swords were set to her satisfaction, Chyrie put the scabbards and mallet aside, laid her boots, tunic, and leggings over a log, and stepped back out into the clearing. A murmur passed from elf to elf as firelight glistened off her amber skin and the full extent of Valann's work became clear.

Starting at the soles of Chyrie's feet, two moondrop vines twined upward around her legs, branching richly around her torso, thinning only at her neck, and shoots trailed down her arms. In some places the vines bore buds or flowers; in others the moondrop berries hung full and ripe. On some prescient whim, Valann had even chosen to depict a cluster of golden berries on Chyrie's belly, which now swelled gently.

Chyrie nodded to the musicians, who began a slow but light beat, waiting for Chyrie to set the pace. Chyrie took a deep breath, engraved the pattern of the swords into her mind, and began to dance.

Valann had taught her the sword dance, as he had taught her so much else. He had thought the swiftness and energy of the sword dance more suited to Chyrie's nature than the more delicate and ethereal dances more commonly danced by elvan women. As usual, he had been right. Like most other beast-speakers, the wild blood was strong in Chyrie, and now it flowed fierce and hot in her veins. Strong and alive she felt,

young and fast and free, her feet carried on the notes of the
music, on moonlight and firelight, on the current of her blood,
on the very wind as she danced. Her feet flickered precisely,
yet ever more quickly, between the shining blades: like all life,
balanced on the sharp edge of the blade.

Now the musicians had her rhythm, and the drums beat
with the hot pulsing of her heart. Firelight flickered yellow
and red off her skin, freely sheened with sweat. The patterns
on her skin glowed like living things, the vines seeming to
flex and coil around her arms and legs, leaves reaching to
cup her small breasts. She felt the wild life of the Mother
Forest reaching up from the earth, reaching for her, reaching
for the children in her womb, flowing through her as it did
whenever she touched the mind of bird or beast. For that one
breathless moment, hanging suspended in time, she *was* the
Mother Forest, she was the dancing feet of the Mother Forest,
she was the Mother Forest made flesh, strong and wild and
ripe with new life.

But she could not hold it, desperately though she tried.
The fatigue and strain of the last few days was weighing
down her limbs; soon her pace would fall off and her feet
become unsteady. She felt a pang of reluctance; better to
go on, better to hold the moment for a few last heartbeats.
But no—one could spoil the dance by clinging to it past its
moment. Regretfully she fell back into her body, back to the
clearing, holding out just long enough for the music to reach
the proper climax, and she leaped free of the blades.

There was a moment, crouching there on the hardened earth,
where the pulse pounded in her ears so loudly that she could
not hear. The first sound she heard, however, was another kind
of pounding—the sound of elvan feet, fists, and sticks striking
the earth and the logs on which they sat as the elves cheered
their approbation. Chyrie grinned, waved an arm weakly in
reply, and stumbled out of the firelight circle, leaving other
elves to collect their swords and return hers.

Suan met her with a bucket of cool water and an absorbent
skin. While other dancers began a new circle, Chyrie washed
as best she could, then simply dumped the rest of the water
over her head before drying off. She reached for her clothes,

only to discover that while she danced, someone had replaced her torn tunic and leggings, stained with travel dirt and dried blood, with fresh garments. The leather was moonlight-soft as Wilding work, but unlike the functional Wilding garments, these were decorated with patterns of marvelously colored dyes in every rainbow shade.

"They are nothing to match your own ornamentation"— Suan grinned slyly—"but we thought it appropriate."

"The plants to make Valann's dyes are rare," Chyrie said, examining the patterns. "We would never have thought of using them on clothing. And you have colors, many colors we have never seen. Val would trade much for such colors if—" Chyrie fell silent. No matter what grandiose schemes for unity Rowan might have, she knew how unlikely it was that Wildings would ever agree even to trade with Inner Hearts. But something that would please Val so much—

"Your dancing was wonderful," Rivkah said quietly. Chyrie turned, and to her amazement, the mage sat alone on the log, her face in her hands. When she took her hands away, the human's face was wet with tears.

"Sharl and the others—they never saw anybody dance without—without clothes," Rivkah murmured, not meeting Chyrie's eyes. "He—they never spent as much time with the elves near us, and even they—they're different. So he—they wouldn't watch. I've got to go now. I just wanted to tell you that—that it was beautiful." She stood slowly, like an old woman, and walked quietly into the darkness.

"I hope you are not completely preoccupied with humans and clothing," Suan said gently when Chyrie continued to stare after the mage. "In truth I think you are better off without either."

Chyrie turned back.

"What are you suggesting?" Chyrie said, grinning.

"That while customs may differ among clans," Suan said solemnly, "surely it is true throughout the forest that we would be most grievously amiss in our hospitality to allow our kins-woman to go lonely to her bed while her mate enjoys the attentions of our ripe women."

Another elf, his height and dark hair marking him as a Moon Lake, daringly traced with his fingertip the butterfly design on her forearm.

"And we would surely offend the Mother Forest should we fail to show one touched by Her blessing every . . . consideration," he said.

"I would not force so unpleasant a duty upon you," Chyrie teased. "Mayhap I will find some elves more eager to entertain a visiting guest."

Suan laughed.

"Were it not for my care of your swelling belly, kinswoman, I would throw you over my shoulder and bear you away in my eagerness," he said. "Will this suffice?" Abruptly he scooped Chyrie up in his arms, and the others hurried forward to help sweep her, shrieking with laughter, over their heads—no mean feat, given the wide difference in height between the clans.

"I am convinced," Chyrie gasped between laughter as they bore her toward the huts. "Indeed I am."

When Chyrie awoke it was still dark; only firelight shone through the chinks in the hut. She was weary indeed—what a day it had been!—but her mouth was as dry as autumn leaves in autumn and she very urgently needed to make water. As gently as she could, Chyrie slid free of the arms around her and crept quietly out of the hut, snatching her clothing from the pile by the door.

In the Wilding village the rule was simply to go at least five hands of paces from the nearest hut and dig a small hole to bury the waste, but in a village as large as this, surely there must be another rule. Chyrie followed her nose and found a privy pit west of the village.

She hesitated outside the village. From somewhere to the north she could faintly hear chanting and could feel the prickle of magic—Dusk and the other Gifted? Something tickled at the wild blood in her, like the touch of a beast's thoughts. Curiously she reached out toward the strange sensation—

—and was suddenly swept away. She was soaring on a hawk's wings, running over the ground with the swiftness of a deer's feet, leaping from branch to branch with squirrels—

—and farther, flowing up from the roots of the trees, gathering strength, the minds of Gifted flowing together to push her outward, insubstantial of form, pulsing with warm green life, bursting out in a hundred directions like wind, like moonlight—

Chyrie hurriedly pulled back her awareness. Touching beast minds was one thing; to brush against the raw power of the forest spirits was something else altogether—something frightening.

Chyrie returned to the central clearing, remembering the large skins of wine she had seen there. The fire had burnt low, but there was one solitary figure sitting there; to Chyrie's surprise, she recognized the slouching figure as Rivkah. Chyrie hesitated, then picked up a wineskin and joined the human on the log.

"Where are the others?" Chyrie asked, pouring two goblets of wine and handing one to the mage.

"Rom and Ria—that's Doria—went back to the speaking hut to sleep," Rivkah said, nodding her thanks as she accepted the goblet. "Sharl is in that one there." She gestured. "He wanted to be alone to think, he said."

"It is late," Chyrie said. "Why do you not sleep?"

"I—I couldn't sleep," Rivkah mumbled. "It could be my last night of life."

"Customs differ," Chyrie said, "but although your transgression was great, *you* undoubtedly will not be killed."

"Why should I be spared?" Rivkah asked bitterly. "I'm the most dangerous to your people."

Chyrie glanced at her sideways.

"Because none of us, Inner Heart or Wilding, would kill a woman with child," she said. "Does your Lord Sharl know you carry his seed?"

Rivkah flushed darkly, glanced at Chyrie, then hurriedly looked away.

"No. He doesn't know. I was hardly sure myself yet." She glanced at Chyrie again. "How did you know? And how do you know it's his?"

"A woman with child has a different scent than one who is not." Chyrie shrugged. "The man Sharl's scent is also upon you, and you said yourself that human mates couple only one with the other. Sometimes, rarely, elvan women choose to keep only to their mates during their time of ripeness. I was doing so, wishing a child of Valann's seed."

"Do you think—" Rivkah hesitated. "Do you think Rowan knows?"

"Any elf with a nose knows it"—Chyrie grimaced—"as surely as they know it has been many days since you last bathed."

"And you're pregnant with twins," Rivkah said slowly. "They made it sound very rare."

"Rare? Unknown," Chyrie said. "At least I have never known such a thing to happen. Well it is known that humans litter like rabbits, but among us it is different. We are fortunate to bear at all. Many of our females never do."

"I see." Rivkah clenched her shaking hands. "And because we took you prisoner, because we kept you from returning to your people's healer, you might have missed that chance."

Chyrie shrugged.

"Having chosen one path, it is useless to speculate what might have waited at the end of another," she said. "An arrow loosed cannot be turned back. You did what you did, and I am with child nonetheless."

"I swear I didn't know." Rivkah covered her face with her hands. "The elves near us are different from your people, and they're very private, very aloof and secluded. I barely managed, through my mentor, to find one from whom I could learn his language by magic, so I could begin teaching Sharl. I swear I had no idea of—of the magnitude of what we were doing. I'm so terribly sorry."

"Your regret would not put seed in an empty womb," Chyrie said sourly. "Nor would it restore life to our bodies if we had been killed violating the boundaries of other clans."

"No. It wouldn't." Rivkah wiped her eyes. "But I had to tell you. Sitting here tonight, watching you dance and celebrate, just as if there were no army coming to march right over us—"

"All the more reason to dance twice as hard tonight," Chyrie interrupted.

"I thought what Sharl was doing was right," Rivkah said miserably. "I thought an alliance was the only hope for both humans and elves. I thought it justified—now I wonder if this whole thing hasn't been a terrible mistake. I wonder if we're not more danger to you than any army."

"Rowan will decide that." Chyrie shrugged. "She is like Valann—she thinks in many directions at once. It must have taken great courage and great wisdom to bring together four clans as she has done. She may well surprise us all with her judgment."

"Valann would like to see all four of us dead," Rivkah said with a sigh.

"Val is shamed that we were captured by humans, and that he allowed himself to be deceived and bespelled," Chyrie said. "He blames himself for my misfortune."

"And you?" Rivkah asked. "I've seen women kill themselves after being violated. They felt shamed for that."

"I am shamed to have been surprised by a handful of gigantic, reeking humans making enough noise to alert every beast in the wood," Chyrie said wryly. "That shames me indeed. But that they forced me, no. I fought as best I could, and that is all I could do. It is more shameful that I was deceived by enemies wearing the guise of friends."

"I'm sorry," Rivkah said again. "I hope that somehow I can make amends. If I live to do so," she added.

"If you fear your fate, all the more reason to spend this night in the arms of your mate, rather than sitting on a log alone," Chyrie said. "Why not tell him of the child? That joy might cheer him."

"You don't understand. It's not that simple," Rivkah said wearily. "He's not my husband. He's titled nobility and I'm a commoner. One day he'll marry a noble lady."

"What has that to do with the child you bear?" Chyrie asked, mystified.

"He's not my husband," Rivkah repeated. "Not my—my mate, you would say, like Rom and Ria. Among my people, it's shameful for a woman to bear a child to a man she's not married to. It would be an embarrassment to Sharl."

Chyrie threw up her hands.

"Why must humans make every matter so complicated?" she demanded. "Go and couple with your man. If you die tomorrow, you have had a night of pleasure. If you live, you will have at least one pleasant memory of the forest, and you can tell him that it was the magic of the Mother Forest that put the child in your belly, and he can blame us. In any wise, tomorrow there will be talk of fighting and death. Let tonight, at least, be a night of life."

Rivkah smiled wearily.

"You seem very wise yourself," she said. "Thank you for listening. And for the advice." She stood.

Chyrie raised her goblet in farewell, picked up the wineskin, and turned back to Suan's hut.

VI

THE INNER HEART village was much quieter in the early morning when Valann and Chyrie met the four humans again in Rowan's speaking hut. Most of the village's elves, sated by the previous night's revels, were still asleep. A few, however, roused themselves to lay a few platters of cold meat, fruit, and nuts in the speaking hut.

Rowan and Dusk looked anything but rested; judging from their drawn faces and shadowed eyes, they had spent a frantic night.

When they had all gathered, Rowan spread out the same map she had shown the night before; now, however, it contained many more clan symbols than it had.

"We managed to contact many clans," she said. "Hopefully they, in turn, will contact others. Some have responded to my request for a meeting. Others"—she glanced at Valann and Chyrie—"have not. I will continue to try, of course. There is nothing else to be done."

Sharl leaned forward.

"With respect, lady," he said, "I am as concerned for my people as you are for yours. Surely you can sympathize with that. Will you allow me to plead that whatever becomes of us, that at least I can send a warning to my folk, as you have to yours?"

Rowan ignored him.

"I fairly took you as my prisoners," she said to Valann

and Chyrie. "You asked the price of your release. Are you prepared to abide by my judgment, both of yourselves and of these humans?"

"We are, Grandmother," Valann said quietly, "under your promise of justice and safety for myself and my mate, and the lives she carries."

"Nothing concerns me more than the safety of your mate and her unborn children," Rowan said quietly. "In the times to come we may all need the inspiration of seeing the blessing of the Mother Forest made flesh to sustain us."

She turned to Sharl.

"That you and your companions trespassed upon lands not your own and upon the sacred ground of the Forest Altars, and that you spilled blood in violation of the peace bond there, I am willing to forgive, for by doing so you preserved the lives of two precious to us," she said. "However, you are charged with abducting and bespelling the Wildings Valann and Chyrie. Honorable capture and ransom are a custom of the forest; however, your actions took place under the guise of food and fire, a very serious offense, indeed. Moreover, by your actions you interfered with the process of reproduction and endangered an elf who was certainly fertile and possibly with child, and there is no more serious transgression known in the forest.

"Your scheming to use Valann and Chyrie as hostages against a battle alliance and trade agreement are another matter," Rowan said slowly. "Though your actions gall me, they violate no law of my people or custom of the forest. You owe no loyalty to out-kin, no more than we to you. Therefore your only offenses are against Valann and Chyrie, and by our custom they are entitled to exact whatever penalty they see fit with their own hand."

Valann smiled grimly.

"A wise custom, indeed!"

"However," Rowan said, gazing sternly at Valann, "as Valann and Chyrie have, as my prisoners, remanded both their fate and yours into my judgment, I will determine your penance, and this is what I have decided:

"That the four humans, Sharl, Rivkah, Romuel, and Doria will return to their city—"

"What?" Valann roared. "Is this the justice you—"

"Be silent," Dusk said quietly, but with authority, "or you will be removed."

Valann glowered, but said no more.

"The four humans will return to their city," Rowan repeated, "under a geas of our making. Under that geas, they will render unto the elves of the Heartwood every assistance, including weapons and supplies, and they will agree to shelter in the city, during any time of battle or disaster, the children, elderly, and infirm of our people, and any females who are ripe or with child for their protection. The humans will not tell their people of this judgment or of the geas, but will act as if of their own accord, and when any conflict is ended, if they still live, will return to the forest to act as hostages against a trade agreement favorable to the elves."

Valann sighed heavily, but nodded.

"I see your wisdom, Grandmother," he said. "I do not like it, but I can agree with it."

"I have not yet finished dispensing it," Rowan said, though she smiled. "And I fear you will like it even less, for I wish you and Chyrie to return to the human city with them."

Val gaped, shocked to utter silence, but Chyrie growled her outrage.

"You cannot be serious," she said. "First they would make us hostages, and now you would! Is this our justice, that we have gained nothing?"

Rowan shook her head, and reached over to touch Chyrie's cheek.

"You are one I would have safe behind stone walls and many swords," she said. "And we must have an envoy among the humans, one who can be trusted. And you are a beast-speaker who can send and receive messages between the two peoples. If you, who must be protected in any wise, will serve that purpose, then another beast-speaker can be spared to remain in the forest and continue our work here. Do you understand?"

"I understand that I must return to stand with my clan," Chyrie said angrily. "I understand that my unborn children belong to me, to Valann, and to their clan, not to you or your people. We are not air and water, to belong to all alike. That I understand."

"Then perhaps you will also understand this," Rowan said quietly. "You are, by your own admission, fairly my prisoners and under my command. Remember that."

Chyrie ground her teeth, but sat back down beside Valann.

"Yes, Grandmother," she said quietly.

"I like this deal no better than Chyrie does," Sharl protested. "My people will have enough problems preparing for war without having to worry about the elves as well."

"I could say the same of my folk," Rowan said serenely. "But that did not trouble *you* when you laid your plans to use us. Now we will use you in the same manner, and if it causes you difficulty, I do not grieve for it."

"What are we supposed to do with them?" Sharl demanded. "None of my people speak their language, any more than they speak ours."

"You learned our language by magic," Rowan said to Rivkah, who looked up, amazed. "Can you teach it so?"

"How did you—" Rivkah shook her head. "I don't think so. My mentor did it, and he's much stronger than me. I know the spell, but it's not my—my area of skill."

"Then Dusk will lend his power to yours," Rowan said, "as well as to ensure you work no mischief with your sorcery. After you have accepted our geas, of course."

Sharl scowled at Valann, who returned his glare. Rivkah glanced tentatively at Chyrie, who sighed explosively.

"You said yourself that the abduction of Valann and Chyrie were the only crimes you would charge us with," Sharl said persuasively. "Romuel and Doria had no part in that. Let them go back to Allanmere free of your geas, and you can do as you like with Rivkah and myself."

Rowan laughed.

"You are truly a leader," she said. "You think as I would— to yet have your people warned with no encumbrances upon them. But I will not have it. To succeed you must still ally with us, and that you will do on my terms or none. And even for your people to pass through the rest of the forest you must have the safe conduct I have bargained with the other clans, and that I will not give unless you consent."

"I am all the hostage you need," Sharl argued. "Let the others go free."

"I will not," Rowan said firmly. "You are too ready to sacrifice yourself, and I do not trust your mage. There will be no bargain. You will all take my geas or none."

"And what of Valann and Chyrie?" Sharl demanded. "What geas will you place upon them?"

"None," Rowan said. "As any beast-speaker knows, you cannot bind a wild one. You can only ask, and pray that it will trust you enough to obey." She looked significantly at Chyrie.

Valann and Chyrie exchanged sober glances.

(What are your thoughts?) Chyrie asked.

(She has a Matriarch's wisdom,) Valann thought. (Her reasoning is sound.)

"We will obey, Grandmother," Chyrie said reluctantly, and Valann nodded.

"And your answer?" Dusk asked Sharl.

Sharl frowned, then sighed.

"We have no choice," he said. "For my people to be warned, I have no choice but to accept your terms."

"That is true," Rowan said serenely. She nodded to Dusk, who poured wine from a small skin into four goblets.

"As you bespelled my kinsfolk's wine, we have done the same," Rowan said. "This is the geas you will accept. You will treat Valann and Chyrie with every respect. You will not seek to harm or confine or restrain them in any way, and you will cast no magic upon either of them except at their request. You will make every effort to make them recompense for your actions against them. You will house and protect any elves we send to you and treat them with every courtesy. You will trade weapons and supplies with us on terms I will set. You will tell no other of your actions against Valann and Chyrie or of this geas, and you will make no effort, magical or otherwise, to break the geas. When the battle is over, if any of you survive, you will return to Inner Heart to act as hostages against the negotiation of a permanent agreement between the forest and the city. Those are the terms I set upon you. Drink, and it is done."

Sharl spoke at some length to his companions in the human tongue, then slowly raised his glass and drank. Rivkah drank with less hesitation, and Romuel and Doria, watching Sharl, also drank. When they finished, Doria said something, and Rivkah laughed wryly.

"She says"—the mage chuckled—"that if we can at least bargain for some of your excellent wine, there will be one thing about this journey she won't regret."

"Let us hope there will be other joyful memories before it is done," Rowan sighed. She turned to Rivkah. "Come, mage, a spell so that my kinsfolk will not be lonely in a place where they can neither speak to nor understand its people."

Rivkah hesitated. "I haven't had much experience with mages combining power," she said.

"I have," Dusk assured her.

"Then—" She glanced at Valann and Chyrie. "You have to ask me to cast the spell."

Valann and Chyrie exchanged glances again, this time more doubtfully.

"I ask it," Valann said at last. "You will cast your magic on me first."

"No," Chyrie protested. "I will be the first."

"You will *not*," Valann said firmly. "You are with child."

"I am your mate," Chyrie said stubbornly, setting her jaw.

"All right. Don't argue. Somebody has to be first, and it might as well be Valann." Rivkah took another swallow of wine to fortify herself. "It should be a little easier this time, because I can give you the language from myself instead of having to take it from someone else. Valann, if you'll stand in front of me—"

Valann reluctantly obeyed, and Rivkah laid one hand on his head, one across the front of his throat. Dusk laid his hands over Rivkah's and nodded.

Rivkah began chanting steadily, her eyes half closed in concentration. Slowly her voice deepened, taking on a sing-song quality. Chyrie felt the tingle of magic growing within her; without warning, she stretched out her awareness for Valann's thoughts as she had a thousand times before, and *reached*.

Magic swirled upward from Dusk, from Rivkah, and into Valann—and from him into Chyrie. Blurred, confused fragments of imagery blinked through both minds like flashes of lightning. Gradually the confusing bombardment slowed as Rivkah's voice raised again, and she stopped.

"That was easier than I thought," she said. "Valann, try it."

"Try what?" Valann asked. He whirled on Chyrie. "If I were to speak," he said, "it would be to chastise this most stubborn of elves. That was a foolhardy thing to do."

"What?" Rivkah asked confusedly. "What did she do?"

"They are mates in spirit, and she a beast-speaker accustomed to casting out her mind," Dusk panted, obviously more wearied than the mage. "She joined him in his thoughts. I felt it. He is right. It was a great risk. I think you have cast two spells for one."

"But why—" Rivkah began.

"Never mind, never mind," Sharl interrupted in the human tongue. "We need to leave as quickly as possible, and if they can understand me now, then the language lesson is over and we can go."

Rivkah glanced at the elves dubiously.

"I understand you," Valann said in the same language, then raised his eyebrows in mild surprise.

"As do I," Chyrie said, then grimaced. The strange sounds seemed to grate at her throat.

"Good," Sharl said, unimpressed. He turned to Rowan. "If you will permit us, then, we must be on our way. My people have preparations to make, no less than yours—more, if we are to fulfill the terms you have set upon us. Will you allow us to leave, so that we waste no more riding light?"

"You may go," Rowan said calmly. "Your riding beasts await you, and we have replenished your supplies of food and drink, and given you gifts and samples of trade goods to take back to your people with you."

Sharl stared at her blankly, then scowled.

"You knew I would agree. You knew it all along," he demanded.

Rowan smiled.

"Naturally I knew," she said. "No true leader of his people could have chosen otherwise. Take that as praise, if you will, for I cannot fault your courage, nor your loyalty to those who look to you for guidance. Now go to them, and think upon us with what kindness you can."

Sharl beckoned imperiously to them, and Rivkah, Romuel, and Doria quickly followed; Chyrie and Valann, however, lingered to walk more slowly with Rowan, while Dusk disappeared on some errand.

"Messages have been sent to the clans between here and the city," Rowan told them. "All but Blue-eyes have answered, agreeing to allow you safe passage."

"But are the Blue-eyes not the westernmost clan," Valann asked, "at the very edge of the forest?"

"Yes, and that concerns me," Rowan said, her brow wrinkling. "Their clan has been most harassed of all by the humans, and at one time, when they lived more to the east, there was an old enmity with us. They are most hostile about their boundaries, and who can fault them for it? But they will not answer our sendings at all. I cannot speak for their behavior."

Chyrie cut a strip of blue-dyed leather from the hem of her tunic and twisted it with the green cord she had worn before, and tied the two around her arm.

"This should suffice," she said. "If the Blue-eyes have at least heard your messages, they know that we but pass through their lands briefly, and no matter how unfavorably they might look upon the humans, they would not molest an elvan woman with child."

"I pray you are correct," Rowan said somberly. "I am half minded to send some of my people with you, but that might be seen as a greater affront, if they still hold hostility against my people. So far as I know, they could have no quarrel with Wilding, and they know the blessing of the Mother Forest you bear, Chyrie. You should be safe enough." She hesitated.

"What troubles you?" Valann asked.

"I would ask something more of you," Rowan said slowly. "Wilding did not answer my messages. I would ask that you add your word to mine, and send a message to your people asking your Eldest at least to hear my words and consider them. I cannot order you to do so, but I ask it."

Valann and Chyrie looked soberly at each other.

"I will send the message," Chyrie said at last, "for you have treated us with kindness beyond all expectation. But I must tell you that if our Eldest heard your words, still he will not agree to join with you. Of that I am certain. But I will ask him as you say."

By this time they had reached the central clearing of the village, where the horses were indeed waiting. Chyrie had to chuckle; each animal had been festooned with garlands of leaves and flowers, designs painted on each horse with colored clay, and brightly colored leather strips woven into manes and tails. The leather tack had been polished to a shiny gloss, and every scratch or tear in the leather skillfully mended. The saddlebags on each horse brimmed with goods, and additional leather sacks and wineskins had been added to the load of the one riderless horse. The humans had already mounted their horses, although Sharl was looking from one decorated animal to the other with a thoroughly disgusted expression.

Elves crowded around Valann and Chyrie, pressing last gifts of flowers, scented herb bags, and small packets of snacks and sweets. Dusk appeared as if by magic; a handsome black-and-gold brighthawk, so named because the large predator often hunted fish in the Brightwater River itself, perched on his wrist.

"I wish you could have stayed longer," he told Chyrie. "Had I not been so busy last night—" He grinned slyly and shrugged. "There will be another time."

He reached out and took her hand, clasped it around his extended wrist. The brighthawk cocked its head inquiringly, fixed its obsidian eyes on Chyrie, then hopped from Dusk's wrist to hers. She had no leather wrist shield like Dusk's, and the brighthawk's talons dug painfully into her skin, but the discomfort was drowned by the feel of the brighthawk's mind—fierce and powerful, but at the same time welcoming and almost soothing, like the soft, comfortable feel of an old, well-worn tunic.

"I raised him from the egg," Dusk said quietly. "He is well accustomed to a beast-speaker's touch and his range is considerable. He will be your companion now. It is my hope that our thoughts may touch through him."

Chyrie gave the hawk a nudge with her mind and it hopped to her shoulder, where the thicker leather provided more protection.

"His mind has the feel of you," Chyrie murmured. She smiled at Dusk. "I am honored, kinsman."

Dusk turned to Valann.

"There is also a gift for you," he said. "Chyrie mentioned that we had found some new colors you did not have. We do not know how you mix your dyes, but we have placed the raw colors in pots in your packs. You will honor us if we one day see our colors in your work."

Valann's eyes widened with eagerness, and he could not suppress an involuntary glance at his saddlebags.

"You could give me no greater a gift," he said quietly. "When next I visit, I will find the time to give some of your folk designs of their own, if they wish it."

"Enough, enough," Sharl growled. "While you spend the day taking leave of your friends, we lose daylight."

Chyrie scowled and Valann sighed heavily, but they led their horse to a convenient stump and mounted, Valann scrambling up first to pull Chyrie in front of him.

"Fare well, kinsfolk," Rowan said, reaching to touch Valann's fingertips, then Chyrie's. "May the road that leads you back to us be a short one. I will not ask that the Mother Forest bless you with rich soil and ripe seed, for it seems She has already done so." She smiled. "Much of our hopes rest with you, my friends. Keep safe and happy."

"And you, Grandmother," Valann said. He clasped her hand. "Happiness and prosperity to you and your people."

Then they had to quickly urge their horse forward, for Sharl, disinclined to wait, was already leading the others back toward the road, consulting a map that Rowan had given him.

"Four days," Sharl grumbled as he urged them as quickly as he could down the narrow trail leading back to the common road. "As fast as we can go on this pitiful trail, it's going to be four days at least." He apparently trusted Rivkah's magic, for now that he had left the village he was speaking the human tongue, apparently as eager to be free of the elvan language as he was of the elves themselves. Rivkah, however, continued to use the elvan tongue, explaining that if they were to live in a city bordering on an elvan forest and hope to foster good relations, she had to perfect her own speech.

"It took you more days to reach the center of the forest," Val said practically. "Why should it take fewer to leave it?"

"On open ground I can make fifteen leagues on a good day," Sharl said disgustedly. "In the forest I'm doing well to travel a third of that, and this trail is by no means straight, either. And nothing is slowing that army, that's sure."

"Nor speeding it," Val said, brushing at the brighthawk's tail feathers as they tickled his nose. "Love, can he not find another perch while we ride?"

"Well for my shoulder if he does." Chyrie chuckled. She prodded the hawk with a thought and he launched himself skyward. "Best he find shelter anyway, for the coming storm may be hard."

"Storm?" Rivkah looked up into the thick canopy of leaves. "How can you tell?"

"Anyone can smell it in the air," Val said. "Even the horses can tell." The animals were, indeed, restless and twitchy.

"I thought they were just ashamed of their ridiculous appearance," Sharl said sourly. "Can you smell how soon we might expect this torrent?"

A loud crack of thunder made the horses dance.

"Very soon," Chyrie said blithely.

"Wonderful," Sharl sighed. "One more thing to slow us down. Rivkah, can you do anything about it?"

Rivkah closed her eyes briefly, then shook her head.

"It's a whole line of storms, coming fast," she said. "It would take ten mages to stop it now."

"Your kind can halt a storm?" Chyrie asked amazedly. "How is such a thing possible?"

"It isn't difficult magic," Rivkah said. "We can cause rain, too, when conditions are right. But conditions are wrong, now, for stopping one. It will likely rain all day and all night."

"Likely," Val said cheerfully. "Late spring is a wet season here. As well it rains now, for we have been over half a moon dry, and the young plants need water."

"I can keep the rain off us," Rivkah offered. "For a few hours, anyway. Maybe long enough to get us to camp for the night."

"That will do," Sharl said distractedly. He spurred his horse to a faster pace, and Chyrie, who had been dispatching a squirrel to the Wildings as Rowan had requested, cried out.

"Enough of that," Val said sharply. "You are paining my mate."

"What's the matter?" Rivkah said, concerned. "I thought Chyrie was healed."

"Kicking your beasts with those metal prongs," Val said. "She is a beast-speaker, and their pains hurt her. Cease that now."

Sharl scowled darkly, but the geas forced him to stop. The horse immediately slowed to a walk.

"You didn't complain before we ran into those Moon Lakes," the lord demanded.

"We used her ability to send messages," Val told him. "She had to keep it secret, lest your mage cast some additional magic to prevent our one hope of rescue."

"These horses," Sharl said between gritted teeth, "are accustomed to spurs. How do you propose I get any speed out of them without it? You see yourself that they slowed the minute I stopped."

"Do you treat your people thus, beating and ordering them without giving reason?" Chyrie said exasperatedly. "Well, it is known that a stag will come to you more eagerly for an apple than an arrow. That is why beast-speakers were given to their clans by the Mother Forest."

She touched one horse after the other, enjoying the unfamiliar feel of their minds; it took her a moment to understand them, but they, like flocking birds, were accustomed to receiving direction from a leader, and immediately responded to her urging to quicken their pace. Sharl yelped in startlement as his mount leaped forward, setting a pace as quick as the quality of the trail and the horse's endurance could reasonably maintain.

"That's a remarkable gift," Rivkah said to Chyrie, dropping back to ride as nearly beside them as the narrow trail would allow. "So that's what Rowan and Dusk meant when they were talking about beast-speakers, and when he gave you the hawk. They do what you say, is that it?"

"They do as I tell them if they are so minded." Chyrie shrugged. "It is much as if you approached a stranger and asked a boon of him—you must give good reason, and perhaps offer something in return."

"But if you feel their pain," Rivkah said slowly, "how do you hunt? And aren't there animals dying all around you every minute in a forest like this?"

"She does not hunt, nor do any hunt in her presence," Val said, folding his arms protectively around Chyrie. "That is the price of her gift. The many small pains and deaths around her, those are like the sound of crickets at night—from hearing them so often, one learns to ignore them."

"That is a part of it," Chyrie said. "The greater pains I learn to close out in reflex, as you would close your eyes if I thrust my fingers at them. But it is no more pleasant for me to keep my mind closed tight than for you to keep your eyes so closed always. I am accustomed to receiving signs, warnings, tidings from the small lives around me."

Thunder crashed again, and a few early spatters of rain trickled down through the leaves. The bird songs changed as the small life of the forest found shelter where it could. Rivkah raised her hand and started to chant, but then stopped, glancing ruefully at Val and Chyrie.

"Not us," Val said sternly. "We will have no more of your magic."

Rivkah nodded and resumed her chant, riding a little forward so that her gesture included the humans and the packhorse but not Val and Chyrie. As the rainfall increased, Chyrie could see the effect of the woman's magic—the bright clay decorating their horse dripped and ran off, but the humans and their horses remained dry, although the horses slowed as the trail quickly grew muddy. Chyrie wondered at them; it was convenient to keep the supplies dry, but Chyrie welcomed the freshness of the warm rain running down her hot face.

Then she chuckled, recognizing in herself one of the mild fevers that often accompanied elvan pregnancy; probably the others found the cooling rain much less pleasant than she did.

The brighthawk screamed above her, and suddenly Chyrie felt herself sharing its eyes, annoyed by the irritating drip of rain on their feathers, their sharp eyes seeking through the brush for small animals fleeing the rain back to their dens, powerful wings beating the air as they gained height, hot blood running fierce as they sighted a rabbit below. Together they dove—

Chyrie broke free just before the hawk reached its prey, quickly shutting herself off from the rabbit's death. Sometimes she could follow through, burying herself in the fierce hunger and joy of the hunter, but today, with new life in her womb, she did not want to feel anything die.

As if in answer, there was a slight stirring in her belly, the faintest flutter of movement under Val's hand where he held her. Val froze for a moment, then his incredulous joy filled her mind as the hawk's hunger had.

The trees, the animals, the thirsty soil, all welcomed the rain like a lover, and suddenly Chyrie felt a part of it all—the new seeds, brimming with life, awaiting only the caress of the rain to make them push up toward the sun; the animals, many of them swelling with life even as she did, or only now calling their mates to couple with them in dens, or nests, or under the warm spring rain; life pulsing warmly up from the earth through the trees until they could not contain their joy and blossoms burst forth at the end of their branches, shouting the glory of the Mother Forest.

Chyrie slid out of Val's grasp and, a little clumsily, dropped to the ground, wanting to feel all that life pulsing under her feet. She trotted alongside the horses for a while until the wild blood surged up through her and would not be contained, and then she ran ahead recklessly, leaping over the roots that crossed the path, her toes squelching through the rich mud, slipping and sliding in the wetter spots.

Her clothing grew sodden and she ripped it off, flinging it carelessly into the brush at the side of the trail. She ran until the breath wheezed loudly through her lungs and pain stitched up her side, trying to keep pace with the fierce throb of her heart, until her body could no longer keep up with the pull of the wild blood to run faster, faster, until she took flight herself. Frustrated, she dropped to her knees on the trail and howled, a free, joyous sound, and the wind howled back at her as a bolt of lightning flashed so brightly that each leaf shone.

Thunder drowned out the sound of the hoofbeats behind her until the riders nearly overran her. The horses slid wildly in the mud or veered into the brush beside the trail, and Val slid from his horse, laughing.

"What in the world?" Sharl demanded, his face crimson with rage and embarrassment.

"Has my vixen exhausted her wild blood for a time?" He chuckled. He threw her sodden clothing over the packhorse's load and pulled a thick fur from the pack.

"Come," he said gently. "You will be chilled, and that is not healthful for a woman with child."

Chyrie was shaking violently, more with excitement than cold, but she let Val help her back onto the horse's back, climb back up behind her, and wrap both of them in the fur as Sharl angrily motioned them forward again.

The horse was warm under her and Val behind her, and the skin, good elvan tanning, easily shed the rain. The storm rumbled on fiercer than ever, but inside the fur, warmth drove out the storm.

Valann slid his hands over her rain-slicked skin.

(They think you are mad,) he thought, nuzzling the back of her neck. (They all think you have gone as mad as a fox with the foaming-mouth sickness.)

(Perhaps I am,) Chyrie thought back amusedly, snuggling closer to him. (What do you think?)

Val chuckled again, and Chyrie caught a flashing vision of how he had seen her—naked and dripping with mud and rain, her sodden hair hanging wildly in her face, a wild beast's expression in her eyes.

(I think I would have liked to couple with you there in the dirt like a wolf and his bitch,) he thought hotly, gently nipping the back of her neck. (And did I not fear the chill of the rain on you after you had run so hard, I would have done it, even while that human Sharl glared down at us and shouted his curses at our delay. I would do it now, would we not tumble off the back of this fleshy mountain like two overamorous squirrels off a branch.)

Chyrie chuckled at the thought, although under Val's caresses she grew warmer than the protection of the fur could account for.

(Even our impatient human lord must stop for the night,) she thought back. She giggled as his fingers found a ticklish spot under her ribs. (Then, if you wish, I will dump a skin of water over my head and roll in the dirt with you.)

"If you will roll in the furs with me, that will suffice," Val said warmly. "And if the storm does not slacken soon, we will have to stop in any wise."

The storm did not slacken; instead, it grew worse, but Sharl pressed on until it became apparent that they would soon be unable to see the road. Even then Sharl wanted to continue, but when they found a likely campsite by the roadside, even Rivkah sided with Val, and Sharl reluctantly gave in.

The camp had obviously been used before, probably by Gray Rock patrols; the stone-lined firepit was useless in the rain, but the cleared areas had grown over with moss, a surface much preferable to the muddy ground. Sharl, Rivkah, Romuel, and Doria set up waxed tents in the clearing of the same odd woven fiber that they wore, but Val and Chyrie moved back farther into the forest and chose some high bushes under which to place their waxed-hide tent, both for privacy and additional protection from the rain and wind.

There was no hope of a hot supper, but the elves at Inner Heart had stuffed their packs with fresh and dried fruits and tubers, spiced dried meat, clay pots of honey, wrapped packets of sap-sugar, and journey cakes of ground meat and fat, dried fruit and crushed nuts. The humans huddled miserably in their tents, shouting at each other over the storm, but Val found their clay firepot and scavenged enough dry bark and wood under trees for a small fire to light the tent and heat spiced wine.

By the light of their small fire, Val took out his dye pots and the new pots that the Inner Hearts had given him, and he exclaimed delightedly as he tested one new color after another.

"These shades will double the number of colors I have," Val said, experimentally blending two powders with some fat and testing a smear against his skin. "There will be no color in the forest I cannot make."

"And what will you do with those magnificent colors?" Chyrie laughed. "There remains little enough skin you have not already covered with designs."

"There is room for several more butterflies," Val mused, eyeing Chyrie's naked body appreciatively. "Some flowers here"—touching a spot on her hip—"and here, and berries here, I think. But first I will go back and enhance the colors on the old designs."

Chyrie stretched luxuriantly on the thick fur they had spread on the ground.

"Can you think of nothing better to use on me than your needles?" she asked teasingly.

Valann smiled and covered his pots.

"A difficult choice," he said. "But for tonight, my new colors can wait."

The storm broke during the night and the sun shone brilliantly on the wet leaves, a thousand new seeds springing into leaf and flower wherever the warm rays touched, and small new mushrooms popping up in the shady spots as if by magic. Val and Chyrie, unlike Sharl, were delighted that the muddy trail caused a necessarily slow pace; there was much to see, and in any event, they were much less eager to leave the forest than the humans. Sharl fumed and Rivkah worried, but Val and Chyrie ran beside the horses much of the time, sometimes stopping to harvest tender new greens for the pot or to nibble as they ran.

The weather held clear for two days and nights, and when they passed through Gray Rock, Swiftfoot, and Spotted Fawn lands without mishap, Sharl's foul mood lifted somewhat. Sometimes the humans would sing road songs, which Val and Chyrie enjoyed immensely, although the humans (with the exception of Doria, who turned out to have a lovely voice) sang with more enthusiasm and volume than skill. Val and Chyrie refused to share the humans' food and wine at night, but after the first night they did share the wild potherbs, seasonings, roots, and mushrooms they had collected as they traveled, and they would sit at the humans' fire for a little conversation before retiring to their own invariably secluded camp.

The third night out from the Inner Heart village, they stopped for the night on Longear land. Before they had more than half unloaded the horses, several of the Longears themselves appeared, hovering shyly at the fringes of the clearing and peering over the bushes, the long, sharply pointed ears for which they had been named twitching excitedly.

It took several minutes of persuasion from Val and Chyrie before the dark-skinned, wiry Longears would venture out from their hiding places and approach, but they clustered around Chyrie eagerly, hesitantly touching her belly with a certain reverence. They had brought gifts of fresh game, but would not place it over the fire until the humans had backed well away. Even then, they would not share the food, but crouched just outside the firelit ring, their eyes reflecting the flames, and murmured quietly among themselves.

"Speak, Longears," Val urged, holding out a wineskin. "What tidings can you give us?"

They ignored the skin of wine, and spoke so softly that Val and Chyrie could not tell which elf was speaking.

"You must not stop on Blue-eyes land," one murmured.

"They have vowed to kill the humans and take Valann and Chyrie as hostages," another said fearfully.

"They want no alliance of the elvan clans."

"They say they will suffer more than any if elf allies with human."

"They are likely correct," one admitted. "The land bordering the western edge is theirs."

"And humans must pass their land to reach the elvan clans."

"And the reverse is true, too."

"They fear all this passing back and forth will frighten away their game." There they stopped, as if waiting for Valann and Chyrie to refute their statements.

"If a human army assaults the forest," Valann said slowly, "every clan in the forest will be disturbed, and all border clans most of all. It is true that some of the game will flee deeper into the forest, for the inner lands will be the least disturbed unless the humans actually penetrate the borders. But it is also true that if the border clans are left without aid and their game moves inward, so too will they move inward, raiding the other clans for food."

"Rowan of Inner Heart proposes an alliance," one of the Longears whispered.

"Such a thing is unheard of."

"Kin are kin, and out-kin are out-kin."

"But if the Mother Forest has sent us a sign, we must listen to Her counsel."

They looked expectantly at Chyrie, and Chyrie turned, troubled, to Valann.

"Rowan is a wise Matriarch," Valann told them. "She sees much that we, younger and less wise, do not, and we go to further her plans as she bid us. But Valann and Chyrie speak only for Valann and Chyrie. We do not speak for the Mother Forest, or even for Wilding. Our Eldest is also old, and he is also wise, and I think he will not agree with Rowan. There are many ways of seeing. We cannot advise Longear how to act."

"Whether Blue-eyes allies with Inner Heart or the humans, or they do not," Chyrie added, "they will still suffer if an army reaches the human city of Allanmere, for the invading humans will doubtless raid the forest for food and timber. And then Blue-eyes' game will flee in any wise, and Blue-eyes will then raid Longear land in turn. That is the way of things."

"We are not strong. If we anger Blue-eyes and they attack us, we will fall."

"If we ally with Inner Heart, what help will we receive against Blue-eyes? Inner Heart is far away, and Blue-eyes is close."

"We have angered Blue-eyes already, by letting you pass through our lands."

(They not only have long ears as rabbits do, but the same cowardice,) Valann thought disgustedly. Aloud, he said, "Longear must decide what they will do. If kin is kin and out-kin is out-kin, then why should Longear concern themselves with Blue-eyes' wishes? Decide for yourselves what is right and what is not. That is why the Mother Forest gave you minds to think."

The Longears whispered together for a long time. At last one of them, an older male with a long white scar running down his face, inched forward, his large brown eyes cast downward.

"Valann and Chyrie have been touched by the Mother Forest," he murmured, barely above a whisper. "They follow the bidding of Rowan of Inner Heart. The Mother Forest would not have blessed them if they were walking the wrong trail. Valann and Chyrie must therefore be doing the will of the Mother Forest. Longear will do the same."

Not waiting for an answer, the Longears melted back into the brush as quietly as they had come.

"Why not just tell them to kill us and be done with it?" Sharl scowled. "You seem determined not to help us."

"We owe you nothing," Chyrie said distractedly. She turned to Valann. "But I like it not, that other clans see us as messengers of the Mother Forest, showing them that they should obey Rowan."

"I don't doubt Rowan is hoping for that," Rivkah said. "She's a clever leader. I'm sure she planned that other clans see you as an example."

"And what are your thoughts about the Blue-eyes?" Val asked, removing his dye pots from their pack. Chyrie obligingly pulled off her tunic.

"We'll use Rivkah's magic to conceal us, just as we did coming into the forest," Sharl said, looking anywhere but at Chyrie. "If it hadn't drained her so thoroughly to heal Valann and—well—"

"And to bespell us," Val said sourly. "You may as well say it."

"Well, yes, and that," Sharl admitted, "she could have been concealing us after we picked up the two of you, and we could have got through the forest without all this trouble."

Val started to retort, but merely frowned and shook his head, and began a new vine branch just under Chyrie's left shoulder.

"Doesn't that hurt?" Romuel asked, and Chyrie almost jumped; to the best of her memory, it was the first time that the burly warrior had addressed her or Val directly. But then, it had only been a few days that she could have understood him if he had.

"The sting of a bee or the prick of a firethorn is more painful," Chyrie said. "I have largely grown accustomed to it over the years."

"How long has Valann been making pictures on you?" Doria asked, fascinated, her fingers picking idly on the small lute she carried.

"He began the night we were mated." Chyrie chuckled. "He said he would make two vines to climb up my body—one for him, one for me. He began very, very late that night, and by that time, I was too weary to feel the prick of his needles."

"Can you fault me for that?" Val smiled. "It had been a trying time for me. We had promised to mate a decade before," he said in answer to Rivkah's curious look. "But Chyrie had not yet passed her trials of adulthood, and we could not couple. And because she had not passed her trials, and was a beast-speaker as well, her mind was yet too open to thoughts around her, and so we lived apart from other Wildings to protect her. The night Chyrie passed into womanhood, that very night we were mated, and I vow she did not stand upon her feet for a hand of days."

"How old were you when you were—mated?" Rivkah asked Chyrie.

"It was the first year of my third decade," she said. "I was slow in reaching my womanhood. Too slow," she added ruefully, "for myself as for Valann."

"Third decade—" Sharl's brow wrinkled. "And how old are you now?"

"I have eight decades and four years," Chyrie said. "Valann has thirty-one decades and six years."

"Thirt—" Romuel gaped openly. "You're over three hundred years old? Rivkah told us elves lived centuries long, but I never believed it."

"Thirty-one decades is not so old," Valann said defensively. "Our Eldest had eighty-four decades, and Rowan must be near that."

"You all look like children to me," Sharl grumbled. "How can anyone tell?"

"The length of hair," Valann told him, touching the coil at the back of his own head. "I saw that Rowan's braid was quite long, and Dusk's, as well. And they had both beaded their braids, and only a Matriarch or Patriarch—an elf of fifty decades or more—may do so."

"But—" Doria gestured at Chyrie's short hair.

"That is a tale." Chyrie chuckled. "Once, not long after we were mated, I was out gathering plants when a bear charged upon me. It would not heed me, though I tried to calm it, and I realized it had the foaming-mouth sickness. There was no time to flee but up the nearest tree. The bear, however, was not too sick to climb after me, and I slipped and fell from the branch I was on—but my hair caught on the limb, and there I hung dangling as that bear climbed toward me. I had to cut through my hair with my knife before I could drop to the ground and escape." She did not finish the story—that she continued to keep her hair short so that when they met other elves, if they stared, Valann could believe it was puzzlement over her short hair, not Val's unusual hairy face and body.

Valann ruffled the short curls affectionately and glanced at Sharl. "How old are you? In humans it seems impossible to tell."

"I'm twenty-six years of age," Sharl said. "Rivkah is nineteen. Romuel is some forty years or so, and Doria is a little younger than that."

"Why, it is no wonder you do not couple, then," Val said amazedly. "You are but children, not of an age to breed. But then—" He glanced at Rivkah, but a quick thought from Chyrie silenced him, and he returned to his work.

"None of us are children," Rivkah said, blushing fiercely. "Girl-children become women at thirteen or younger. But our lives are shorter, less than a century."

"You see, that is why they litter like rabbits," Chyrie told Valann. "They must be dying constantly. Soon there would be none if they did not breed in huge numbers. Certainly they must couple more among their own people and in their own place than they have done here."

"All this," Sharl mumbled through gritted teeth, "is unimportant." He spread out the map Rowan had given him. "Valann, do you think we can cross the Blue-eyes' territory in one day's ride?"

Val sighed and put down his needle to take the map.

"If we ride quickly and do not delay," he said, "we should be able to pass. We are not far from the Longear border. But it will rain again tomorrow. If it should storm as it did before, we will be hard-pressed to pass completely through Blue-eyes lands."

"Allanmere is less than half a league from the forest's edge," Sharl said. "We can easily reach it if we can just win through this last distance."

"Rain will render my spell less effective," Rivkah objected. "I can make us invisible to the Blue-eyes' sight, but they'll see the tracks our horses make in the mud. A storm would cover our sounds, though," she mused, "and wash away our scent, if their noses are as sharp as Valann's and Chyrie's."

Chyrie looked up surprisedly at Val, then touched her own nose.

"Our noses are not sharp," she protested. "They are shorter than your own."

"I'm sorry," Rivkah said, changing to the human language. "I was careless with your language. I only meant that your sense of smell is much keener than ours."

(Apparently, or they would forever be vomiting from their own foul stench,) Chyrie thought to Valann, who diplomatically said nothing.

"Home," Doria sighed longingly. "I want a loaf of hot bread and butter and a mug of ale as deep as my arm is long."

"A proper bed and two days to sleep," Romuel said wistfully.

"A hot bath and fresh clothing"—Rivkah smiled—"and a big fire in the fireplace."

"Good solid stone all around me," Sharl agreed, "and, please Evandar, sensible folk to deal with. Well, wish on, my friends, and may your eagerness urge you on faster tomorrow. We should all get what rest we can in preparation."

Val had scowled once at "sensible folk," but he quietly put his needles and pots aside, running his hand over the new vine on Chyrie's shoulder and healing it.

"Go on to our tent," Chyrie told him, glancing at Rivkah. "I will not be long."

Rivkah, too, remained at the fire after the others had retired, moving to a closer seat where they could talk quietly.

"You have not yet told him," Chyrie said. "Is that why you do not couple with him, fearing he will see the signs upon you?"

"Your wits are as keen as your nose," Rivkah said wryly. "I'm afraid to tell him. So much troubles him already. Finding out he's going to have a bastard child won't help."

Chyrie shook her head at such an odd dilemma; then her face cleared.

"Go and couple with the man Romuel," she said, "and many other men when you return, and then Sharl can believe that the child is not of his seed."

Rivkah stared amazedly at Chyrie, then laughed until she had to knuckle tears out of her eyes.

"I'm sorry," she gasped. "I know you mean well, Chyrie, but trust me when I say that it would trouble Sharl much more if he thought I had lain with other men than him, and even more yet if he thought I was pregnant by another man."

Chyrie scowled.

"I think I will not like your city," she said, shaking her head again. "The Mother Forest made males to make seed and females to bear it, and the planting of such seed is a joyful act. Why must that be such a difficult thing for humans? If I could fill my belly so easily as human women, I would see myself truly blessed."

"Chyrie—" Rivkah hesitated. "Have you ever thought that your child—children—might not be fully elvan?"

Chyrie looked down at the ground.

"I have thought upon it," she said. "Valann says that like may only breed with like, but I know he is troubled as well. Only the passing of time will show us the truth. I pray only that my children will be healthy and whole, and whatever the Mother Forest has seen fit to make them, they are a precious gift to me."

Rivkah reached out to cover Chyrie's small hand with her own.

"Your courage shames me," she said. "I'll tell Sharl now." She turned and walked out of the light of the dying fire.

There was another flutter of movement in Chyrie's belly, and she laid her hand on it, pensively.

"A precious gift," Chyrie repeated softly. "May I be strong enough to bear it."

She stood and walked slowly back to their hidden tent, where Valann's warmth waited to comfort her.

VII

"CAN YOU GET the horses to go any faster?" Rivkah shouted over the thunder.

Chyrie shook her head, and Valann shouted back in answer.

"They are already sliding in the mud," he called. "They dare go no faster on this trail."

Chyrie slumped back tiredly against Valann, letting him hold her up. She had sent the brighthawk ahead to scout the trail until the rain became so heavy that the bird rebelled; since then she had enlisted whatever squirrels or deer she could coax out of their various shelters, and she was dividing her attention between her makeshift scouts and the horses. Never before had she attempted to so jump from one animal's thoughts to another, and it was horribly difficult and disorienting. Sometimes she lost all sense of who was truly Chyrie, and it took the strength of Val's familiar thoughts to pull her back.

It was well after midday by her estimation, although by the darkness it could be midnight instead, and they had been forcing the quickest pace the horses could manage since first light. At first she and Valann had demurred to be concealed by Rivkah's magic, but Sharl had answered logically that if they were visible, then they might as well all be. Chyrie might still have argued, but Val reluctantly sided with Sharl, saying that Chyrie's unborn children must not be endangered, and Chyrie had given in.

Rivkah had cast her spell before they left Longear lands. Chyrie herself felt no different, and when she looked back she could see the others clearly enough, but there was a tingly feeling in the air around her, and to her amazement, when she looked through the eyes of her hawk or other animals, the trail was empty but for the branches that mysteriously bent aside and the tracks that appeared, as if by magic, in the mud.

The mage herself looked pale and wan this morning. Sharl was quiet and drawn, and ignored Rivkah steadfastly except to give her sharp-voiced orders, never looking in her direction. In petty revenge, Chyrie had had the hawk fly over him once or twice and drop its waste upon him.

Twice already they had passed Blue-eyes patrols. The Blue-eyes were not fools, and they had loosed arrows and spears at the invisible travelers; Blue-eyes, however, had little knowl-edge of horses and could not gauge their targets, and so far no one had been struck except for a slight graze to the rump of the packhorse. The horses were quickly tiring, however, and there was no way to tell how much forest yet remained to cross. Valann and Chyrie had taken the lead, since their sensitive eyes could more readily find the trail in the darkness.

Chyrie cast out desperately with her mind and found the brighthawk. She had to promise it a fresh rabbit at the soonest possible opportunity, but at last it soared above the canopy of the forest, striking out westward, diving occasionally as the lightning became too threatening.

What the brighthawk saw both encouraged and dismayed Chyrie. They were indeed near the western edge of the forest, and not far beyond that was the human settlement Sharl called the city of Allanmere, perched on the edge of the Brightwater River almost at the edge of the swamp. It was a frighteningly large collection of stone heaps of varying sizes—presumably dwelling places of some kind—surrounded by an enormous stone block wall, only partially completed, and that was in turn surrounded by a deep water-filled ditch. Strange and unfamiliar animals moved through this "city," and the sheer number of stone huts indicated an unthinkable number of humans living therein. At the northwest corner of the city was one stone structure larger than the rest—so unthinkably large, in fact,

that Chyrie wondered if it was not actually several houses
built one atop the other.

The brighthawk was as eager to abandon the place as Chyrie,
and it quickly retreated back into the trees to land and dry its
feathers. Chyrie sighed and, with some difficulty, fit herself
back into her own body. There would be no more need for
scouts now.

She was too tired now to speak aloud, but she silently
told Val what she had seen, and he turned to shout back to
the others. He had no more than gotten the first few words
out, however, when an arrow whizzed by perilously close to
his face, and a perfect rain of them followed immediately—
apparently the sound of their voices had let the Blue-eyes know
how far from the ground to shoot.

There was nothing Val and Chyrie could do but be silent
and make themselves as small as they could on the back of
the horse and ride on; the humans all had shields, behind
which they crouched as they rode, but Val and Chyrie had
none. Doria cried out as an arrow sank into her unprotected
leg, and Val and Chyrie's horse trumpeted as another creased
the top of its neck. A perfect rain of Blue-eyes arrows followed
the sounds, and Chyrie heard Valann gasp. Before she could
turn, however, an arrow thudded solidly into her hip, and more
frightening still, another grazed her belly; instinctively Chyrie
bent forward on the horse, pulling Val with her, protecting
her unborn children with her own body and Valann's. She
heard another scream from somewhere behind her, and she
silently begged the horses for more speed; suddenly the forest
parted ahead of her, and then they were in the open field, the
horses gaining new strength from the firmer footing and sight
of home.

Sharl's horse thundered past them, the human lord now
without his shield and clutching his shoulder, from which a
broken spear shaft protruded, but Chyrie had no thought at the
moment except for her mate.

(Love, do you live?) she thought anxiously, and was reassured
as Val tightened his arms around her.

(An arrow only grazed my cheek,) he thought back. (The
woman Doria, however, was sorely hit, if I saw correctly.) He

did not touch the arrow in her hip, but Chyrie felt his healing sense move through her. (Can you ride, love, long enough to reach the human village?)

Now that her desperate fear for Val was gone, Chyrie could feel the grinding pain of the arrow tip rubbing against bone. A slow burning was spreading outward from the wound, and she remembered, knowing Val did also, that many clans poisoned their battle arrows.

(I can ride as long as I must,) she thought firmly. (It is but a short distance, and I think the man Sharl has ridden ahead to see us welcomed with all speed.)

Rivkah was shouting something at them, signaling for them to drop back behind her. Chyrie slowed their horse to let Rivkah pull ahead, realizing that regardless of what Sharl might be doing ahead of them, better if a human led them into this human city.

Lightning flashed again, illuminating the broad plain brilliantly. Suddenly frozen with wonder despite their pain and fear, Valann and Chyrie stared at the huge space around them, and the same thought flashed through both minds.

(How large the world is!)

Another flash lighted their way, and they saw with mixed relief and dismay how close the city was. From the air, Chyrie had not realized just how tall the half-built wall was—in the places where it appeared completed, it stood at least five times as high as the horses' heads.

There was a gate set into the wall they were approaching, but it stood open now, and Chyrie gaped again as she realized that the huge wall was a third as thick as it was tall. Sharl was waiting for them just past the gate, in the center of a crowd of humans, some armored and some not, all talking excitedly.

Rivkah reined her horse to a stop at the gate, motioning to Valann and Chyrie to do the same. Romuel followed close behind, carrying Doria—an arrow protruded from her left side, just below the ribs, in addition to the one in her leg—and behind him, Doria's horse and the packhorse. The humans came running to take Doria and to help Rivkah and Romuel from their horses, but when they saw the elves, they fell suddenly still and silent, a few drawing weapons.

"These elves are my guests," Sharl shouted over the thunder and rain.

Those humans with drawn weapons slowly sheathed them, but they still stayed well away, jumping back when Valann ripped out an arrow that had hit the saddlebag behind him, then slid down from the horse. Rivkah hurried forward to take Chyrie and carry her gently to Sharl, where Doria already lay on the muddy ground.

"The arrows are barbed and must be cut free," Val told Rivkah. "The spear is not, but I believe all are poisoned." He touched the tip of his tongue to the head of the arrow in his hand, then grimaced. "*Karsha* berries. It is a slow poison and not difficult to treat."

"There are mages at the keep," Sharl said, pressing a cloth to the wound in his shoulder, "but it's across the city. It'll be quicker for us to go to the mages than to send for them."

"Doria doesn't have time," Rivkah said, gently probing the area around the arrow. "And I exhausted my magic protecting us."

"Valann—" Sharl began, but Val ignored him, carefully cutting the leather away from the arrow in Chyrie's hip.

"Hurry," Chyrie panted. "The poison must not spread to my womb."

"No!" Romuel seized Valann's shoulder. "You have to heal Doria! She's dying!"

Valann threw Romuel's hand off, not sparing the energy to reply. He glanced at Chyrie, his knife ready, and she nodded; without further delay, he sliced deeply into her hip.

Romuel reached for Valann again, but his hands froze, shaking, as the geas restrained him. He turned to Sharl, his face purple with rage. Rivkah chanted desperately, trying to raise some last wisp of magic, but to no avail.

"Do something!" Romuel shouted. "Chyrie can wait for help. Doria can't."

Chyrie ground her teeth as Val cut deeper, both of them ignoring the humans—Chyrie from pain, Val from concentration—and with a last searing cut, the arrow came free. Immediately Val pressed his hands over the wound.

(It was deeper than I thought,) he told her, even as his healing power flowed through her. (This may speed your children more, if what Dusk said was true.)

Chyrie might have told him as much; she could feel her belly swelling, as if her unborn children sucked in his healing magic like water, and the small lives within her moved fiercely, almost hurting her. But as soon as she felt the burning of the poison subside, she pushed his hand away.

(The rest can wait,) she thought. (Go to Doria.)

Val scowled but obeyed; the human woman was hardly breathing now, and Val shook his head.

"She is wounded in her vitals," he said. "If I cut for the arrow it will kill her. I can stop the poison and the bleeding and give her a little strength, but I have not enough power left to do more."

He pressed his hands carefully around the arrow; sensitized to his healing as she was, Chyrie could almost see the power flow out of him. Doria arched upward, gave a last sigh, and was still. Romuel stared blankly, unbelievingly, as the rain poured into Doria's unseeing eyes, until Valann gently closed them. The warrior sat quietly in the mud beside his wife, holding her hand, until Rivkah gently drew him away.

When Valann turned away, his hands were shaking with exhaustion and his face was gray.

"I did what I could," he panted, almost falling as he crawled back to Chyrie. "But the arrow was lodged in her vitals and the poison had gone to her heart."

"If you had gone to her first—" Sharl began hotly, but Rivkah laid her hand on his arm.

"Help me with Sharl," she said to Romuel. "There's nothing more to do for Doria. They're bringing a cart now."

Drained as he was, Val received no help from the humans standing by and watching as he made a pad of absorbent leather and dressed Chyrie's wound. By the time he was done, the humans had carefully pulled the spear out of Sharl's shoulder and were helping him to a cart filled with hay, harnessed to four horses.

"I cannot wrap your wound tightly because of your belly," Val said regretfully, "nor stitch it here in the mud and rain, and it must yet be cleaned more thoroughly. Why did you stop me before it was healed?"

In answer, Chyrie took his hand and pressed it against the now prominent bulge of her belly.

"I did not know what harm it might do them," she murmured. "I felt as if I might split open, they grew so quickly. I will heal, as generations of Wildings have healed, and there was no need to risk them."

That Valann could accept, and he retrieved one of their waxed-hide cloaks to give Chyrie some shelter from the rain. Sharl was carefully helped into the cart first, and Doria, now wrapped in a blanket, was also lifted in, but only Rivkah came back to help the exhausted Valann lift Chyrie onto the damp straw.

Valann and Chyrie had begun to appreciate the speed with which a horse could travel and still carry a rider; however, they had never ridden in a cart over a road before and found the bumpy ride less impressive. The jolting speed caused Chyrie to grind her teeth—only Wilding discipline kept her from crying out—but neither she nor Valann suggested that the cart be slowed; at the moment Chyrie wanted nothing in the world more than to get out of the rain, and Sharl had not yet had his poisoned wound tended. Despite her pain, Chyrie addressed a moment of prayer to the Mother Forest—first for her unborn children, and then for Doria's spirit, that it might pass safely to the roots of the Mother Forest and there dwell in peace.

At last the jolting ride stopped, and Chyrie saw the huge stone building that she had seen through the brighthawk's eyes. From the air she had, she realized, gotten no true idea of the immense size of the structure. The entire number of Rowan's people would have occupied only a small part of it, and Chyrie could see that it, like the wall, was still incomplete, judging from the tumbled stone and half-built rooms occasionally illuminated by the lightning.

An astonishing number of humans poured out of the huge open door of the stone building. Someone had apparently ridden ahead from the gates, because several of the humans had brought out litters. They hurriedly lifted Sharl onto a litter while Romuel lifted Doria's still form onto another, but hesitated until Rivkah glared at them sternly; then they gingerly helped Chyrie and the utterly exhausted Valann onto a litter together at Valann's fierce insistence.

Even from her supine position, Chyrie could see and wonder at the winding stone halls and stairways, lit by torches set into sconces along the walls. The stone was still rough and new.

A door opened and they were carried into a huge room. A fire was burning in a place recessed into one wall, and thick furs were strewn over the stone floor. A few windows showed that the storm outside continued unabated.

"What is this place?" Valann asked wearily. "In all this huge stone mountain is there no place where my mate and I can rest?"

"This will be your room," Rivkah said, appearing beside them. "I came to see you settled in. Sharl—" she hesitated. "Doesn't need me right now." She turned to the other humans. "You can go."

The other humans set the litter down quickly and fled with amazing speed. Valann struggled to a sitting position, motioning to Chyrie to remain where she was.

"How many others stay here?" Valann asked warily, looking around.

"In the keep? About a hundred when I left," Rivkah said. "Now, I don't know. Some who were living at the keep have built their own houses, probably, but more have come."

"No. In this place," Valann said, gesturing around him.

"This room?" Rivkah looked surprised. "This is your room, for you and Chyrie. Nobody else will stay here but you. Come on, I'll help you to the bed, and then I'll bring Chyrie. One of our healers will be here soon, as soon as they know Sharl is in no danger and Romuel—well, they'll give him a sleeping potion. I'll stay until the healer comes."

"No." Val stood slowly, shaking his head. "Leave us be. Only see that our packs are brought. I have medicines in them."

Rivkah sighed wearily.

"They're there," she said, pointing to a corner where the leather sacks rested. "May I at least carry Chyrie to bed for you? You're very tired, and if you drop her, she could start bleeding again." Val looked inclined to deny her request, but Chyrie shook her head at him and he reluctantly stood back.

Chyrie would not have recognized the bed as a bed; she had never seen a sleeping place raised up on a heavy wooden frame, surrounded by heavy hangings. The bed itself was larger by far than the last woven-switch camp they had had. She gasped, too, when Rivkah put her down on it—the thing was unexpectedly soft, and she sank down deep into it.

"If you're sure I can't bring one of Sharl's mages—" Rivkah said tentatively.

"You can leave us be," Val said firmly.

"All right. I'll come back in the morning, then. Romuel will need a friend to talk to." Rivkah hesitated by the door, as if she would say something else, then simply stepped out.

"Leave it, love, for tonight," Chyrie said as Val walked shakily to retrieve their packs.

"I will not," Val returned. "Your wound is not clean, and I will see it bound at least, lest you make it bleed anew."

Chyrie sighed; she was exhausted and wanted nothing more than to sleep, but she submitted to Val's ministrations and let him gently work off her wet clothes and toss them with his in a corner.

Despite their weariness, however, they could not sleep. The noise of the storm and the pain in Chyrie's hip distracted them both, and the unfamiliarity of the soft bed and the stone walls around them made it even more difficult. At last they shared a skin of wine, piled the furs into a thick heap on the floor, and settled there before the fire. At last the wine and the warmth lulled them to sleep.

"I hope you're not going to sleep on the floor as long as you're here."

Rivkah's voice startled them both awake. Val immediately leaped to his feet, sword in hand; Chyrie started to do the same, then cried out involuntarily as the movement caused a flare of pain in her hip.

Rivkah stood smiling a little, not only at Val's actions, but because the two maids who had come with her had stood gaping for a brief moment at Valann's and Chyrie's nudity, then fled with crimson faces. Rivkah looked very different this morning, still tired and sad, but much cleaner, and her grimy traveling tunic and trousers had been replaced by a gown of rich blue that complemented her fair skin and hair.

"Would you like to come down to breakfast," Rivkah asked, "or shall I have something sent up?"

"We will go," Val said, looking at Chyrie, "if you will allow me to finish healing you."

"But—" Chyrie began to protest.

"With the poison gone, there is no need for me to hurry," Val said patiently. "Dusk said that it was very strong healing that affected the unborn. I will heal you slowly and with great care, so that it does not reach your womb."

"Very well, then," Chyrie agreed.

True to his word, Valann did heal her slowly and carefully. He was growing in his ability, Chyrie realized, just as she had never thought that she could jump between so many animal minds as she had in the forest. Then she felt a pang of guilt. If his healing had improved so in the course of a few days frequent use, he might likely have become a Gifted One in their clan—had not her beast-speaking sensitivity driven them to live apart.

"We found you some clean clothing," Rivkah said awkwardly. "I'm afraid all we had that might fit is, well, children's clothing, for us. But the maids will look at your old clothes and see what we can have made."

Chyrie scrambled over eagerly, wincing a little as her newly healed muscles twinged, to examine the garments. They were made of woven fiber as the humans wore, and Chyrie marveled at the unfamiliar texture. There did seem to be a rather large stack of garments, however, some white, some colored; several of the tunics, seemed unusually long.

"Those are gowns," Rivkah told her, indicating her own gown. "Women wear them."

(How does anyone run and hunt in such a garment?) Val marveled privately.

Chyrie formed a very amusing mental picture of the idea and chuckled, then cast the gowns aside.

"I think not," she said. "Tunic and trousers will suffice, and better accommodate my belly as well."

Rivkah hesitated, but said nothing as Valann and Chyrie sorted through the garments for size, at last finding suitable sets and donning them.

"How light they are," Chyrie marveled.

"Well, you're only actually wearing half." Rivkah grinned rather embarrassedly. "We wear undergarments under our clothing—that's the white ones." She jumped backward in amazement as Valann nonchalantly lifted the hem of her skirt to look underneath.

"Surely you want some food now," she suggested.

"I could eat three deer, a wild pig, and five rabbits," Val said, "and then come back for more."

"And I could eat twice as much," Chyrie groaned. "These small wolves in my belly demand a full share and more."

This time Val and Chyrie took more of an interest in the twistings and turnings of the keep. The stone labyrinth might have daunted most newcomers, but they had developed an almost unfailing sense of direction and memory for trails.

"How fares the man Romuel?" Chyrie asked as they walked.

Rivkah was silent for a moment.

"He and Doria had been married—mated, if you will—for many years," she said. "He's—he's very angry right now, angry at Valann and at all elves. It's best if you avoid him for a time. Anger is his way of putting grief aside for now."

"I do not hold any human in kind regard," Valann said slowly, "but I wished no harm to the woman. I would have saved her if I could, but to choose between healing her and my mate, and my mate with child—"

"I understand," Rivkah sighed. "And I know how important children are to your people. Even Sharl understands—well, somewhat. But Romuel loved Doria very much, and he has no great love for any elf now. It's no different from the way you felt, Valann, about us. It's unfortunate. Most of the people who were there last night have no fondness for the elves, either, and they'll talk. It's not going to help matters. Well, there's nothing to be done about it for now. Come, here's the hall."

Valann and Chyrie had thought their quarters were enormous, but the size of the main hall stunned them to silence. The huge hall rated two fireplaces, one at each end, and was brightly lit by hanging groupings of candles. The heavily carven table that ran the length of the hall was so long and wide that Chyrie suppressed an urge to jump atop it and run down its length. Sharl sat alone at the far end of the hall, but a huge repast had been laid.

Sharl nodded at Valann and Chyrie and glanced briefly, coldly at Rivkah, then gestured at the food.

"Be welcome," he said shortly.

It was a poor invitation by elvan standards, but Valann and Chyrie were too hungry either to be suspicious of the food or to stand on ceremony. The chairs were so low that, seated, the elves' eyes barely peeped over the top of the table; however, when Sharl, exasperated, motioned to a servant to bring cushions, Valann and Chyrie simply climbed onto the tabletop and, despite Sharl's glare, seated themselves there. They looked curiously at the plates and forks, but had no idea what to do with them; in the elvan manner, they helped themselves from the platters as they liked and shared a mug of wine.

Chyrie discovered that the humans' bread was much different from the rather tough and chewy rounds of stone-baked nut flour bread that the elves used to scoop up soft or liquid foods. This stuff was shaped in rounds and flat-bottomed cylinders, and was exquisitely crispy outside, meltingly soft inside. Another wonder was cheese, soft and white in bowls or golden in wheels, melted by the fire and scraped onto a plate to smear onto the wonderful bread or crumbled and biting to nibble with the fruit.

(This wine is abysmal,) Valann thought sourly, even as he reached for more. (It tastes as if it was trod out with unwashed feet.)

(Given the general state of cleanliness among the humans I have seen and their apparent aversion to water,) Chyrie thought wryly, (I would not doubt it. And the mead is far too harsh. But this foamy urine-colored liquid is good, though I was doubtful to taste it at first. Say nothing. Sharl, too, is angry at us.)

"We need communication between the city and Rowan," Sharl mused, "as to how many soldiers and weapons, and of what kinds, each of us has, and what other resources each of us has and requires. I think the best way to do that is for the two of you to see the keep and the city and relay information to Rowan, but I can't spare the time to take you myself. I have to supervise labor on the wall and other fortifications, and deal with the shipments coming into the city."

"I'll show them the keep and the city," Rivkah offered. "It's probably not wise for them to wander around alone, with the way the people—" She glanced uneasily at Valann and Chyrie. "Well, until the mage companies arrive from the west, I could—"

"Do that, then," Sharl said shortly, turning back to his food.

Rivkah flushed miserably and turned to her own plate, only picking at the food.

(Why is he angry with Rivkah?) Val asked Chyrie.

(Humans are impossible creatures,) Chyrie told him. (Sharl is angry because Rivkah is with child and they are not formally mated. There is more, something to do with Sharl being the Eldest in Allanmere, but I did not understand Rivkah's explanation. Perhaps their Eldests are not permitted to mate.)

(That does not explain why he would treat Rivkah unkindly,) Val protested, reaching for more cold roasted fowl.

(Why do *you* treat her unkindly?) Chyrie countered. (Of the four humans who wronged us, only she honestly seems to wish to make amends.)

Valann scowled and made no reply. Chyrie smiled to herself and took another round of the wonderful bread.

"How many live in your city now?" Valann asked Sharl.

"At last counting, some four thousand," Sharl said. "But more are coming quickly—warriors and mages from the west, and soon there will likely be refugees from the north, fleeing ahead of the army. I expect six thousand or more in the city by the time any sizable force arrives."

"Six thousand," Val marveled. "Likely there are scarce more than that in the Heartwood, and we have dwelt there for many centuries."

"I expect Allanmere to one day grow to ten times its population," Sharl said proudly. "With its location on the river, it should one day be a great trade city."

Val glanced sidelong at Chyrie.

(With trade roads to be built through our forest, no doubt,) Chyrie thought. (Our people will likely have some comment to make on that matter.)

(Now they number no more than we,) Val cautioned. (Now their leader is geas-bound to us. Now we can easily say no. One day, when a different Eldest leads them, when they are ten times our number, our no may mean nothing to them.)

(Then Sharl, in his attempt to make this alliance, is aiding our cause in disclosing his numbers and armament,) Chyrie mused. (It is well for us to have this information and to assess the skill of his warriors, to tell our own Eldest as well as Rowan.)

"How many of your folk are able to fight?" Val asked Sharl.

"Now? Less than a thousand with any skill," Sharl said. "There are likely two thousand more who can pick up a weapon and try—farmers, craftsmen, and the like. The rest are women, children and the old. They can sometimes be useful in a battle, carrying arrows to the warriors, tending the wounded, and so on, but that's about all."

"Do your women have no skill to fight?" Val asked, surprised. "The woman Doria carried a sword."

"Romuel and Doria came from Keralon, a city to the west, several years ago," Sharl said. "There are more women who choose to train as warriors in the western lands. The custom is growing here, but more slowly. I know it's different among the elves."

"We are all taught to fight," Val said. "Most particularly our women, for those who ripen and those who are with child are most precious to us, and if the weapons of their clan cannot protect them, then still their own skill may save them. Only the very youngest of our children and the physically feeble do not fight, and all but infants are able to assist the warriors as you said. If there are six thousand elves in the Heartwood—and I cannot say whether there are more or less than that—there are but a handful who cannot use either weapons or Gifts, or both, to defend themselves, although of course some are more skilled than others."

"How many do you think might come to the city for shelter?" Rivkah asked him.

Valann shrugged.

"It is difficult to say," he said. "I know only of Wildings, and they will send no one. But Rowan spoke of ripe females and those with child also. They will be able to fight, however, at least with bows."

"I will gladly test my skill with a sword against any human's," Chyrie said hotly.

"It may well come to that," Valann said somberly. "And if it does, I will thank the Mother Forest for your skill, which is the equal of any I have seen. But you and the lives you carry are the hope of the forest. *You* must be kept safe."

(If you think I will be coddled in some safe place like a newborn—) Chyrie thought fiercely.

(Both armies together, elf and human, are not mighty enough to keep my she-fox in a corner,) Val thought wryly. He reached over and tapped her swelling belly. (At the same time, I know you will protect these young ones as fiercely as that same she-fox her pups, and to guard them, you must guard the womb that carries them. We will speak of this later.)

(At some length,) Chyrie replied, although, like Valann, her face was calm; the humans had no place in their quarrel.

Rivkah noticed that they had stopped eating, and frowned a little.

"If you're done," she said, "we can go now."

"Very well." Val slid off the tabletop, again ignoring Sharl's irritated glance, and waited. Chyrie followed—but not before she snatched another piece of bread and a chunk of cheese.

"Your lord is as sour as your wine," Chyrie complained as they walked down several flights of steps. "Both could bear much improvement."

"Sharl's very worried," Rivkah said quietly. "He's worked so hard to bring these people here, to build this city, and he's desperate to protect them. Our defenses are less than half finished, most of our people are farmers who know more

about handling a hoe than a sword, and the elves who live
less than half a league away and control the entire forest are
as much enemies as friends. He has reason to be a little bit
sour right now."

"He has thousands of people who have followed him to this
place and who honor him, he has wealth and territory, and a
woman is bearing his child," Chyrie said. "Among the elves
he would have much reason to celebrate. It is said among elves
that 'He who seeks only thorns on the flower will never smell
its sweetness.' "

"That's a good saying," Rivkah said remotely. "I wish you
elves wouldn't seek only the thorns in humans."

Valann and Chyrie looked surprisedly at Rivkah, then each
other, then laughed rather embarrassedly.

"It would seem that we sometimes dispense our wisdom
more freely than we follow it." Chyrie chuckled. "Thank you
for reminding me of that."

"This place is huge," Val marveled as they descended yet
another set of stairs. "And that it has all been built from pieces
of stone—"

"The great hall, where you ate this morning, was the first
part of the keep to be built," Rivkah said. "It's taken five years
to build it, and as you saw, it's not finished yet."

"Where did you get so much stone?" Chyrie asked curiously.

"From under the city," Rivkah said. "Most of the buildings
in town are going to have wonderful cellars. And tunnels
between them. And subcellars. Maybe we'll attract better vint-
ners." They all chuckled at that.

"I'll show you something that should interest you," Rivkah
said, opening one of the doors along the hallway. "It's something one of our mages discovered when we were cutting deep
into the stone."

An odd smell came from the room, rather like the odor of
the bird eggs Chyrie sometimes ate—strong, but not actually offensive. A wave of warm, moist air billowed out the
open door.

Interestingly, the only thing in the room was a circular
depression set into the floor, and the depression was filled
with bubbling water.

"There are springs of hot water deep down under the city," Rivkah said. "The mages sensed it when they probed the ground, and they used magic to bring it to the surface. There are three here in the keep and two more in the city, plus some under the moat, and Sharl plans dozens more. The bubbles are from something in the water, not boiling heat."

Chyrie knelt on the edge of the pool and tentatively dabbled her fingers in it.

"It is very warm," she admitted. "What do you do with these pools?"

"We bathe in them," Rivkah said. "Except for the one in the kitchen, where we get water for cooking and washing. There are pipes in the side. The water comes up from the bottom, and the old water flows out."

"You bathe in *hot* water?" Valann asked curiously, also touching the bubbling liquid.

"Indeed we do. It's very pleasant," Rivkah told him. "Even before we had these springs, we heated water for bathing. Now we have to cool water in the cellars when we want cold water, and unfortunately there's this smell. But it's worth it."

"I want to try it," Chyrie exclaimed, starting to draw her tunic over her head.

"Wait, wait," Rivkah said, laughing. "If you want to try the bathing pool, fine, but why don't you wait until tonight? If you want to see the rest of the keep and the city, you'll see more by day."

Chyrie grudgingly pulled her tunic back down, the more reluctantly because of the image she had caught from Valann of other water sports that might take place in the bubbling pool.

"I'll show you the keep's watchtower," Rivkah said, leading them up several flights of stairs. From the top floor of the keep, they passed through another door into a narrow, cylindrical room containing only a spiral stone staircase that wound up, and up, and up, ending in a platform and a ladder leading through an open trapdoor at the top.

Rivkah mounted the ladder first, a little awkwardly because of the gown, and Valann and Chyrie scampered up quickly after her. At the top of the ladder and through the trapdoor was a stone platform ringed with a short, crenellated wall of stone blocks. Rivkah motioned them to the southeast portion of the wall, and the elves stared, silent with amazement.

Chyrie had seen the city once before from far above, but her view had been limited by the storm. Now all of Allanmere stretched out before them, sparkling in the sunlight with last night's rain.

They could never have conceived of a village so huge. Inner Heart, which had shocked them with its size, was but a few paltry huts compared to this. And these huts, some large, some small, were all of stone—some thatched, some topped with sloping roofs covered with what appeared to be scales, like a fish. Besides the wall around the city, there was a second wall around the keep, with smaller towers of its own.

"Why are they all of stone?" Valann asked.

"Several reasons," Rivkah told him. "First, we couldn't get timber from the forest, because the elves attacked us every time we tried. Second, we had more stonemasons than carpenters. And third, we were sitting on all this good stone; why not use it? Besides, the stone buildings will last much longer and are safer from fire."

"Why do some of the buildings have scales on top?" Chyrie asked.

"Some people are trying baked-clay tile roofs," Rivkah said. "They're sturdier than thatch and seem to last longer. We'll see. Again, it's an idea to protect from fire."

"Those other towers are not as high as this one," Chyrie said, pointing.

"That one isn't quite finished yet," Rivkah said, following her gaze. "When they're all done, there will be one on each corner of the city, two smaller towers at each gate, two more towers on the south and east walls, and one on the north and west. Sharl plans a system of docks to the west, too, and there's an opening there now, but I'm sure he'll simply have it walled up. The fewer gates to have to defend, the better."

"You are wrong," Valann told her. "The approaching army is mostly afoot, some on horses. They will not travel by river, and you have left little bank between the wall and the water.

No force of any significance could gather there. It would be simple to make that small area inaccessible from the other land without walling it up. Neither will they win through the swamp, nor would your people if they had to flee. Had you an opening onto the river, you could cast nets for fish to feed your people and have an additional source of water, as well as an egress for escape, if necessary."

Rivkah stared at him.

"That's very canny," she said. "I didn't think you would be so knowledgeable about warfare."

Valann smiled grimly.

"Wildings have fought off raids from neighboring clans many, many times. None have yet defeated us, and we have won lands from two other clans. Fools do not win battles."

"I'll tell Sharl what you suggested," Rivkah said. "It may cheer him."

"It seems strange to build your keep in this place," Val said, sniffing the air. "There must be times when the smell of the swamp is strong, especially after the spring floods."

"Yes, but this is the safest place, in the corner of the swamp and the river," Rivkah said. "The keep was the beginning of the city, as I said, and at one time everyone stayed here."

Chyrie ignored the conversation, staring to the west at the forest looming cool and inviting there. This high openness made her almost as uneasy as the closeness of stone walls around her had, and a pang of homesickness brought tears perilously close.

Val sensed her unhappiness and folded his arms around her from behind, caressing her rounded belly.

"Where is your friend the brighthawk, love?" he asked. "Can you feel him from here?"

Chyrie reached out and touched the brighthawk almost immediately.

"Yes," she said. "He stayed in the Blue-eyes' lands, waiting."

"Why didn't you bring him?" Rivkah asked.

"You cannot take a wild thing from the forest and make it happy within walls," Val said absently, and Chyrie knew he longed for the forest as much as she did. "In any wise, your people would likely have shot him from the sky for their supper."

Chyrie leaned back against Valann and closed her eyes, reaching out to touch the brighthawk more fully. Through the bird's mind, she reached back to Inner Heart, experimentally, to see if she could in turn touch Dusk.

The Gifted One's answer was firm and immediate, like the clasp of a warm hand in hers.

(I am pleased to finally meet you in thought,) Dusk told her, (and doubly pleased that you left the forest without harm.)

(I cannot say without harm,) Chyrie thought wryly, telling him what had transpired when they passed through Blue-eyes lands. (There will be no safe passage there for any. You must send those whom you would shelter here by another road, north or south of Blue-eyes lands.)

(But how could they attempt to harm you?) Dusk asked, horrified. (You were wearing plainly the mark of a woman bearing child, and they knew of you already.)

(The humans hid us with magic,) Chyrie told him. (The Blue-eyes did not know they were shooting their arrows at Valann and myself. Perhaps if Rowan tells them that they nearly cost us our lives, it may aid her in her negotiations with them.)

(But how do you fare?) Dusk pressed. (Are your unborn ones safe?)

(They are safe enough to fair burst my belly when it pleases them,) Chyrie thought amusedly. (Still, I wish for a healer of our own people here. Valann trusts no human mages.)

(He is wise, for they know nothing of the ills of our kind,) Dusk told her. (A bird can eat berries that will poison a squirrel, and it may be so with human and elf. Without doubt a healer or perhaps even a Gifted One of one of the clans will come to the city to minister to those who shelter there. Until then Valann can tend you well enough. But you must eat much meat, especially the liver and the heart. Your body will guide you.)

(Thank you, Gifted One,) Chyrie thought. Reaching the brighthawk over such a distance was wearying enough; the unaccustomed task of touching Dusk through the bird made it doubly difficult, and she could feel her hold on the bird slipping. (I will contact you again soon.)

Valann gently eased her to a seat on one of the low notched-out blocks of the wall, Rivkah hovering worriedly nearby.

"Are you well, love?" he asked.

"It is difficult to touch a mind from such a distance," Chyrie panted. "And I have never reached through one mind to touch another. But I am glad to find I can do it. At least we will have some contact with the forest."

"You must not do it often, if it wears upon you so," Valann fretted.

"Every endeavor is difficult at the first," Chyrie said when she recovered her breath. "It will become easier with practice. Ooof!" She pressed her hands against her belly. "You both need not kick so. I will do no more now."

Val touched her belly, his face lighting with joy as he felt the strong movements beneath his hand. He pressed his cheek against the bulge and laughed.

"Little warriors, the both of them," he exclaimed. "They are kicking my face."

Chyrie glanced at Rivkah, noting her wistful expression, and laughed, took the woman's hand, and pressed it to her belly.

"My younglings do not know elf from human," she said, grinning. "They will kick and strike anyone they can."

Rivkah laughed, too, but her eyes were very moist, and she turned away quickly, one hand pressed to her mouth.

"How long do humans bear their offspring?" Val asked as they descended the tower.

"Nine moons or a little more," Rivkah said. "I likely have seven moons left."

"Dusk said I would bear in six to seven moons," Chyrie sighed. "But that was in the forest, before Val healed me again. Now I do not know how many moons are left, but I cannot think it will be many. I only wish they had been born before battle comes to your city."

"So you would be fit to fight?" Rivkah guessed.

"Were my mate but breaths from bearing, she would be fit to fight." Val laughed. "What fights more fiercely than a mother beast with young?"

"No," Chyrie said somberly. "So that if I were slain, my children might yet live."

That sobered everyone, and Rivkah diplomatically diverted the subject to more cheerful territory.

"So I conceived before you," Rivkah said, "and we bear our children more quickly, but you'll bear months before I do. Magic's a strange thing. Soon every woman in the land will be running to the healers, begging them to speed their bearing."

"I think not," Valann said. "As Dusk said, it is a dangerous thing to do, avoided except in direst necessity. He would not have so warned us were it not dangerous indeed."

Rivkah's brow wrinkled.

"But—" She glanced at Chyrie. "What do you think it's done to your children?"

"I cannot know until they are born," Chyrie said serenely. "But they move strongly, and that is a good sign. They are no ordinary children in any wise, being two." She shook her head. "I can tell you one real danger—had they grown any more quickly, they might well have split my belly wide, and I do not jest when I say it."

"It might be best if we tell no one else in the city about the effects of such healing, then," Rivkah mused. "The only humans who truly know are Sharl and myself, and Romuel and—" She stopped abruptly.

"Will there be a death ritual held?" Chyrie asked. "We would wish Doria fair journey."

Rivkah was silent for a long moment, then spoke hesitantly.

"There's a—a ceremony tonight," she said. "It might be best if you don't attend. Romuel is very upset, and—and others might not feel kindly toward you."

Valann raised his eyebrows.

"Would Romuel and the others not be comforted by our respect for his mate, our recognition of her courage?" he asked.

"I don't think he would see it that way," Rivkah said gently. "Trust me, you would only make him angry."

"Then we will not go," Valann said. "We would not add to his pain."

Chyrie laid her hand on Rivkah's arm, halting her.

"The healing that might have saved Doria bought life for me and for my children," she said. "There is a debt between us."

"There is no debt," Valann growled. "It was my choice, and I would choose the same again. If there was debt, it was her debt to you for wrongs that might have cost you your chance to bear child."

"There is a debt between us," Chyrie said again. "One day there will come a way for me to repay it."

Rivkah squeezed Chyrie's shoulder.

"That's kind of you," she said, "but I don't think there's anything to repay. Whatever Rom said, Ria was a warrior, and a brave one. She'd have given her life to save a pregnant woman, human or elf, if the choice had been hers."

"As would any elf in the forest," Chyrie said. "But she did not make that choice."

Rivkah was silent for a long moment, then asked lamely, "Would you like to see the wall?"

"Indeed we would," Valann said. "I would like to see how it is built."

Rivkah took them outside the keep to examine the wall more closely. Although the walkway was wide enough on top for four men to walk abreast, they could not walk the entire circumference of the city there because of the many incomplete sections. Most of these partially built sections were being worked on by crews of burly human men who stopped to stare with curiosity and hostility at their observers, but Rivkah led Val and Chyrie past these places to the east wall, where, she said, they could see how the magical portion of the construction took place.

The journey itself was an interesting one—an education to herself as well, Rivkah added, as she had been out of the city with Sharl for some months, and a great deal of building had taken place since then.

"That northern part, nearest the keep, houses four temples already," Rivkah said. "We've brought in people from so many different lands that I'm afraid we have quite a mixture of beliefs. Sometimes I think everyone who steps into the city

brings a new set of gods with them. Sharl thinks that one day
we'll have twenty temples here."

"Temples?" Valann asked curiously, mouthing the unfamiliar word. "Oh, sacred places, such as the altars."

"Something of that kind." Rivkah indicated another turning
in the muddy road. "One day this road will all be stone, too.
Over there, just south of the keep, we've already begun to build
houses for the minor nobles, who want to live nearest the keep.
In case of danger, of course, and for convenience in visiting.

"Merchants are building shops on the east side of the city,
and in the center is the market," Rivkah continued. "It's only
a small market now, but Sharl has left plenty of room. I don't
know how we'll ever fill it. From the market south on both
sides are only a few homes now—a good many of the common
folk live on farms outside the city proper—but a tavern or
two are moving in, and there are barracks for our soldiers
and boardinghouses, too, for the mercenaries and labor that
Sharl's brought in. And south of all of that are the guildhalls,
where the craftsmen are."

They had come to a group of several large, rectangular pits
in the ground. Men were working at the bottom of the pits,
cutting out large blocks of stone. Walking between the pits
was a man dressed in ordinary rough clothes, but holding a
short rod of what appeared to be bone. As soon as a block
was completed, the man would hold the rod between his palms,
chant a short incantation, and the block would rise steadily
through the air to a waiting wagon.

"We have six mages who do nothing but work on the wall
and the buildings," Rivkah said, "and another three who work
at the keep itself. Each set of three is a team, two lifters and a
bonder. Sharl paid a good sum to bring in stoneworking mages
from as far west as Bridingham. Come, I'll show you the wall
being built."

Rivkah guided them to a place on the east wall where several
crews were working. Whenever a wagon would arrive, another
plainly dressed mage floated each block into place on the
wall, and human crews would make small adjustments to
place each block exactly, chiseling away any rough edges.
When a large enough section was so fitted, a second mage

would step forward and chant another spell, to no visible effect.

"That other mage bonds the blocks into place," Rivkah explained. "Each block melts a tiny bit into the blocks around it. It protects the blocks from weathering, and it's incredibly hard to break. Besides that, the wall's smoother—harder to climb, that is."

"It seems as if the mages do most of the work," Val commented.

"Not really," Rivkah told them. "The mages can do their work much faster than the masons can cut the stone, so most of the time the mages are just waiting for blocks to work with. Sharl's ordered every available man into the rock pits to cut block, with only a few masons to each pit to supervise. That way they can cut more stone at a time, and the mages move between the pits. Come, I'll show you the wall and the gate towers."

Valann and Chyrie followed Rivkah, scrambling over piles of loose rock and dug out dirt, to the structure of the wall itself. The humans stopped work, glaring at the elves and murmuring angrily to each other.

The wall was solidly built, tapering from almost six human heights wide at the base to a little over two at the top. The walk at the top of the wall faced against the stone battlements, with wood-shuttered breaks and narrow slits through which arrows could be shot. At intervals this pattern was broken by stone hoardings jutting out past the wall, but these were too incomplete for Val and Chyrie to examine.

Two cylindrical towers, also set somewhat out from the wall, flanked the gate, and the wall walk penetrated the towers to pass straight through. Each tower contained a few guards' quarters and stairwells leading up to high watch platforms at the top. Valann and Chyrie were fascinated with the gigantic wheel and chain that raised and lowered the heavy iron portcullis that could close off the gate if the heavy wooden doors were breached.

In addition to these precautions and the arrow slits, the walkway floor over the wooden gate and the portcullis was slightly recessed and covered with a hinged wood slab. Under the slab, the stone had been replaced by a wide-meshed metal grid. Rivkah explained that this grid would let the guards pour down boiling water or heated stones on anyone trying to breach the gate, and that the hoardings would have similar grids.

Chyrie pulled herself up to peer out through one of the arrow slits, grimacing at the feeling of confinement that gazing through the narrow opening gave her. This was her first chance to have a good look at the water-filled moat outside the wall, and she could see that that, too, was being worked on by human crews, apparently widening the waterway. The forest seemed terribly distant, and she hurriedly brushed away tears before Valann could see them.

"With such defenses, how can you fear any army?" she asked.

"This wall isn't so impressive as all that," Rivkah told her. "If the elves were going to attack us—if *all* the elves in the Heartwood would attack us together—how would you go about it?"

"We would not." Chyrie shrugged. "You have nothing we would want."

"Well, assume you *did* want to," Rivkah said patiently. "How would you do it?"

Val sat down on a block of stone to consider.

"Attacking the wall would be foolish," he said. "I would send archers in boats across the river to the west side, to shoot anyone who tried to come through that opening for fish. Other groups would similarly watch the south and east gates. That way no one could leave the city, either to flee or to seek food. Our Gifted Ones would attempt to use magic against the city, but there would be no necessity for a determined attack, as long as we could keep your people confined in the city."

"A siege." Rivkah nodded. "But these barbarians won't be able to do that. Unlike the elves, they don't have boats and they don't have a forest to feed them—I doubt the elves will be any more willing to let them hunt or forage in the woods than they let us. They can cut us off, though, even without boats. It may come down to a question of who has more food, them or us. They do have magic, according to rumor, primitive but powerful. Our own mages may be kept busy just countering that. Sharl hopes we can outwait them, that they'll become so low on supplies that they'll retreat, believing the city not worth the trouble of waiting."

Valann and Chyrie exchanged glances.

(They will *not* retreat,) Val thought grimly. (Instead they will attack the forest in force, for we have no stone walls, and there is more food to be had in the forest than in this city as well. The city will tempt them like a tasty nut, but if its shell proves too tough, they will turn to the forest to feed their hunger. First Blue-eyes will fall, then the frightened Longears—this is Sharl's way to press us for aid, even under the geas, for he can sit secure, taking no action himself, while this army descends upon the forest.)

(This is news for Rowan's ears,) Chyrie thought. (Under the geas, if we call to him for assistance, he must order his people to render it.)

(And we are here to ask,) Valann thought. (Another example of Rowan's forethought. We must keep alert to these plans.)

"I would be interested in seeing your weapons," Valann said aloud to Rivkah. "Some clans in the Heartwood are tall enough to use human-sized swords, but some, like Wilding, are not."

"Here in the city we have only human-sized swords," Rivkah said. "But the weapons coming from Cielman were made smaller, and they should arrive in a few days. I'll show you one of the guard armories, if you like."

The guard barracks were south, and Valann and Chyrie were able to view Allanmere's market. There were a few stalls, farmers and craftsmen selling their goods to the nobles and to each other, but Rivkah said that Sharl someday expected a huge market, when Allanmere became a more prominent stop for merchant trains and when river trade became more feasible.

There were only a few guards at the barracks when they arrived.

"Most of the guards are doubling as stone cutters or other laborers," Rivkah explained. "Others are training the farmers in weaponry and helping them bring their goods into the city for storage."

One of the guards had to be persuaded to open the armory, and did so reluctantly, watching Chyrie and Valann intently as he did so. The small room held numerous weapons on racks and suits of armor of various kinds on stands.

Valann and Chyrie poked at the armor curiously, chuckled over the bows, and openly admired the swords and daggers. Some of the largest swords were almost as long as Chyrie was tall, but she found a long dagger that served her as well as a sword, while Valann experimented with a heavier short sword.

"These are of excellent make," Chyrie said ruefully, drawing her own age-thinned blade for comparison. "The metal is stronger, and doubtless it holds a better edge. It is a fine blade."

"Take those if they suit you," Rivkah suggested. "Most of our guards use the crossbows and longer swords, and it's best if you have time to practice with an unfamiliar weapon."

"Here, lady, you don't mean to be giving them our weapons?" the guard protested. "Those puny imps would be no good in a fight, and like as not run us through as soon as an enemy."

"I think I'd disagree with you on both points," Rivkah said ruefully.

Valann touched one of the crossbows. "This is an unusual design," he said.

"Show him how it works," Rivkah told the guard. He gave her a rather surly look, but picked up the crossbow and a couple of bolts and took them to the door of the barracks. He gestured wordlessly to a post across the road, loaded the crossbow, and just as casually sent both bolts thunking solidly into the indicated post, much to the dismay of a passerby. The burly soldier retrieved the bolts—he had to wrench them mightily out of the post—and returned them and the crossbow to the armory, still without a word.

"A marvelous weapon." Val nodded. "It almost compensates for the pitiful bows your people use. If there is indeed a trade between our two peoples, you must have the elves make new bows for your people. Yours would snap like dry twigs at a good draw, for all your warriors are stout with muscle."

"Valann made my bow with his own hands," Chyrie said proudly. "I have seen few better, even made by those who live by such trade."

"Ah, but my mate can fletch an arrow so skillfully that it flies straight as a sunbeam and swift as a hawk's dive," Val returned.

"I used to be a fair shot with a bow," Rivkah said shyly. "But I know I could be better."

"Then in exchange for these weapons, and perhaps others, and partners to try them against," Chyrie said, "Valann shall make you a bow and I your arrows, and we shall instruct you with them." She elbowed Valann, who looked inclined to protest. "Shall we not, my mate, so that she may defend her own unborn?"

Val sighed, but nodded.

"I cannot argue with the defense of a mother and her unborn," he told Chyrie. "But you are a sly she-fox, there is no doubt."

(I will provide more persuasion when we can be alone,) Chyrie thought coaxingly, taking Valann's hand.

Valann chuckled and squeezed her fingers.

(I will be most difficult to persuade,) he thought. (It will take some effort on your part.)

(I would have it no other way,) Chyrie returned.

"Can we not return to the keep now?" Chyrie asked aloud. "Two small wolves live in my womb, and if I do not feed them, I vow they will kick their way free."

Rivkah looked up at the sun, surprised.

"I'm sorry," she said. "The midday meal is long past. We'll stop at an inn and pick up something to keep you until supper. I'm hungry myself."

The concept of an inn mystified Valann and Chyrie, but the hearty bowls of stew and dumplings, crusty loaves, and meat and vegetable pies set before them suited them well, and Chyrie professed a fondness for the cellar-cold beer with which they were served.

"That's one advantage of cities." Rivkah laughed, accepting her second meat pie. "Here, you don't have to catch it first."

"But in the forest I would choose a younger stag for its tenderness," Valann returned, chewing with some vigor at a lump of meat in the stew. "But I am wrong. This is not venison."

"That's beef," Rivkah said, gesturing at the stew. "The pies are pork."

"If you will insist on so much conversation," Chyrie said, snatching the last pork pie, "there will be all the more food for me."

Rivkah laughed and indulged Chyrie by buying sweet seed cakes for each of them, and they returned the more merrily to the keep. There they found Sharl in a less pleasant mood, stalking the long great hall angrily.

"There you are!" he shouted, apparently at Rivkah, when they entered. "Six new mages arrived today, including your own teacher, and you're the one who knows where they should be and what they should be doing! I've had guards looking for you for hours, and I'm late to meet with my advisers already!"

Rivkah's jaw trembled and her cheeks flushed red, and she started to speak, but Chyrie touched her arm.

"Do not let him speak to you so," she murmured to the mage, and Rivkah took a deep breath and squared her shoulders.

"I'll attend to the mages," she said quietly. "And I'll help you in any way I can—when you can speak to me as a friend, not a slave." She turned back to Valann and Chyrie. "Come, you can try the bathing pool, and you can dine with me and with my mentor in his quarters tonight." She glanced briefly at Sharl. "There you can expect polite conversation."

Valann chuckled, carefully under his breath.

(So the rabbit can bite,) he thought to Chyrie. (Why you choose to befriend this human woman I do not understand, but we will yet have much amusement of it at Sharl's expense, or I am much mistaken.)

(Sharl is no different from the leader of a pack of wolves,) Chyrie thought, (playing games of dominance and intimidating everyone he can. A leader must find a better way of dealing with those who do not enjoy such games.)

"Wait." Visibly calming himself, Sharl walked over and took Rivkah's hand. "I'm sorry. I've let my worries make me harsh these days." He smiled for what seemed the first time since Valann and Chyrie had seen him, an engaging, crooked grin that made him suddenly handsome. "I was angry when you told me—" He glanced at the elves.

"They already know," Rivkah said gently. "Chyrie knew before I was even sure myself."

Sharl nodded.

"They are a perceptive folk," he said wryly. "Rivkah, in another time, at another place, I might not have been angry at all. I might have been glad. At the time when you told me, it was just another worry. Can you understand?"

"Of course." Rivkah smiled. "Now, go meet with your advisers. I'll take Valann and Chyrie back to their rooms, get the mages settled, and then I'll join you."

Rivkah showed them back to their quarters and reminded them how to reach the closest bathing pool, and then left them to their own devices. This suited Valann and Chyrie perfectly, and they took two skins of wine from their packs and retraced their steps to the bathing room.

"There are some advantages to this human city," Val admitted, tossing his clothes in a corner and testing the water with a toe. "At least they do not have to melt snow in the winter for water."

"And in the heat of summer they have no cool lake or stream to swim in and to chill their wine," Chyrie reminded him. She, too, dipped a foot in the bubbling liquid. "Bathing in hot water. I would never have thought of such a thing."

Valann grinned mockingly at her.

"I see you still sit outside the water," he teased.

"As do you." Chyrie laughed, then shrugged and slid into the water, yelping at the unfamiliar feeling of hot water closing around her and the tickling of the bubbles. Val quickly followed.

(Chyrie.)

Surprised, Chyrie lost her footing briefly and slipped under the water; Val hauled her back up, and she let him hold her while she answered Dusk's call.

(I am here.) Dusk was not as strong a beast-speaker as she was, but he had worked with the brighthawk longer, and his call was strong and clear.

(There is news,) he told her. (You should tell the humans that a small party of human raiders, clothed and armed as the ones at the altars, attacked the Dawn's Edge clan only hours ago. Word has only just reached us.)

(What of the Dawn's Edges?) Chyrie asked, alarmed. Dawn's Edge was not far north of Wilding. (How did they fare?)

(Two were slain,) Dusk thought. (Most of the humans were killed, but some fled back out of the forest. The incident has much frightened many clans, and several who refused to join their force to ours have now reconsidered. Many wish to send some of their folk immediately to the city to be sheltered. Blue-eyes will not join us, nor agree to give us passage, and Western Heart, to the north of Blue-eyes, say the same, but the Brightwaters to the south have now promised both. The first elves from the Brightwater clan should reach Allanmere in two days, with others following soon after.)

(I will alert the humans and tell them of the raid,) Chyrie promised. (If you could send a map such as Rowan made, showing the locations of the clans and those who have allied with Inner Heart, it might be of assistance.)

(I will send an owl with the map tonight,) he promised.

(Each elf who comes to the city should bring his or her bow, if they use them,) Chyrie told him. (There are bows here, but a child could make better. Wine would be welcome, and it would be wise for the elves to also bring as much food as they can carry. There are few stores in the city, and should the food run low, well that our people have their own.)

"Chyrie," Val murmured, drawing her attention back from the forest. "Tell Dusk to send pots of poisons for arrows and blades."

(A good thought,) Dusk replied when Chyrie relayed the message. (I will send our best poisons, and their antidotes as well, and also salves and potions. The Dawn's Edges say they will send their Gifted One, as she is a ripe female. She is an exceptional healer and known to be well versed in plant lore, both poisons and medicines. What of the weapons the lord promised?)

(Some mages have arrived here, but the weapons for our people have not yet come,) Chyrie told him. (I will see that they are sent to the forest as soon as they arrive.)

(Then I will contact you again as new tidings arrive,) Dusk thought, vanishing from her awareness.

Chyrie quickly told Val what Dusk had relayed to her, and Valann frowned in consternation.

"Sharl said we could expect the barbarians to arrive in less than two months," Chyrie said. "But why do they attack now?"

"These are but small advance groups," Valann said thoughtfully, "such as the one Sharl and his people pursued into the forest. But it may well be that they will arrive sooner than expected. Sharl must be informed of this."

"Now?" Chyrie sighed, clinging to Valann.

"Are you not wearied by your conversation with Dusk?" he asked, grinning.

"No, for it is he who sent his thoughts out, as I did this morning," Chyrie said. She ran her hands down Val's skin, warm in the water. "Must we go now to warn Sharl?"

"He said he was going to meet with his advisers," Val said, nuzzling the back of her neck. "Perhaps there is no need for us to rush immediately to him."

Chyrie turned to him, then grimaced when her belly interposed itself between them.

"Soon I shall be too heavy and round to couple," she groaned.

Valann laughed.

"Not so very soon," he said. He lifted her with one hand, taking advantage of her body's buoyancy in the water. "And should you become too heavy, then we must simply find another pool of water."

He tossed her suddenly away from him, letting her splash resoundingly into the deeper water, and she emerged sputtering; before she could protest, however, he covered her mouth with his.

"Two days," Sharl groaned. "I had no idea they'd start arriving so soon. Nothing's prepared. Where am I going to put all those elves?"

"We can't put them anywhere except the keep," Rivkah said unhappily. "The people are too hostile."

"Our room alone would hold many," Valann said reasonably. "We are not like your people, to desire so much empty space and solitude, and we do not require raised beds for comfort. A few rooms such as ours would likely hold all the clans will send, and this is the safest place in the city for them."

"My advisers are in an uproar," Sharl said grimly. "This is moving too fast for the people. Some of them will likely flee westward, abandoning their lands and the city. They have reason to hate the elves, and this sudden invasion, if you will, is going to cause problems. I thought I'd have more time to ease them into it. I'll have to have a gathering in the square and address the people as soon as I can arrange it, tomorrow if I can."

"Perhaps news of an alliance with the elves would reassure them," Rivkah mused. "There's been some unrest simply because of that hostility. I've heard folk talk of leaving for that reason alone."

"Why would they leave?" Chyrie asked, surprised. "This is their home."

"You don't understand," Sharl told her. "Most of the people haven't really had time to settle here. They came for the promise of good land and the possibility that one day this would be a prosperous trade city. It's all a gamble to them. There's no assurance to them that the city will be here for their children, no promise of continuity. Why shouldn't they gamble on another, more established city?"

"That is the question you must answer for them," Valann said patiently. "You brought them here, believing this would be a great city, and they believed because you did. You must make them see that you still believe, and they will believe with you. If you wish them to stand firm and put down roots in this soil, you must show them that you, too, will do so. Do you understand?"

Sharl frowned, then slowly nodded.

"I think I do," he said. He turned to Rivkah, sighing.

"I've always been better with swords than words," he said. "And I've never been skilled in dealing kindly with people. I've always relied on you for that. Will you stand with me tonight?"

"Of course." Rivkah smiled, taking his hand.

"And tomorrow," Sharl said slowly, grinning crookedly, "when I can arrange for a priest, will you stand with me as my wife?"

Rivkah's smile faded, and the color drained from her face.

"You can't mean that," she said. "It would ruin your chance to make a marriage alliance with another city."

Sharl shook his head.

"The alliance we need is with our forest neighbors," he said, "and I want you to help me get it. It's your choice, Rivkah. I couldn't ask for a stronger High Lady at my side. But whatever you decide, I'll declare your child my heir. I owe the people of this city that much hope." He took her hand. "And I owe you much more than that."

Valann groaned, utterly disrupting the mood. Sharl and Rivkah glanced irritatedly at him.

"You speak as if you were making a treaty," he scolded Sharl. "Tell her you love her and then put her on the floor and prove it."

Sharl looked back at Rivkah, raising one eyebrow challengingly.

"Well?" he said.

Rivkah laughed.

"Very well," she said, forcing her face into a more serious expression. "I'll marry you, Sharl, whenever it can be arranged. But I'll *not* be tumbled on a cold stone dining-hall floor for the servants' amusement. And you must meet with your captains to tell them the news, and arrange a town meeting tomorrow. I'll start dispatching messengers to the farthest farms."

"They will make a fit pair," Valann said disgustedly as he and Chyrie left Sharl and Rivkah to their planning. "They both would rather talk than couple, even on the night they pledge to be mates."

"And now we will likely get no evening meal," Chyrie sighed, "and I am *very* hungry."

Val chuckled.

"You have eaten five times today already," he said. "Those young ones are more ravenous than a bear after his winter's sleep. Come, we will find the place where their food is prepared and get our own meal."

Rivkah had not shown them the kitchens, but the elves had only to follow their noses, reasoning correctly that if the lord ate hot food in the dining hall, the place where that food was prepared could not be too distant.

Valann and Chyrie, accustomed to preparing food and seeing it prepared over open fires, could never have imagined a place like the kitchens. The barrage on their senses—smells of numerous foods and smoke, the confusion of numbers of humans hurrying here and there, and the clamor of noises—almost made them retreat, but curiosity and hunger were stronger, and they marched boldly in.

Preparations for dinner were in progress, and at first the humans were too busy to notice their guests. When the first woman shrieked and dropped the bowl she had been carrying, however, all work stopped, and the humans stood staring in silence at this unexpected invasion.

"We would like food," Valann said, a little uncertainly.

Several of the humans glanced worriedly at each other, and a few murmured together; finally one of the younger males nerved himself to come forward.

"Do you wish your dinner in your quarters?" he said very slowly and rather loudly, as if to make himself better understood.

"Why carry it so far?" Val asked, surprised. "We will eat here if there is a place for us."

There was another moment of awkward silence, then hurriedly servants rushed to clear off space at the end of one of the tables, while others brought platters, goblets, and bowls. This time Val and Chyrie allowed the servants to pile up cushions for them to sit upon, for sitting on the table would have obviously taken up their work space.

"This is good food," Chyrie said cheerfully, reaching for a second joint of fowl. "I admit it surprised me, how fine human food can be." She looked dubiously, however, at the wine. "Have you any beer in this place?"

The young man who had spoken to them quickly poured tankards of cellar-cold beer, and the humans rather self-consciously returned to their work, not without frequent glances at the elves. By the time Valann and Chyrie had had their fill, the wary glances were occasionally interspersed with amused and even proud grins at the enthusiasm with which the elves attacked the food, and the uneasy servility had been replaced by a kind of jovial competition over whose preparations found the most favor with their guests.

As Valann and Chyrie expected, there was no invitation to join Rivkah and her teacher; Chyrie speculated that hopefully Rivkah's teacher was being similarly neglected. They took advantage of their quiet evening to pay another visit to the bathing pool, and then took some wine—their own—and a couple of furs to the top of the watchtower Rivkah had shown them. They had been afraid that there might be night guards on the watchtower, but there were none; either they were all occupied elsewhere, or Sharl did not yet see the need for constant vigilance actually within the city.

They made themselves a comfortable seat on the wall in one of the cut-out niches, lining it with the soft fur, and settled there, one behind the other. From this height, the city seemed to sparkle with lights. The glow of fires in the streets and at hearths, torches, and lanterns all produced the illusion of a swarm of fireflies settling over the buildings.

"It is beautiful," Valann admitted, wrapping warm arms around Chyrie. "Look, they have created their own forest— a forest of stone and light."

Chyrie leaned back against him, enjoying, as always, the feeling of his hard chest against her back. The city *was* beautiful by moonlight, but it was a beauty that troubled her— a forest, yes, but of cold, dead stone. Fireflies, yes, but not living things. Despite the huge number of lives in this city, the city was a dead place feigning life.

"I do not want my children born here," she murmured. "Not in this place. Please promise me that."

"Yes, they must be born in the forest." Valann kissed the back of her neck. "And you should be among our own people when your time comes upon you in any wise, although I fear no healer in the forest knows any more than I do about bringing two children at one birthing."

Chyrie felt a gentle tug at her mind and looked toward the forest, recognizing Dusk's touch. Her keen night vision picked out the approaching owl, and she gasped—this was a great-grandfather owl, absolutely huge. There was no question of holding out her arm for this gigantic bird; Valann and Chyrie scrambled off the wall and stood back to give it room.

The ancient owl was so pale a gray as to be almost white. It did not land, but flapped ponderously down close to the top of the tower, dropped a packet, and rose laboriously again, this time making a circle of the city. Chyrie knew that in this darkness, there was little danger among the night-blind humans that one might try to shoot it, and doubtless Dusk wanted his own look at the human city.

"It is the map he promised," Chyrie said, unfolding the skin. Many more clans had been marked from the preliminary map they had seen in Rowan's hut.

Val was silent for a long moment.

"I have thought on this," he said. "Do you think we are wise giving Sharl this map? From it he will know the location of each of the clans, something we have kept hidden even one clan from the other for so many centuries. He can guess our numbers as well. Should we trust the humans with this knowledge?"

Chyrie gazed worriedly at the map. The Wilding marker seemed very visible, very prominent on the map. She thought about how few the Wildings were, how vulnerable they were there at the edge of the forest, easily accessible, bounded by hostile clans who would slay them if they tried to flee deeper into the forest.

"It is too late for caution," Chyrie said slowly. "Rowan did not conceal her map from the humans, and we ourselves showed her where to mark Wilding upon it. Now we can betray only out-kin. We must trust in the geas to protect us after this conflict, should these humans have an inclination to make use of this knowledge."

"What you say is true. We will give him the map, but not at this moment." Val rolled the skin again, and they resumed their cozy seat on the wall, watching the great owl turn back toward the dark blur of the forest.

Val rubbed his cheek against her short curls. "I know why you never let your hair grow, love."

"Because it is cool and easy to care for." Chyrie laughed, shaking her head so that her hair danced over Valann's face. "Because I enjoy tickling your nose."

"Because I am blessed with the kindest mate who ever took pity on a man embarrassed by his overabundant fur," Val corrected. "But let it grow, love, if you wish, for in but a few months our kinfolk will be staring at our two children, and they would not see us if we were dyed blue."

"What of one dyed every color the Mother Forest has ever created?" Chyrie teased, pushing up the sleeve of her tunic to display his latest rainbow-hued butterfly. "Am I not your silent boast of the extent of your gifts?"

"It is yours I envy," Val said, in a tone so serious that it surprised Chyrie. "The wild blood in you is what first drew me to you, love. Sometimes through you I feel as though I touch the Mother Forest Herself."

"Do you?" Chyrie turned to him and smiled. "At this moment I only wish you would touch me."

Valann slid from their seat and lifted her carefully down to the waiting furs.

"Nothing"—he smiled back—"would please me more."

VIII

CHYRIE SHIVERED AND stepped uneasily closer to Valann. She could never have imagined so many humans in one place. Massed together there in the marketplace, they looked like an army.

Sharl waited for the angry shouting to die down before he continued.

"These elves are only envoys," he said. "There are whole clans in the forest who are joining us as allies. Other clans who refused are changing their minds. There are still some who do refuse, but we'll work with the clans willing to help us. It is still my hope to forge a lasting peace with the elves, and it isn't a vain hope. My journey through the forest, and these envoys at my side, they prove it."

"They've killed many of us," a man shouted, "including your own guard. Why should we trust them?"

"As I said, there are certain clans still hostile to us," Sharl said. "They are angry at us, just as you would be angry if someone came onto your land and stole your livestock or trampled on your crops. The forest is their land, and when we hunt there, we are taking *their* livestock, the food from their children's mouths. When we cut down the trees, we're taking their shelter and their protection. They've only protected their land, just as I want to protect ours."

A thoughtful murmur ran through the crowd, but another man stepped forward, and Chyrie recognized Romuel.

"If we can't hunt or cut timber," he shouted, "how will we survive? We need game and fruit to store against a siege. We need wood to build some of the fortifications, for our very homes, for fires. We can't go on burning dung and river drift forever."

"We'll burn peat," Sharl said. "I've had men cutting peat at the swamp's edge for many months now. We've been burning it in the keep, and it burns well. Not hot enough for a forge, but wood doesn't burn that hot, either. For that we'll need black rock from the north, and I've already bargained for a large load to arrive within days. We'll build your homes from stone, as we've been doing, and stone won't burn down if our enemies shoot a fire arrow into it."

"And what of food?" a woman called. "We can't eat stone. If the city is besieged, we'll starve, and now you say the elves are sending more mouths for us to feed."

"The elves who shelter here will bring their own food," Sharl answered. "There's still good hunting on the plains west of the river, and there's fish in the Brightwater. I've been told that the elves who come to us will earn their keep helping us to fish and hunt, those who can, and even standing as bowmen in battle. Some are healers, and others have other magic they will use on our behalf. Some have skills they will teach us. They're a brave folk, and I'm proud to have them stand beside me."

"And how do you know they won't turn on us?" the woman demanded. "How do you know they won't take our city themselves, once they have a foothold in it?"

Sharl chuckled.

"I'll let them answer that themselves," he said, pushing Valann and Chyrie forward.

Chyrie gaped, shocked to silence, but Valann faced the woman squarely.

"We have lived in the forest century upon century," he said. "Had we wanted a stone city, we could have long ago built one. We do not wish to live here any more than you wish to live in the water like a fish. And we will not turn on you because we do not wish to trade one enemy for another. We wish only to protect our people and keep our homes, even as you do. Even those clans who will not ally with humans would not harm any of you, if you would keep from their lands and leave them be."

"I've met with the leader of the elvan alliance," Sharl said. "She's a wise leader and has dealt with me fairly and honestly, and I believe she will continue to do so."

"And what if you fall?" a man shouted. "What will become of us then?"

"Then my lady will lead you," Sharl said, "and after her, my heir." He seized Rivkah's hand and pulled her forward. "This very hour we will be wed on the steps of the keep. I will give you a High Lady, my people, and I will give you an heir. What will you give me? Will you give me the loyalty you swore when I brought you here?"

There was a moment of stunned silence. Then a "Yes!" came from somewhere near the back of the crowd. Another joined it, and another. Slowly the cry built, as resolution replaced the doubt and anger on the people's faces. Some joined hands; others lifted their children high, and finally most of the crowd were cheering. Valann and Chyrie hurriedly retreated to Sharl's carriage before the humans swarmed upon Sharl and Rivkah, lifting them over their heads and carrying them, laughing, to a wagon full of hay and tossing them in. Dozens of humans clustered around the wagon, pulling it toward the keep.

(What an odd thing,) Chyrie thought, frowning. (Why should they not doubt him now, simply because he will mate Rivkah?)

(Because now he has a mate and child to protect,) Valann told her. (They see that he risks as much as they. A man alone may spend his life cheaply if he is foolhardy. You know that nothing fights more fiercely than a beast defending the young in its den.)

Because of the mass of people going before it, the carriage took longer to reach the keep and could not get through the crowd at the gate. The carriage driver shrugged and tied the horses at the wall, resigned.

"Now we will miss their mating," Chyrie said disgustedly, "although we are in some part responsible for it. I cannot push through that crowd of humans, nor see over their towering heads."

"Then we will find another way," Valann said. "This wall was made to keep out large-footed humans, not nimble tree-climbing elves, and we can descend from one of the towers and go around the crowd."

Valann was right; doffing their boots, the elves found ample fingerholds and toeholds on the stone block wall, and despite its height soon reached the top. Sharl and Rivkah were already on the steps of the keep with a strangely robed human male, presumably the priest, but the ceremony had not proceeded, as Sharl and Rivkah looked worriedly around them. At last Rivkah spotted the elves atop the wall and pointed, laughing.

"There you are!" Sharl shouted. "Come down and stand with us!"

Valann nudged Chyrie, pointing to the hay-filled wagon sitting just inside the wall not far away. Chyrie nodded delight-edly, and they ran across the walkway to the appropriate spot. Valann leaped first, shouting with laughter as he bounced on the loose hay; then Chyrie followed, gasping with joy as, for once, she flew in her own body. The hay smelled sweet and fresh, but it was scratchy and managed to insinuate itself into her hair and clothing, and Chyrie brushed vainly at herself as Val pulled her around the crowd to Sharl and Rivkah's side.

The human ceremony made little sense to the elves; while they understood the words the priest used, the usage itself was confusing. It was certainly like no mating ceremony Chyrie or Valann had ever seen.

(They speak much of lands and duties,) Chyrie thought, scowling. (Why do they say nothing of the joys of mating, the binding of spirits? Are they such grim folk that for them there is no pleasure in mating, only purpose?)

(It cannot be so joyless as all that,) Val returned, (or they would never mate. You can see that they are happy from their faces. Later you can ask Rivkah what pleasures are found in mating for the human folk. I wish only to get out of this press of humans. They smell unclean, and they look at us as we look at out-kin patrols, despite Sharl's words.)

Sharl repeated his promises after the priest, then Rivkah. Chyrie turned to gaze at Valann, clasping his hand.

(Two hearts that beat as one,) she thought, remembering the day of their mating, the smell of the sweet oils that had been rubbed into her skin and the flowers strewn about them. (Two bodies, one spirit.)

(We are the seedlings of the Mother Forest,) Val replied. (Warm rain, rich soil, and ripe seed; the blessings of the Mother Forest on our mating.)

(May our children be many as the leaves of the tree,) Chyrie thought, grinning as she touched her belly. (May the sun shine bright upon them.)

The priest had finished his long list of stern reminders to Sharl and Rivkah of the many duties and responsibilities associated with their mating. He intoned some final blessing, and the people began to cheer and shout, startling Valann and Chyrie very much. Masses of humans rushed forward to embrace Sharl and Rivkah, and Val and Chyrie hurriedly retreated around them and inside the door of the keep, peering out cautiously around the sturdy wooden doors.

"I, too, do not enjoy such crowded gatherings," a light voice said, startling them even more. They turned to confront a gray-haired human male, short and slight, a few wrinkles around his eyes and mouth betraying his age.

"Forgive me," the man said, breaking into a sunny smile. "I am Loren, a friend of Rivkah's."

"Her teacher?" Chyrie eyed the man with new respect, seeing nothing to distinguish him from other humans. "We are honored . . . Grandfather," she said a little hesitantly. The human word did not carry quite the same connotations as its elvan equivalent. "I am Chyrie, and my mate is Valann."

"And I'm Loren. Oh, I said that already, didn't I?" He grinned even more widely. "Rivkah promised to introduce me to the two of you, but things as they stand, I thought I'd leave her be and simply introduce myself, and ask if you might care to dine with me this evening. I imagine the happy bride and groom will be—ah—dining privately, and likely supping in their quarters as well."

"The first night we were mated"—Val chuckled—"we forgot to eat entirely."

"For two days," Chyrie added.

Loren laughed delightedly.

"You are so wonderfully different from the elves near Cielman," he said. "Come, let us leave this joyful crowd to themselves."

"Only a moment," Val said. "We must wish them well."

It meant another difficult push through the crowd, but Val and Chyrie finally managed to make their way back to Sharl and Rivkah.

"May your joy go deep as the roots of the Mother Forest," Val said, nodding to Sharl and Rivkah.

"May your children be many as the leaves of Her trees," Chyrie finished. She pulled Rivkah down for a hug. "My heart sings for you," she whispered into the human woman's ear.

Loren was still waiting for them, and he escorted them back up to his own quarters. Unlike Val and Chyrie's spacious room, his quarters were divided into three rooms: a sitting room, a sleeping room, and a sort of study. Servants appeared, laying a hearty supper in the sitting room, and Loren fussed over the meal until Val and Chyrie felt amusedly at ease with him.

"I would have come south with Rivkah and Lord Sharl," Loren chattered, "but they were traveling fast, and an old crow like me would only have slowed them down. Besides, when you reach my age, you want to travel a little more comfortably. And of course there were the other mages to bring, too. So tell me," he said, switching to heavily accented and rather clumsy Olvenic, "have my studies proved worthwhile?"

"I believe the elves you have met speak a slightly different tongue than we, Grandfather," Valann said diplomatically. "Perhaps it would be wisest for us to converse in the human tongue for your convenience."

"How very kind of you." Loren beamed at them. "You know, I'm really quite sorry the elves hereabouts aren't on better terms with the city. It's a terrible pity. There was an elvan village only a few leagues from Cielman, but they were so very aloof, you know, we never saw them except through our merchants, and even they weren't allowed into the city itself; they had to set up stalls outside the walls and do their trade there. Hardly profitable. I was so hoping the elves here would be more friendly. I wanted so very much to learn about elvan magic, you know. And now I hear that the humans and elves hereabouts don't get along at all. But you're rather different from the northern elves, you know," he continued thoughtfully. "Rather—if you don't mind my saying—smaller, really."

"We are Wilding," Valann told him. "Wildings are small in stature. Many other clans are taller, much taller, and colored differently. There will be elves from many clans coming here soon."

"Wilding. How interesting, how very interesting." Loren smiled. "And I don't suppose either of you are mages, or Rivkah would have told me."

Valann and Chyrie exchanged glances.

"We have few 'mages' as the humans mean," Chyrie said slowly. "Valann is a healer and I am a beast-speaker, and those are gifts given to few elves, but there are many such gifts. Our Gifted Ones are those who have been given many such gifts, or whose gifts are exceptionally strong. I have seen Gifted Ones who are likely what you would consider 'mages,' but I think they are somewhat different. I cannot explain it, I fear."

"Do you suppose any of these elvan mages might come to the city?" Loren asked wistfully.

"I do not doubt it," Valann said. "Many clans will be sending females with child to the city. I know that the Gifted One of the Dawn's Edges, a healer, will arrive soon, and surely there will be others."

"How wonderful, how very wonderful," Loren said delightedly. "But tell me, my lovely Chyrie, whatever is a 'beast-speaker'?"

"The Mother Forest has blessed me with the ability to touch the minds of Her creatures," Chyrie said. "It is an especially useful gift for sending messages over long distances. Even the youngest-minded beast can carry a message in thought to another beast-speaker, and follow simple commands if they choose to do so."

"How marvelous!" Loren exclaimed. "And can you do that with any animal you like?"

Chyrie raised her eyebrows.

"If there are beasts I cannot touch, I do not know," she said. "I have never met such a creature."

"Well, let's see, shall we?" Loren peeped into his pockets as if searching for something. "Weeka? Where are you hiding, Weeka, my pet? Come out, little one, and say hello to my new friends. Aha, there you are!"

The tiny creature he withdrew fit comfortably into his hand, and Chyrie and Valann leaned forward curiously. The creature had a golden-furred body rather like a squirrel's, but its front and rear paws, if they could properly be called such, more resembled tiny hands. Its furry tail also resembled that of a squirrel, but curled dexterously around Loren's wrist. Its head was rounder than a squirrel's, and set rather differently on its neck, and its eyes were large and bright; somewhat large, mobile ears, tipped with furry tufts, twitched nervously as the little creature hugged Loren's fingers tightly.

"Come, Weeka, don't be shy," Loren chided. "They won't eat you; they've already had their dinner, and one little chirrit is too small to make a decent meal anyway."

Weeka chattered nervously, a high-pitched chuckling sound, but hopped off Loren's hand and edged a few fingerlengths closer to the elves, eyeing them dubiously.

"Can you speak to my little one?" Loren asked Chyrie eagerly. "She's my familiar, and chirrits are rather intelligent anyway for their size."

Chyrie frowned a little worriedly—she had never seen such a beast in her life—but reached very gently for the creature's thoughts. Both she and the chirrit jumped a little, startled, as Chyrie touched a mind more sophisticated than she had ever sensed in a beast—more like sharing silent speech with a clever child, Chyrie realized, than touching an animal.

"Chrrrrrreeee!" the little creature gurgled, leaping forward. Before Chyrie could react, it had scampered up her arm and into her hair, its handlike paws wound tightly into her short curls and its tail tickling her neck while it leaned over her forehead to peer down into her face.

"Did—did it speak?" Val asked incredulously, reaching to help Chyrie as, laughing helplessly, she tried to disentangle the chirrit from her hair. "Did it say my mate's name?"

"Indeed she did speak, didn't you, Weeka, my little one?" Loren laughed. "Come down, Weeka, come down at once, I say! Oh, dear, when she's this excited, sometimes she makes droppings right where she is. Behave, mischievous little monster!"

Chattering affrontedly, Weeka allowed Valann to coax her down out of Chyrie's hair, but settled herself adamantly next to Chyrie on the table, giving Loren a very "So there!"-sounding chirp as she did so.

"Trying to make me jealous, eh, my pet?" Loren said, shaking his finger at the chirrit. "But I couldn't be more delighted. Oh, what a pity, what a pity I can't just walk right into the forest and meet all these wonderful folk," he mourned.

Val grinned wryly.

"Had *you* been the first of humankind met by our folk," he said, "likely we would have permitted it. It is an unfortunate truth that most humans have brought swords to our forest, not smiles. But how did you come to bring with you such a curious creature?"

"Weeka is my familiar," Loren said. "I can hear her thoughts, a little, and she can hear mine, and sometimes I can see what she sees. It's a special spell, very difficult, where a mage puts some of his magic into his familiar. Weeka was a gift to me from a friend, a mage who lives far to the west. But do tell me, however did you meet Rivkah? She's always been my very finest pupil. I knew she'd do something wonderful one day."

This time Chyrie and Valann exchanged glances more soberly.

"She and Sharl came upon us when we were being attacked by barbarian humans," Chyrie said slowly. "They fought bravely to help us, and Rivkah healed my mate. We came to the city with her to speak for our people, and she has made us welcome."

(Well spoken, if incompletely,) Val thought ruefully. (But we will keep our peace as Rowan bade us.)

"A fight and a rescue! How wonderful," Loren exclaimed. "And now the lord wants an alliance. Very sensible. I'm glad Rivkah's finally gotten him to marry her. He might have done it long ago if his father hadn't gone on so about marriage alliances. I said, 'Marry the girl, and nobility be damned'—

didn't I, Weeka?—but no, young folk these days can't see what's right there in front of their noses—"

A polite mental nudge distracted Chyrie from Loren's ramblings, and she recognized Dusk's touch through the brighthawk.

"Please excuse us," Chyrie interrupted, standing and pulling Valann with her. She patted her rounded belly. "These days I seem to seek the privy every hour."

"Oh, of course, of course," Loren said hurriedly. "But come and see me again soon, or perhaps I'll come see you, or Rivkah and I might come—"

Chyrie hurried out, pulling Val with her.

"Is something wrong?" Val asked as they climbed the stairs to the watchtower.

"I think not," Chyrie said. "But Loren is a kindly man, and he would have wanted to come, and I did not like to refuse him."

As it was only midafternoon, they could actually see the brighthawk, a mere dark speck in the distant sky.

"Does Dusk have news?" Valann asked.

Chyrie touched the brighthawk's mind and shook her head.

"No, I think he only wished my attention," she said. "A moment."

She settled herself comfortably with Valann in their seat on the wall and looked out through the brighthawk's eyes, immediately seeing why Dusk had called to her; the brighthawk flew over a small group of elves, mostly children and women, some of the latter swollen with pregnancy. Most carried packs, while others dragged travois laden with sacks and bundles.

"It is the Brightwaters," Chyrie murmured to Valann. "Dusk wished to alert me to their arrival, so we could see them kindly met at the gates."

Val said nothing, and Chyrie pulled back her awareness to look at him. He was staring at the brighthawk, and the expression on his face reminded Chyrie of the aching hunger she had felt, looking at the forest through the stone slits of the wall.

Daringly, for she had never attempted such a feat before, she *reached* for Valann's thoughts and the brighthawk's at

the same time. For a moment her perceptions fragmented into
a host of confused images, and her mind seemed to stretch
between her mate and the brighthawk, like a bowstring pulled
too tightly, almost at the breaking point, but then Valann was
with her, astonished and a little frightened, as they soared
together far above the ground. Gradually Chyrie grew more
comfortable with the unfamiliar sensation of touching two
minds at once, and discovered in Val's presence a kind of
anchoring, giving her an unaccustomed feeling of security and
strength.

She nudged the brighthawk higher, and they climbed together, powerful wings beating the air, until the elves below them
were mere ants moving on the ground.

(Oh, love, never could I have dreamed this,) Val sang in her
mind. (By the Mother Forest, how can I hold such joy?)

(You are my strength,) Chyrie replied, urging the brighthawk for one last upward push. (Let me be your wings.)

Suddenly she released the brighthawk and it dove, screaming
its pleasure, wings folding tightly against its body. The wind
whistled by them and the earth spun below, reeling drunkenly
closer and closer, as the elves looked up in amazement—

—then their wings caught air and they curved sharply, only
just missing the top of the first elf's head, arching back into the
sky. The brighthawk silently but strongly protested this unaccustomed recklessness, and Chyrie, strained by the feat, had no
strength to argue; reluctantly, she abandoned the brighthawk's
mind and pulled Valann back with her to the watchtower.

They sat panting raggedly against the stone, both of them
sheened with sweat, until Valann mutely folded Chyrie into
his arms and squeezed the breath out of her, and Chyrie could
feel his tears wetting her cheek.

(There are no words to thank you for such a moment,) Val
thought, too shaken to speak. (Oh, love, how can you bear to
return from such a flight? My soul cries for joy, and my blood
burns—)

His grip became even stronger, and his mouth took hers
almost savagely. For a moment Chyrie reveled in his ferocity,
the fire in her matching his; then a moment of sanity was hers
and she pushed him away hard, almost stunning him as his

head smacked against the stone blocks. Brief anger flashed through his eyes, and he snarled and reached for her again, but Chyrie scrambled backward, reaching for his thoughts, at the same time trying to calm the fierce heat in herself.

(Valann, you are not a beast,) she thought firmly. (It is the wild blood you feel. You must not let it rule you. I will couple with you and gladly, but you must calm yourself, or you will hurt our children. Do you understand?)

Valann took a ragged breath and then flung himself away from her, pressing his face against the stone of the wall, clenching his hands until she saw blood trickle there. At last she felt him calm a little, and she went to him, holding him close.

"Forgive me," she murmured. "I should not have done that without warning you."

Valann took a deep breath and leaned his head against her.

"Forgive *me*," he said. "I did not know how heady a wine a beast's mind can be. I fear I became drunk upon it."

Chyrie smiled.

"That is not always an ill thing," she said, chuckling. "I remember the first time I touched a wolf, and when we coupled I clawed you so that it looked as if you ran bare-backed through a bramble patch, but you swore I had never pleased you more." She sighed regretfully. "I would gladly share the wild blood with you, but I have grown so large that it might be a danger. We must have more care."

Val nodded, holding her tightly until their breathing quieted.

"No wonder you are my fierce and hungry she-fox." He laughed, nuzzling her neck. "I have not burned with such a fire since my passage from child to adult. How do you bear it?"

"I was many years learning to master the wild blood," Chyrie reminded him. "And still sometimes it masters me, as well you know."

Valann raised himself on an elbow to look at her.

"How did you do it?" he asked. "How were you able to share that flight with me?"

Chyrie shook her head.

"Like skill with a bow or sword, I believe my gift grows with use," she said. "I would not have dared such a thing before. But the times have made me try feats I might never have dreamed of otherwise, and I saw how you longed to share my wings. It was not so draining as I might have thought, and there will be many other flights, but you must learn to master yourself afterward, and not only for my safety."

"For a time I was not myself," Valann sighed.

"And that is the danger," Chyrie told him. "Just as I take Chyrie into the body of the hawk, so, too, do I bring back some of the hawk with me. Sometimes I hardly know what I am. Sometimes you are all that brings me back."

"Then I bless the Mother Forest for making me your mate," Valann said lovingly, "for this world would be a sorry place without you, my she-fox. Come, let us go and greet the Brightwaters, for your smell dizzies me and I am not certain of myself."

"Very well," Chyrie sighed resignedly. "But tonight you must doubly compensate me for your afternoon flight."

"Love, if I am granted my wish, not one life in the keep will sleep all the long night for our cries." Valann chuckled.

At that moment the trapdoor raised, and Sharl's irritated face appeared.

"My guards tell me there's a group of elves approaching," he said. "I'd appreciate it if, since I've had to postpone my postnuptial celebrations, you'd take the trouble to come with me to welcome them."

"We were just coming to do so." Valann smiled. "And if you tell us which rooms we should use, you need not accompany us."

"I can't send you through the city alone," Sharl said annoyedly. "We'll take the carriage, and some wagons for our guests."

Rivkah was waiting with the carriage, dressed in a simpler gown, and from the contented expression on her face, Chyrie speculated that although their "postnuptial celebrations" might have been interrupted, they had not entirely been postponed.

Val and Chyrie were suitably impressed by the difference a speech and a wedding had made in the people. As they rode through the city, humans stopped what they were doing to stare at the elves, but their curiosity no longer seemed so hostile. Some waved cheerily, and others called greetings.

Valann and Chyrie had entered the city through the east gate initially, but as the Brightwaters were following the river, this time the carriage took them to the south gate, where a considerable crowd was waiting.

Unlike the east side of the city, this section of the wall had been completed, and there were no work crews here, but the gate towers and wall walk were now crowded with guards and peasants, all staring at the small band of elves approaching.

Sharl climbed down from the carriage.

"It appears my guardsmen have forgotten their instructions," he shouted angrily. "My orders were that the gates were to be opened to any elves seeking shelter, and wagons brought to meet them. I don't recall saying anything about standing over closed gates and staring like frightened rabbits, nor yet allowing every citizen in town onto the guard wall."

The guards hurriedly herded the peasants down from the wall and rushed to open the gates, most of them murmuring some embarrassed apology as they passed near Sharl.

About sixteen adult elves and as many children were waiting outside the gates; to Valann's and Chyrie's surprise, some of them were Longears and Southwinds, the lanky Longears and fair-haired Southwinds easy to spot among the dark-haired, sturdily built Brightwaters. The Brightwater with the longest braid coil, a light-skinned woman heavy with child, stepped forward expectantly, and Val and Chyrie, aghast at their own poor manners, hurried to join Sharl and Rivkah at the gate.

Sharl started to speak, but Chyrie touched his arm and shook her head, and it was Val who stepped forward.

"I am Arrin, of the clan Brightwater," the Brightwater said. "I come to share your fire at the invitation of Rowan of Inner Heart, bringing with me these kinfolk of Brightwater, and of clan Longears and Southwind."

"I am Valann of Wilding," Val said. "I make known to you Chyrie of Wilding, my mate, and Sharl and Rivkah, the Eldest of the Allanmeres. On their behalf I ask you to share our food and fire, and be made welcome among us."

"We are honored to share your food and fire," Arrin said a little dubiously, glancing at the humans crowded around. "May joy and friendship be our contribution." Then she added, "We have brought food and wine for our keep, and gifts for the Eldest of the Allanmeres."

"Your friendship is the greatest gift you can bring us," Rivkah said graciously. "My lord and I have dreamed of the day that our two peoples could stand together on these streets."

"I must apologize for my ill-mannered citizens," Sharl said, glaring at the guards. "They seem to have forgotten how to treat guests to our city." He added in the human tongue, "Some of you come over here and help, or do you think it speaks well for our city to let women and children load their goods into a wagon unassisted while healthy men stand gaping by?"

Several of the guards sheepishly put down their weapons and obeyed, a few even unbending so far as to lift children into the wagons.

"Rooms have been prepared for you at the keep," Sharl told the elves when they were settled in the wagons. "Val and Chyrie tell me that you are accustomed to sharing living space. If anything is not to your liking, you have only to tell us."

"Has a Gifted One come before us?" Arrin asked worriedly. "Some of us are near our time of birth."

"Dusk has told us that Dawn's Edge is sending their Gifted One," Chyrie said.

"Dawn's Edge!" Arrin exclaimed. "It will take many, many days to travel from there, perhaps as much as half a moon, and we have not even a healer among us."

"My mate is a healer," Chyrie told her. "And there are humans with healing magic."

Arrin glanced at Sharl and Rivkah doubtfully, but said nothing more.

"We should ride with the others," Val said as Sharl turned back to the carriage.

"No," Sharl said. "I need to speak with you both."

Reluctantly they climbed back into the carriage. It took some maneuvering to turn the carriage and the wagons around in the crowd, but it was finally accomplished, and thankfully not too many of the people tried to follow the wagons back to the keep.

"Why did you interrupt me?" Sharl demanded. "It was my place to greet them, not yours."

"You did not know the proper words," Valann apologized. "The welcome of food and fire you heard Dusk speak was—was not appropriate for the welcome of guests. Greetings are important to us, and doubly so, I think, when meeting out-kin. A careless word might have caused great harm."

"I see." Sharl frowned. "I'd gotten the impression your people didn't stand much on ritual."

"We do not," Valann said. "But what—rituals—we have, they are honored among us."

"Are there any other customs we should know?" Rivkah asked anxiously.

"It would be a kindly gesture to share food with the elders when they arrive," Valann suggested. "The ones who bead their hair. Arrin is one such. And you must accept the gifts they bring. It would be an insult to refuse them."

"Shouldn't I be the one giving gifts?" Sharl asked. "Among my people, it's usually the host who gives, not the guest."

"You must not," Chyrie cautioned him. "Gifts are for the showing of respect. As they have come to you for sanctuary, it is their place to honor you, acknowledging your leadership in your own lands. To give them gifts would be a sign of weakness, an attempt to buy their favor."

"I see." Sharl turned to Valann. "Thank you, then. It seems that when I deal with elves, it might be best to have the two of you present, to keep me from making any other mistakes."

"We will speak to them tonight," Valann said. "They must make allowances, too, in your place." He grinned. "And you and Rivkah must have peace in which to celebrate your mating."

"Too late," Sharl said wryly. "I think the mood is lost."

"Oh, I don't know." Rivkah laughed, leaning over to nibble at his ear. "I'm a very resourceful person. I'm sure I can think of something."

Over the next seven days, groups of elves arrived almost every day. At first Sharl tried to place each clan in separate

rooms, but he quickly found that his caution was unnecessary;
squabbles between even enemy clans seemed to cause no
hostility at all when both clans were on equally unfamiliar
territory. He also found that beds, or even cots, were unnecessary. Some clans brought sling beds, which could be hung
from two hooks on the walls, but most, like Val and Chyrie,
preferred to simply pile furs on the floor. The only problem,
it would seem, were the children.

The infants and toddlers were no bother at all. Schooled
from birth in the necessity of quiet unobtrusiveness, they rarely
cried, even when hungry or injured, and tending them seemed
to be a communal affair; whenever an infant needed attention, the closest elf, even if from another clan, cared for
it.

The older children, however, were another matter. Accustomed to running the forest in small packs, mostly doing
exactly as they pleased, the elvan children made themselves
at home in the keep, and, gradually, in the city, running the
halls, wall tops, and streets, hiding in corners and bursting
out to startle the unwary, and poking their noses into whatever interested them. At first it was a nuisance, as nothing
short of a locked door could keep them out of a room or
an area, but gradually Sharl realized that the children were
accomplishing what no amount of speeches or examples on
his part could. The citizens might shout and complain when
shrieking packs of younglings dashed through their shops or
homes, but it was good-natured complaining, for a child was
a child, human or elf, and even the surliest citizen saw little
harm in them. It was not long before human children began to
show up in these elvan child-packs, and soon the two groups
were inseparable, causing twice as much havoc as they would
have apart.

The adult elves proved more aloof, keeping to their quarters
or the keep's gardens for the most part—understandably, since
the majority of them were heavily pregnant, ill, or extremely
old. Loren immediately installed himself among these elves,
appointing himself their entertainer whether they wanted him
or not. He could usually be found in their quarters or with
them in the gardens, casting small magicks to amuse them,

goading the irritated Weeka to do tricks, and chattering away at a furious pace, never minding that most of the elves could understand little or none of what he said. His friendly eagerness, however, was impossible to resist, and a few of the elves began coming to Val and Chyrie shyly, almost ashamedly, to learn a few words of the human tongue. Loren's own command of Olvenic, however, quickly improved.

Val and Chyrie soon found that the arrival of the elves meant the end of their free time. When they were not serving as interpreters between the elves and the keep's servants or assisting Sharl and Rivkah in dealing with their guests, Chyrie was sending or receiving messages from Dusk, and Valann daily exhausted his healing, circulating among the infirm elves until a Gifted One could arrive.

Several wagons laden with trade goods and foodstuffs arrived in the middle of the week, to Sharl's and Rivkah's relief, and to the delight of the elves. There were five wagons filled with crates of swords, daggers, metal spears and arrowheads, axes, and even shields and chain armor in varying sizes to accommodate the slightest or the tallest clans. Chyrie relayed this news to Dusk, who promised that if guards could convey the wagons to the edge of Brightwater lands, elves would come to collect the goods and distribute them throughout the allied clans.

Mercenary groups, both warriors and mages, had also begun to arrive. The building of the fortifications speeded dramatically with the additional labor, but the number of troops arriving also meant building additional barracks and rooming houses. Another priority was introducing all new arrivals to the growing number of elves in Allanmere, and instructing them on their expected behavior when dealing with the elves.

Lua, one of the Southwinds, was the first of the visiting elves to bear her child, a healthy daughter. Fortunately it was not a difficult birth, since no Gifted One had yet reached them and the elves were reluctant to be attended by human mages or midwives. Sharl, in a rare burst of insight, held a great feast in the main hall to celebrate the first elf born in Allanmere, and Rivkah and Loren entertained them with dazzling illusions. Lua, proud of her baby and not a little awed by the elaborate occasion, named her daughter Shara.

The next day, on Rivkah's urging, Sharl had messengers proclaim throughout the city that the first elvan child had been born in the city, and that in celebration, every citizen of the city would receive a one-in-twelve reduction of taxes for that year. Sharl had agreed reluctantly, arguing that with the upcoming war he would need all the revenues he could get, but he was gratified, in the end, by the warmth this gesture generated between the elves and the humans.

Meanwhile, however, Valann worried. Even in the week since they had arrived in Allanmere, it was becoming apparent that the many demands on Chyrie's time, and the equally heavy demands of her unborn children on her body, were wearing harshly on her. She ate prodigiously, but her cheeks grew more hollow and her eyes were shadowed deeply, and despite her weariness, she slept badly or not at all.

"Sometimes she vomits in the mornings when she wakes," Valann confided to Rivkah. "It frightens me."

"You worry too much," Rivkah chided. "I vomit in the mornings, too. It's not uncommon."

"In thirty-one decades," Valann grumbled, "I have never known a healthy female to vomit in the mornings, whether or not she was with child. I pray a Gifted One will soon come. I have the healing power, but not the knowledge and experience of a Gifted One."

Another seven days passed, however, before Jeena, the Dawn's Edges' Gifted One, arrived with a group of nearly fifty elves. Jeena had brought another Gifted One, however, from North Ridge, and there were two other healers in the group as well.

"It is a pity I could not find another beast-speaker to ease your burden," Jeena said when she had examined Chyrie. "Unfortunately that gift is most often held only by very powerful Gifted Ones, and they cannot be spared by their clans. I do not agree with Rowan and Dusk that you should be here. I think you should return to the forest immediately."

"Now, wait a minute," Sharl protested.

"The Gifted One of the Wildings is not more skilled than you," Val argued.

"No. You should not return to Wilding," Jeena said, shaking her head. "There was another attack against the northeastern edge of the forest, a stronger attack. They did not engage Wilding, but it cannot be long, and you must not be endangered. I think you should return to Inner Heart, where there are now several Gifted Ones to tend you. You would be safe there as long as there is still one elf in the forest able to raise sword to defend you."

"She was nearly killed coming here," Rivkah protested. "Surely the trip back would be very hard on her, if not actually dangerous."

"I cannot go back to Inner Heart," Chyrie said. "As you say, there is no other beast-speaker to take my place here, and we cannot send and receive tidings from the forest without a beast-speaker."

"Yours is no ordinary pregnancy," Jeena said sternly. "That you carry two instead of one, that they have been so unnaturally speeded, that your health is affected, Chyrie—these things concern me deeply. Your children are drawing too heavily upon you."

"What could Dusk and the other Gifted Ones do for me that cannot be done here?" Chyrie asked practically.

Jeena shrugged.

"I only feel that you would be healthier among your own. But it is your life, and your unborn children, and if you are bound to stay, I will do what I can for you. There are potions that will help. Valann, come here, and I will show you a thing."

Val obeyed, and Jeena laid her hand on Chyrie's belly, placing Val's hand over her own.

"Feel what I am doing," Jeena said. "If I allow but a little healing energy to flow, her children drink it like a thirsty deer drinks water. I do not know whether it is because they are two, or because of the magic used upon them so soon after their conception, but they are drawing the very life from Chyrie. I will show you how to replace it."

Jeena cupped one hand behind the back of Chyrie's head and the other over her heart; at her direction, Val again placed his hands over hers.

"Ordinarily I give life through the navel, the seat of life," Jeena said. "But I believe that would speed the growth of her children. Focus your energy at these two points whenever she wearies unduly. She must sleep, if we have to potion her to do it, and she must eat much red meat, as Dusk told her. Air and exercise will benefit her, but she must not become overtired. I will check her daily."

"I've never seen anything like that," Rivkah said, awed. "Our mages have been studying how to combine power, transfer power to each other, for years, and you do it as matter-of-factly as breathing."

"Believe me," Jeena said wryly, "it is hardly that easy, and it takes a Gifted One many decades to learn."

"How long will it be until I bear?" Chyrie asked in a small voice. Jeena was obviously highly skilled, and her concern worried Chyrie in turn.

"Perhaps three moons, or even sooner," Jeena said. "Surely no longer than four. I cannot be certain because the presence of two lives confuses me. Their sparks of life are very strong indeed, like those with strong gifts." She smiled. "You may be the first elf in the long history of the Heartwood, Chyrie, to give two Gifted Ones to your clan."

"I will be more than content to give two healthy children to my clan," Chyrie said wryly.

"Can you tell if her children are male or female?" Sharl asked Jeena curiously.

Jeena raised her eyebrows.

"One is male, one female," she said. "Why do you ask?"

"I thought they would like to know." Sharl shrugged. "Most human parents would."

"It is not important to us," Chyrie said surprisedly. "I had never thought to ask." She turned to Rivkah. "Is it a concern to you? Perhaps Jeena could tell you the sex of your child, if you wish it."

"I'd like that," Rivkah said shyly. "If Jeena wouldn't mind."

Jeena touched Rivkah's belly, still almost flat, and smiled.

"You will bear a son," she said. "He is small still, but very strong. Soon he will let you know what a fierce little warrior he is."

"A son," Sharl breathed unbelievingly. "I'm to have a son!"

"I suppose I'm to eat lots of red meat, too." Rivkah grinned.

"Rich red meat is good for any woman bearing child," Jeena agreed, "but your body asks for berries and fruit."

"A son!" Sharl repeated.

"You will not have your son unless you feed your mate," Jeena said gently.

"Feed her? I'll have a feast prepared!" Sharl laughed. "Two feasts! A dozen!"

"We only just had a feast," Rivkah reminded him. "Be reasonable. We need to store food against a siege, not squander it."

"Some of the Brightwaters say they have a better kind of net," Sharl remarked. "They've got half the elves weaving cord. They say we can triple the number of fish we catch."

"Then we'll feast on fish when the catch triples." Rivkah laughed. "Come now, Sharl, and get out the map you drew, and have Jeena show you where the attack was, and estimate the number of soldiers. I want to talk to Crystal, the other Gifted One, about this elvan talent for sharing magic."

Jeena and the humans withdrew, and Valann and Chyrie, by silent agreement, sought their favorite quiet spot on the watchtower. Valann had half lied to Sharl when he told him that elves were accustomed to sharing their living space; for most elves it was true, but Valann and Chyrie had spent the better part of their lives living apart from the Wilding village, favoring the privacy and solitude of wide patrols and temporary camps. Now, with other elves sharing their room, Val and Chyrie usually sought the quiet of the watchtower in the evening. They had even taken to keeping their small clay firepot and some wood on the tower, so that Valann could continue the designs he was adding to Chyrie's present ornamentation, even after the daylight was gone.

"Jeena's words troubled you," Val guessed, cuddling Chyrie close on their favorite seat.

"This is an ill place, she was right in that much," Chyrie said, shivering. "I miss our kin, I miss the forest, I miss the feeling of green things around us. And every day I close my mind tight to the kitchen servants wringing fowls' necks or the stable hand kicking a dog. And I fear . . ." She fell silent.

"What do you fear?" Valann asked gently. "Tell me."

Chyrie ran her hand pensively over her belly.

"I fear that the children in my womb have human blood in them," she said slowly. "I fear that the violence done to me, or the magic used on them, has turned them awry. I fear that I might die in childbirth, or in battle, and never live to see our children born."

"For a woman bearing two healthy children, you are somber tonight," Val chided. "Jeena and Dusk have assured you that all is well with your children, and there is a forest full of warriors and strong stone walls between you and danger."

"I could die," Chyrie persisted, turning to Valann. "Many females die in childbirth, and they bear only one child, not two. What would you do if I die?"

Valann frowned, taken aback by her intensity.

"You and I are one spirit, love," he said gently. "Do you remember the day we were mated, when our souls first came together? How could I live without my soul, my fierce she-fox? I guard nothing with more care than your life, for it is my own as well."

"And if you died?" Chyrie's eyes were large and frightened. "What would I do?"

"Why, you would not let me die." Val laughed. "You are so determined, my sword dancer, I believe you would pull my spirit back from the roots of the Mother Forest Herself to stay with you. Come, why this fear tonight?"

"I think of our people," Chyrie admitted. "They live so close to the Dawn's Edges, who were attacked."

"Then send your brighthawk to our Gifted One tomorrow," Val suggested. "See how they fare, and warn them again. Perhaps some of our kin will come here to shelter."

"But it is so far," Chyrie protested. "The brighthawk will not wish to fly so far."

"He flew from Inner Heart to Blue-eyes," Val said practically. "It is no farther from Inner Heart to Wilding."

"But it is far from Blue-eyes to Wilding," Chyrie said. "I do not think I can touch the hawk from so far away."

"Then you will tell Dusk, and he will send a bird to them in your name," Val said. "You are becoming like the humans, hoarding worries as a squirrel hoards nuts against winter hunger." He pulled her closer and nuzzled the back of her neck. "Come, I know how to comfort you."

"Love, can we not stay here tonight?" Chyrie asked, turning in her seat to slide her hands under his tunic.

"Why not?" Valann smiled. "We can couple here in the sky like two hawks on the wing."

Chyrie said nothing, but sighed and pulled him closer.

IX

THE SUN PEEKED shyly over the forest, staining the sky purple, then pink, then orange. Chyrie sat quietly on the battlement, watching the sun rise, while Val snored softly on the furs. When the sun was high enough, she called the brighthawk.

The bird responded sluggishly, having fed heavily the evening before, but at Chyrie's urging it rose and flew northeast, its powerful wings lifting it higher to coast on the wind.

The air was still cool and crisp with morning dew, and the sun shone on the leaves below with that special brightness that only late-spring sun seems to give, and Chyrie thought poignantly that a flight had never been sweeter. She had flown birds before, although rarely anything as large as the brighthawk, but she had seldom gone above the green canopy of the forest. From such a height, she could marvel at the huge green expanse of the Heartwood, not flat as it always seemed to her, but rolling in gentle hills and valleys, broken here and there by stream, and in one place by the shimmering expanse of Moon Lake.

It was becoming more difficult to hold the hawk now. The hawk was not used to flying so far, and Chyrie was already far past the greatest distance over which she had ever tried to maintain rapport with a beast. She pressed the brighthawk harder, poured more of herself into the bond between them, feeling her link to her body grow weaker as she did so. For a moment she was frightened—she had heard stories of foolish beast-speakers losing their minds into the minds of some beast they touched—but her resolve strengthened her, and she pushed on.

Suddenly warm strength flowed into her, and far behind her she could sense Valann's presence. Reveling in her sudden feeling of power, of free flight, Chyrie *reached* back and pulled Valann in with her, drawing him in a breathless rush over the miles.

(You are as reckless as you are bold,) Valann thought, even as his joy poured over her like fresh water. (I thought you said this was dangerous.)

(Last night you said I was hoarding worries,) Chyrie teased. (Now you call me reckless. But with you here with me, I could fly to the end of the world and back.)

It seemed they *were* flying to the end of the world. Never having concerned herself with the rest of the Heartwood, Chyrie had had no idea it was so vast. The hawk was built for speed, not endurance, and it became more restive as it tired.

(The brighthawk must rest,) Chyrie thought regretfully. (I feared as much. I do not know if I can maintain the contact long enough. We must find another.)

Val hesitated, having never made the jump from beast to beast, and Chyrie sympathized; she had done it seldom enough herself. The brighthawk was tiring, however, and it was plain that it would oust them from its mind soon in any event.

They were over Black Feather lands now, slightly east of the altars. Chyrie cast about with her thoughts and found a spot-tailed hawk; it was smaller than the brighthawk, but still large enough to range a good distance. Before Chyrie could take time to doubt her ability to move both herself and Valann from the brighthawk to the spot-tail, she determinedly gathered her energy and *reached,* pulling Valann with her.

For a moment the world whirled around her as she was pulled tight, this time between her own body and the brighthawk's, the spot-tail and Valann, but her will was stronger than the confusion, and she held on grimly until she was looking clearly out the spot-tail's eyes.

The spot-tail, preying only on the smaller life of the forest, never traveled above the trees, and unlike the brighthawk, it had not been raised to accept a beast-speaker's control so easily, so Chyrie did not try to force it higher than its inclination. Still, it flitted through the trees at an amazing rate, and within a short time Valann and Chyrie joyfully recognized the familiar landmarks of Wilding territory.

They flew past a wide patrol, and Chyrie felt her own and Valann's delight as they recognized kin; but there was no beast-speaker among the patrol, and so after lingering long enough to drink in the familiar voices and faces, Chyrie turned the hawk west toward the Wilding village.

Unlike the Inner Hearts, Wildings did not build their homes on the ground, preferring the safety of woven-switch huts hung from sturdy branches or cradled close to the trunks of the great trees. Also unlike the Inner Hearts, there was no central firepit; the more secretive Wildings preferred the small braziers for light and heat, and built small, closed stone-and-clay ovens on the ground for cooking. Chyrie did not pause, but prodded the spot-tailed hawk directly to the hanging hut of the Wildings' Gifted One.

Riuma was in his hut, as usual; the Gifted One had a weakness in his eyes, and the light hurt them, so that he seldom went out by day. When Chyrie coaxed the spot-tail past the half-open leather flap that hung over the opening to the hut, Riuma looked up from the paste he was grinding in a clay bowl, his large, dark eyes wondering.

"What have we here?" he asked, putting the bowl down slowly so as not to frighten the hawk. "Hello, little flier. Who visits me today?"

(Greetings, Gifted One,) Chyrie thought. (It is Chyrie who visits you, and I bring my mate Valann with me.)

(Chyrie, and Valann, too!) Riuma thought, his eyebrows raising. (But the Inner Hearts sent word that you had gone to the human city far to the west. When did you return to the forest?)

(We have not returned, Gifted One,) Valann told him. (My mate has grown strong in the use of her gift.)

(Strong indeed, to come so far, and to bring you with her,) Riuma agreed. (But how do you fare? The Eldest was enraged when he heard what befell you two, and it was only fear of our lands being seized by humans that kept him from sending every fit warrior to your aid.)

(We are well,) Chyrie thought. (Were you told—)

(That you are with child, doubly so?) Riuma shook his head. (I was hard-pressed to believe such a thing; but who would invent a lie so fantastic? And then I received your own messages, and those I could not doubt. Would that you could return to us. I fear for you.)

(Rowan thought it a blessing from the Mother Forest,) Valann thought doubtfully.

(It may be so,) Riuma thought, shrugging. (But little in this life is given for nothing, and for a blessing on our people, it may be Chyrie who pays the price. Can you not come back, little one, that we can protect you and tend you?)

(Our word was the price of our release from Inner Heart,) Chyrie thought regretfully. (And Rowan wisely saw the need for a beast-speaker in this place.) She hesitated. (Is there no hope that the Eldest might send some of our people here for safety?)

Riuma shook his head.

(There was a meeting of the clan,) he told them. (He would not ally with Inner Heart, but he put the choice to our females who were ripe or with child that they might journey to the city for safety if they would. Each chose to stay, to stand in defense of our lands. Only last night our patrols at the forest's edge saw many humans to the north—near Silvertip lands—and soon it will come to battle.)

(How many humans?) Chyrie asked quickly.

(More than fifty, less than a hundred.) Riuma shrugged. (Who can count the fish in a school?)

(Would that we could add our swords to yours,) Valann thought angrily. (But we were given no such choice.)

(It may be as well you are where you are,) Riuma told him. (As Rowan said, Chyrie must indeed be protected. Her kin will fight the more strongly for knowing she and the lives she bears are safe, and that every human who falls to our swords will be one less to threaten her.)

(But tell us the tidings of the clan,) Chyrie thought eagerly. (What has passed since we left on wide patrol?)

(Your mother is well,) Riuma told her. (Leean is with the wide patrol who saw the humans. Jire, Mera, and Riss all bore healthy younglings, two females and a male. Mera has mated Arel. No one has returned to the Mother Forest since you left.)

The hawk was growing restive, unaccustomed to a beast-speaker's prolonged presence, and Riuma felt its resistance.

(You must go before you hurt this little brother,) he thought. (But before you go, Chyrie, there is something I wish to show you.)

His thoughts reached out to hers, and Chyrie could only helplessly admire his skill, for he touched her as gently as a mother might clasp her child's hand.

(Come with me,) he thought. (This is a teaching that the Gifted One before me gave to me, and today I will give it to you.)

He drew her gently away from the hawk and Valann, away from the hanging hut until they flowed into the tree itself, as easily as water flowed into a cup. Chyrie marveled at the slow pulse of life she felt, like the beat of a distant drum, sweet, warm life flowing upward from the roots to meet quicker, brighter life flowing down from the leaves.

Inward Riuma and Chyrie flew, through the concentric layers of the tree toward its center, and yet farther in and farther beyond that, until they touched a bright spark of burning life at the very heart of it all, and Chyrie felt a shock of—recognition?

(Follow an oak back to its very beginning and you find a seed,) Riuma told her as they bathed in the warm glow. (Follow a man back to his very beginning and you find a seed in a woman's womb. This is the door to the heart of the Mother Forest, the seed from which begins all life. If you looked deep within yourself you would find such a seed. That is the seed to which we all return, that we may grow once again. From this seed comes the life that feeds us, and a Gifted One learns to use this strength. You have felt the touch of it when you dance, when you touch the mind of a beast, and this is because at those times you touch the Mother Forest. Just as an acorn is the beginning of an oak, its leaves are its outer limit, and we—

you and I, Chyrie, and every one of our kind, and each beast and bird, and every living thing that grows in the forest—we are the leaves of the Mother Forest. Do you understand?)

(I am not certain,) Chyrie thought hesitantly. (But I feel the truth of what you say.)

(Then that is enough,) Riuma told her. (Remember your way to this place when you need the Mother Forest's strength, and She will give it gladly.)

(Why do we not go closer?) Chyrie asked eagerly. (I want to touch it.)

(That is the caution you must take,) Riuma warned her. (Those who return to the heart of the Mother Forest come here so they may grow again as a new life. Take care not to touch the seed, or you may lose yourself in the soul of the Mother Forest. You have felt this danger in the minds of beasts. Do not let the promise of life you feel here blind you to that danger. Now we must return.)

They surged up through the earth, through the tree, and Chyrie settled again gratefully against Valann's comforting presence. The hawk was more than restive now; it was fighting desperately, frightened, and Chyrie held it just long enough for a last farewell touch with Riuma, then released it, glad of her renewed strength to pull her and Valann back over the great distance.

She fell back into her body as painfully as if she had fallen from a great height onto stone, and for a moment she could only lay where she was, panting helplessly while every part of her body screamed agony at her. Gradually her eyes creaked painfully open, and the blurred images above her slowly resolved into Jeena's and Rivkah's worried faces. The softness of furs under her and the stone ceiling above her told her that she had been moved back to their quarters.

"There you are," Jeena said crossly. "What a foolish thing you have done. You are stiff as a tree limb and your mate is even stiffer, and you frightened a human guardsman near to death when he found you both on the watchtower unconscious and hardly breathing. Sharl and Rivkah were utterly terrified. A word of warning to one of us might have saved them much grief."

"A word of warning and I would have spent the day trying to dissuade her," Valann said hoarsely, raising himself on one elbow. (Are you well, love?)

(Only stiff from lying long without moving,) Chyrie assured him. (And my little ones—oof!—are telling me it has been far too long since I last ate.)

"You must tell Sharl," Chyrie told Rivkah, "that a Wilding patrol saw between fifty and a hundred humans just north of Wilding lands last evening. It will come to battle with Silvertip if they enter the forest. Silvertip are strong, but they are few."

"Has Silvertip allied with Inner Heart?" Valann asked.

Jeena shook her head.

"Few border clans chose the alliance," she said. "Perhaps it is because the boundaries of their lands are the most abused, and they are more protective of their territory."

"Their boundaries will be abused indeed," Rivkah said darkly. "They'll be the first and hardest attacked. We must find a way to win their cooperation. We need their eyes, and they need our assistance."

"Send them weapons as a gesture of goodwill," Val suggested. "Neighboring clans can leave the weapons just within their boundaries."

"Those few wagonloads of weapons aren't going to go very far among a whole forest of elves," Rivkah said doubtfully.

"It is the gesture that is important," Valann said, Jeena nodding agreement. "Most clans' strength will lie in hiding in the trees and picking off the humans with bows or spears, and a stone tip to arrow or spear will kill as easily as steel when a sure hand sends it forth. They will set traps as well. Most clans have swords and daggers should it come to close fighting, although they are old and worn and poorer in quality than those you bring. It is the promise such fine weapons represent that is their value, the promise of future benefit that any clan can understand, and the trust shown by the city in arming those who have been its enemies."

"You speak as an Eldest." Jeena chuckled.

Valann smiled back warmly.

"But for you, Matriarch, I likely *am* the eldest in this city," he said.

"Sharl has more to learn from you than he thinks he does," Rivkah sighed. "When I told him what you'd said about the river wall, he just laughed—until his advisers and his commanders all told him the same thing. The problem is that he's rarely been on the *defending* side of a war."

"That is not Valann's and Chyrie's concern now," Jeena said gently. "They must eat and rest. They might have paid a great price indeed for the tidings they brought you."

Rivkah reluctantly took herself off in search of Sharl after ordering the servants to bring food to the elves' quarters, and Val and Chyrie could do nothing but let Jeena confine them to their furs, although it was only midafternoon. It seemed to take forever for the food to arrive, and when Chyrie's stomach rumbled so loudly that it resounded through the stone room, several elves laughingly delved into their bags for trail food.

It seemed strange to be resting in the middle of the day, but Val and Chyrie were too tired and weak for anything else. Loren came to pry every detail of the story out of them and entertain them with Weeka, and the other elves turned a simple supper into a minor festival. The celebration changed focus and tone when one of the Longears began her childbirth, but Chyrie prevented Loren from embarrassedly leaving, assuring him it would be many hours before Naura bore.

Afternoon turned to evening and evening to night, broken only by the arrival of more food and by the unexpected arrival of Sharl to question Val and Chyrie closely—how many humans had the Wildings seen, and exactly where, and which way were they moving, and how were they armed, and were they all afoot, or were some on horseback—until Naura screamed, and Sharl blanched and hurriedly retreated.

"Are all elvan births this difficult?" Loren asked hesitantly as another hoarse scream sent Weeka scurrying for his pocket.

"This is not a difficult birth," Chyrie said, raising an eyebrow. "Jeena says Naura is fully opened and will bear soon now. I have seen many women of the Wildings whose bones will not give to allow the youngling to pass, and it must be cut from them. That requires much preparation and strength of our Gifted One, and still some die; and even if the mother survives, she can rarely bear again. Jeena tells me her people, who are larger, more rarely have such troubles, but Longears are narrowly built. Naura is fortunate to bear so quickly." Chyrie sat up as Naura's cries changed tone. The elf was squatting now, her face tight with concentration, a fierce joy in her eyes.

"Every midwife I've ever seen has chased men out of the room," Loren said hesitantly. "Are you quite certain it's—I mean, I wouldn't want to intrude—"

"Males share in the planting of the seed," Chyrie said, scrambling to her feet as Naura gave one last cry. "Why should they be barred from seeing it come to fruit?"

They waited expectantly for the infant's cry. Then Jeena stood and glanced around, covering her eyes with one bloody hand. As one, the other elves turned silently away and quickly occupied themselves with other tasks. Chyrie and Valann glanced at each other soberly, and Chyrie pensively folded her hands over her belly, and they sat back down on the furs.

"What's the matter?" Loren asked, still standing. "Did she—"

"Hush," Valann said softly. "Sit down."

Loren sat slowly.

"I don't understand," he said. "Why don't—oh. Oh, my." He fell silent as Jeena walked past, a small, leather-wrapped bundle in her hands.

"Turn away," Valann hissed, then in a completely normal voice said loudly, "Is there more wine?"

"Here is another skin." One of the Brightwaters brought it over. She handed Valann the wineskin, touched Chyrie's cheek sympathetically, and hurried back to her kin, who busied themselves vigorously with the arrow shafts they were carving. Naura wiped the last blood from her thighs and tottered back to where the other Longears had laid their furs, and curled up alone in a corner.

"Shouldn't someone take care of her?" Loren asked in a whisper. "Or comfort her, or—"

"Chyrie, some of those bits of meat on a stick would not be amiss," Valann said. "And some of that cheese you like so well might be pleasant with it."

"I will ask for more," Chyrie agreed, getting up and going herself instead of calling a servant.

When Chyrie was gone, Valann leaned close to Loren, speaking barely above a whisper.

"It is an ill thing to talk of the unspoken, especially in the presence of a female with child," Valann murmured. "Ordinarily our women go to be alone with the Gifted One when they bear, and with their mate if they are mated. To bear one of the unspoken is a thing of shame, so out of kindness we act as if she has not done so. Treat Naura no differently, but you must not speak to her of—it."

"What's an—unspoken?" Loren asked, equally furtively. "You mean the child was born dead?"

"It is dead," Valann said, noting Loren's frown at the subtle difference of his answer. "Unspoken are born—awry. Now, I beg you, speak no more of it. You shame Naura and invite ill upon the others with child, and Chyrie is already greatly fearful."

"Well!" Loren looked away and patted through his pockets as if searching physically for something to say. "Well. Ah, Weeka, there you are, my pet." He kissed the little creature's head, then whispered in its ear. The chirrit chattered excitedly as he put it down, then scampered off in Naura's direction.

Chyrie returned with a basket of food, Jeena with her. Jeena patted Chyrie's shoulder as she sat down beside Valann, and the Gifted One returned to Naura's pallet. The Longear woman was sitting up now, absently cuddling the chirrit.

"I saw Sharl in the hall," Chyrie said, determinedly cheerful. "He was engrossed in Rowan's map, he and several of his warrior leaders. Tomorrow he says I must contact Dusk again and see what news has come from the north Heartwood and whether his weapons have been received. He says that soon he will dispatch a small company of warriors to guard the narrow pass between the forest and the river, and wishes to treat with the Brightwaters for their assistance also, since the company will be stationed beside their lands."

"You mean *on* our lands," Moondrop, one of the Bright-waters, said as she joined them. "We often cross that narrow open land to reach the river, where we fish and harvest sword-leaf plants for their sweet tubers and their fibrous leaves."

"The Brightwaters claim lands outside the forest?" Valann asked amazedly.

"Why should we not?" Moondrop countered. "No other clan has sought to contest our right to them, not until these humans arrived. We had a sure source of fresh food, even in winter, and water in the driest summers. Now because of these humans passing back and forth, we must creep furtively to the river where once we ran freely. Our Eldest says that it is to our gain now to deal with the humans, so that we can openly reclaim passage to the Brightwater to sustain us."

"How will the humans on the Brightwaters' land communicate with the city?" Valann asked Loren. "They have no beast-speakers among them."

"We use messenger birds," Loren told him. "They're trained to fly back and forth and carry written messages. Usually such companies will have a mage with them, too, to send a message by magic in case of an emergency, although that's very draining. Rivkah and I together developed a spell to be cast upon an object, which will later return directly to its owner's hand upon pronouncement of a command word. It's much an improvement on the message spell, yes, indeed, although not so flexible in usage."

"That is very interesting," Jeena said, joining them. "Our weakness in the forest—if you would call it that—is that we have no real means of long-distance communications other than our beast-speakers, and they are limited by the speed of the beast that hosts them. We have no means of transporting objects unless a beast-speaker can coax a beast to bear it. I would be eager to observe such magic."

"Why, I would be more than honored to teach you the spells," Loren beamed.

"Spells later." Sharl stood in the doorway of the room, his face tight with worry. "Valann, Chyrie, I need you on the watchtower now."

"They cannot go now," Jeena said. "They are too weak still."

"I'm sorry," Sharl said. "This can't wait."

"We have had many hours to rest," Chyrie told Jeena. "It is enough."

Valann, Chyrie, Loren, and Jeena followed Sharl up to the top of the watchtower again. Rivkah was there, staring off into the distance, and on the battlements beside her was a huge owl Chyrie recognized as the same one Dusk had sent to bring the map.

(Dusk?) Chyrie thought at the owl.

(Praise the Mother Forest you are safe,) Dusk replied. (I have tried to reach you a dozen times this eve, and you did not answer.)

(I am sorry,) Chyrie thought. (Other matters occupied me, and I did not feel your call. What has happened?)

(Look north and east,) Dusk thought grimly. (You can see it for yourself now.)

Chyrie looked northeast and gasped. Far away on the horizon was a red glow.

(Surely that is not fire?) Chyrie thought, horrified.

(It is fire,) Dusk thought quietly. (Well over a hundred humans have camped just east of Dawn's Edge. The Dawn's Edges, thinking the humans were but few, attacked those who came too near the forest, and the humans retaliated with fire. It took many of the Gifted Ones here to stop the fire before the entire forest could burn. The flames are dying now. The Dawn's Edges have retreated deeper in the forest, those who live.)

"Love." Valann's voice cut through Chyrie's horror. "Sharl asks you what tidings Dusk brings, and why the sky glows with fire."

Chyrie tersely told them what Dusk had said, holding her link to Dusk with difficulty because of the distraction and her weakness.

(More clans have agreed to join us,) Dusk told her. (Many have sent messages begging for assistance, for some of the human weapons, for shelter for those who cannot fight. There will be many arriving at the city now. We are trying to concentrate the Gifted Ones here at Inner Heart where we can join our power together, and what beast-speakers we have are moving to the borders to act as our eyes and ears. Our warriors are being dispatched to every allied clan near the forest's northern and eastern edge. Can the humans suggest any strategy?)

Again Chyrie relayed the message, and this time it was Rivkah who answered.

"By the time any of our troops reached the northeastern edge of the forest, they would be useless," she said. "But there *is* something we can do. Chyrie mentioned that elvan mages haven't mastered weather magic. It's still spring, and the air is good and moist. It won't take much to bring a good heavy rain, perhaps enough to last for days, with luck. That would make the forest harder to burn, and possibly slow the army's pace. The trick will be keeping the rain from becoming a heavy storm, or the barbarians might try to take shelter in the forest, even despite the inconvenience of striking camp in the middle of the night and facing the elvan defense."

(It is a good thought,) Dusk returned eagerly, when Chyrie relayed Rivkah's suggestion. (I do not think the humans will try for the forest, for they have many wagons now filled with goods, and those will be impossible to bring into the forest. Tell your lady to bring any rain that she can, and if it storms, then may the lightning strike among them.)

"Should I send for the other mages?" Sharl asked, hesitating by the trapdoor.

"There's no use," Rivkah said regretfully. "I've only worked with a few of them, and I haven't tried joining my power with theirs yet." She turned to Loren. "Master, if you would, though—"

"Oh, of course, of course," Loren said hurriedly. "Let me get my bag from my quarters, my dear, and you can start the fire. It won't take me but a moment." He scampered down the ladder with surprising nimbleness for his age.

"I, too, will join you," Jeena said quietly, startling them all.

Rivkah hesitated.

"Forgive me," she said, "but I haven't worked with you before, and your type of magic is so different—"

Jeena held up a hand, silencing the woman.

"I have joined my will to that of others many times," she said. "It is my kin's land, and indeed their lives, you work to save. I will not fail you."

"All right, then," Rivkah said. "I'll welcome your help."

Glancing to Valann and Chyrie for permission, Rivkah kindled a small fire in the firepot. By the time she was finished, Loren had returned, a leather sack slung over his shoulder. He rummaged through this sack, extracting several smaller pouches, some of the contents of which he ground together in a small metal bowl. When everything was prepared to his satisfaction, he nodded to Rivkah, and the three of them knelt beside the firepot, Rivkah taking Jeena's hand.

"Let them cast their spell," Sharl told Chyrie. "While Dusk is here—well, such as he is—I want you to update this map Rowan sent me. I need to know which clans have allied with Rowan now, where they are, and where these so-called beast-speakers are stationed."

Chyrie grimaced—she had been curious about the weather spell, and she was already tired and drained—but saw the sense in what Sharl asked and obeyed. She soon found that as difficult as it had been dividing her attention between touching Dusk's thoughts while conversing with Sharl and Val, it was far more difficult to do so while attempting to read a map in the dark and pen characters upon it. Val had no strength to lend her, being unaccustomed to beast-speaking and even more drained by the morning's adventure than she, and by the time she was finished, she was utterly exhausted, barely able to remind Dusk of the expected torrent of rain and watch the owl fly away before she all but collapsed in Valann's arms.

Rivkah, Loren, and Jeena had finished, too, and were watching for the result of the spell. Already the air was heavy, as before a storm, and Chyrie could see clouds gathering to block out the stars. A low rumble could be heard, and even as they watched, a few flashes of lightning lit the clouds.

"I'm sorry," Rivkah said. "Jeena gave me more power than I'm used to working with. I think we may have built something bigger than we thought."

A tremendous gust of wind whistled over the watchtower as if in agreement, almost snatching the map from Sharl's hands, and ashes swirled up from the firepot.

"We'd best get under cover," Sharl said. He glanced at Val, who was wearily trying to lift Chyrie. "I'll get her. The wind is stiff and that ladder's steep." He lifted Chyrie carefully and, to Valann's grudging relief, was able to cradle the elf in one arm as he climbed down the ladder.

Chyrie was asleep before Sharl reached the bottom of the ladder.

When Val and Chyrie awakened the next morning, it was still storming violently outside. As elves in the Heartwood tended to do, the elves sharing the room with them were huddled sleeping under their furs to wait out the storm, but both Jeena and Naura were missing. Val and Chyrie hurried down to the main hall, where they found Rivkah breaking her fast alone. The mage brightened considerably at the sight of the elves, and eagerly invited them to join her; the elves were no less eager to scramble to their usual seats on the table and eat heartily.

"Sharl's meeting with the Brightwaters," Rivkah said. "He never came to bed last night, stayed up talking with his generals. He personally took nearly two hundred soldiers this morning to be stationed between the forest and the river, and several more supply wagons. Jeena and Loren rode out with them—Loren wanted to meet the Brightwaters' Gifted One—and they took another elf with them, one of the Longears, I believe. Sharl said they would meet whatever elves were coming to the city and bring them back in the wagons."

Chyrie looked soberly at Valann.

"It is perhaps best that Naura goes back to her people," Valann said. "Here it would be painful for her to see other women bear."

"What are you talking about?" Rivkah asked puzzledly.

"Nothing of significance," Chyrie said quickly. "Will Sharl be returning tonight?"

"I hope so," Rivkah said, glancing down at her food. "This is no weather for them to be traveling, much less camping. Sharl said they'd come back with the wagons as soon as the troops were settled, but that may take some time in this storm."

"If the rain slows Sharl and his men," Valann comforted, "it also slows the invaders." He shook his head. "It is unfortunate, but I doubt that the Brightwaters, however kindly inclined they may be, will allow two hundred humans to camp within the forest on their lands, nor yet supply them with food and wood for fires."

"We've solved the firewood problem, at least," Rivkah said, brightening slightly. "Come and look."

Val and Chyrie followed her to the closest of the hall's two fireplaces. To their surprise, the fire there was fueled not by wood, but by stacked blocks of some plant material, judging from the smell.

"It's peat, cut from the Dim Reaches," Rivkah explained. "Sharl had men cutting it even before we left for Cielman. It has to be pressed and dried before it can be used, but the cutting and pressing is simple labor, and it can be dried quickly with such a simple spell that even apprentice mages can handle that job. A great load of black rock arrived, too, only two days ago—our very first ship trade. There's plenty for the forges, and in a pinch we can burn it in our fires, too. The peasants are saving and drying droppings, too, from the horses and livestock, and bringing it to the city."

"How can we be of help?" Valann asked. "No elves will likely arrive until the wagons return, and there is no need to wait for Dusk's call, for Chyrie will feel it."

"You exhausted yourselves yesterday," Rivkah said doubtfully. "Perhaps you should rest today, especially Chyrie."

"If I need not fly a hawk across the Heartwood, to me that is rest," Chyrie said wryly, taking another piece of bread to sop her stew. "We are a folk not accustomed to sitting idle while others labor. Surely there is some small help we can give, and there are few in the rooms above us who could not perform some tasks to be of use."

"It's hardly weather for a strong man to be laboring outdoors, much less pregnant women and children," Rivkah said slowly, "but surely there's light work that can be done indoors. What do you suggest?"

"The Brightwaters, as Sharl said, are skilled at making nets and lines for fish and eels," Valann said. "Let them continue to do it. Even the children can assist in that. I have seen many of the elves carving bows and arrows; let them work with your weapons-makers to improve the quality of your own bows. Even those with few skills can sort feathers for fletching arrows or whet blades. I am not as skilled as Jeena in herb-craft, but I know many healing salves and potions that can be made against future need. Chyrie is skilled at drying and potting foods for later eating; she can instruct your people in such preparations that there will be more food in the city."

"You're right," Rivkah said, chagrined. "Sharl and I didn't realize we were neglecting a work force under our very roof. Let's go put your friends to work."

To Rivkah's surprise, she found the elves not only willing, but eager to find tasks to occupy their time. Even the oldest elf could fletch and tip arrows, and many of the women, early in their pregnancy or simply known to be fertile, could exceed most human women in strength and energy. The Brightwaters, down to the youngest child, showed themselves to be every bit as skilled at making and mending nets, fish traps, and lines as Valann had said, and could turn almost any small scrap of metal into sharp barbed hooks as well.

The storm actually worsened, rather than slackening, and Sharl, Jeena, and Loren, together with nearly fifty more elves, returned late that night, all of them thoroughly soaked but happy. Loren and Jeena were enthused by the possibilities of elvan and human magic, each very different in nature, being used to complement each other. Sharl was pleased that the Brightwaters had received him kindly and were even glad of his troops camped near the forest, providing a human wall between them and the invaders.

Unfortunately, he told Rivkah, the Blue-eyes were adamant in resisting any contact with either the humans or other elvan clans. The Brightwaters' envoy had come running back from their lands, arrows whistling after him. Worse, the Blue-eyes had made a raid on Longear lands, stealing a good quantity of their preserved food and killing two Longears. This attitude, Jeena added, was far from isolated; many clans who had refused to join Rowan's alliance were striking savagely at neighboring clans who had, fearing that the allied clans might join forces against them.

"How can they feel that way?" Rivkah protested. "The storm we created helps every clan in the forest, not just those who are working with us."

"Remember that we do not use weather magic," Jeena reminded her. "It is spring, and it is storming. Few elves in the Heartwood would credit you with that."

"No gratitude is owed to out-kin," Valann added. "They will not ask you for help, nor thank you for it." (Any more than we did,) he added in thought to Chyrie.

"You can't mean to say you still agree with your people that it's better to fall alone than stand with us," Sharl demanded.

"It is better to stand with kin than with strangers," Val said adamantly. "It is better to die free than live enslaved or obligated to another. Our thoughts have not changed."

"But you've been so much help to us," Rivkah argued.

"You have treated us as kindly as you could," Chyrie said gently. "But you are not our clan, and this is not our land. We came because our word to do so was given, and because I must protect the lives I carry within me. If we must be here, then it is well to do what we can to ensure that we survive. But given the choice, and only myself to consider, I would return to my kin without a moment's delay, even to die there."

Sharl shook his head disgustedly.

"Well, against your will or not," he said, "at least you've made yourself useful, I must admit that, and so have the others. Rivkah told me what you've done today. It had never occurred to me, putting pregnant women and children and tottering elders to work, but what they've done is amazing. If only more of our people could see what your folk are accomplishing—" He shook his head again silently.

"What?" Rivkah pressed. "There's trouble, isn't there? What is it, Sharl?"

"It's Rom," Sharl said quietly. "Just when I thought I'd gotten the folk settled down, he's got them stirred up again. Yesterday when a group of elves arrived at the gate, people were shouting insults at them. A few even threw stones. The guards had quite a time getting them under control so the elves could pass safely."

"What are you going to do?" Rivkah asked softly.

"What can I do?" Sharl said bitterly. "Arrest him for spreading rumors? Hang him for fanning coals that were already lit? He was one of my best guards, even saved my life. Doria's dead, Rivkah, and I'm to blame, but Rom sees it as the elves' fault. I don't know what to do. I can't even send him back to Cielman, not past that army. I've set him to supervise the guards on the keep's wall, away from the people and from the gates where the elves arrive. I don't know where else to send him, unless it's to the swamp to dig peat like a common laborer."

"Rom isn't causing the problem, only aggravating it," Rivkah comforted him. "The people will come around once they see how willing the elves are to help us all."

"I doubt if there's time to change their minds," Sharl told her. "Even with the rain, it can't be more than a few days before the advance force of that army reaches our garrison. We could be seeing combat here in a week or less. We'll be fortunate just to finish the fortifications and get the last of the people and the food into the city in time."

The next days were as frantic as Sharl predicted, even despite the rain that continued to pour down with only short and infrequent breaks. Families arrived from farms to the south and west, bringing wagons filled with every portable item they owned and driving their livestock ahead of them. They were met at the gates by guards who recorded that farm's mark and the number and type of livestock, which were then herded to the city pens. Any grain or preserved food the farms brought was carefully logged as well, and stored in the large storage buildings Sharl had had built for just this purpose. The families were then directed to lodging and assigned work in the city.

Every available person was sent to work on the still incomplete fortifications, despite the weather. The teams of mages were now supplemented by hand labor, hauling blocks from the stone pits to the wagons with horses and chains, and from wagon to wall. The hand labor went much more slowly, but every block set in place meant one more obstacle between the invaders and the city.

Those who were not working on the fortifications were directed to the Potters' Guild, where roof tiles were being formed and baked to be used in place of the flammable thatching, or sent to the large open kitchens to dry or pot meat and vegetables. Even the children worked in the stone pits, gathering in baskets the small loose stone chips, which could be heated red-hot in huge caldrons on the walls and poured down on the invaders below.

The rain-soaked city seemed to have fallen into frantic and muddy chaos, and indeed there was a certain air of fearful hurry about the workers; but Sharl could consult his records and determine how many blocks had been set on the wall, how many barrels of pickled fish had been stored, or how many score arrows had been tipped and fletched on that day, and how many people could be moved from the pottery sheds to the nets for the next day.

Contrary to Sharl's prediction that the wagons he had brought back contained the last elves who would come to the city, elves continued to arrive. Guards had to be diverted to escort duty; while most of the city folk accepted the elves' presence and even admired their willingness to help with any task they were set, there were still many who hurled insults, if not rocks or offal, at every elf they saw. The elves now worked only in the keep or its grounds, or in places where there were guards watching.

The elves' quarters grew crowded, but no one complained; Sharl, frantically busy, did not notice the state of affairs until some of the servants shyly came forward, offering to share their own quarters so that the extra rooms could be given to the elves. There were now so many pregnant females, infants, and sick or crippled elves that Jeena, Crystal, and Lusea, a Gifted One recently arrived from the Black Feather clan, were kept constantly busy, and Valann, Loren, and often Rivkah with them.

There were births almost every day, and sometimes more than one. Rivkah and Loren were horrified to learn that nearly one infant in four was stillborn or "unspoken," but the elves seemed resigned to it. When Jeena or Lusea quietly carried away the pitiful little wrapped bundles, the mothers would grieve alone in silence for a few hours, carefully ignored by the others and comforted only by the Gifted Ones, then go on with their business as if nothing had happened. None now returned to the forest, however, for with the imminent approach of the barbarian army, it was far too dangerous for a weakened elf to attempt the journey.

Jeena's own bearing was long and difficult, but she survived, as did her healthy son. She confided in Chyrie that she had felt in her unborn the potential for malformation, but that a careful course of diet and potions, together with carefully applied healing magic, had remedied the problem. Her words came as a relief to Chyrie, especially when Jeena assured her that she had sensed no such problem in Chyrie's children. Chyrie needed such reassurance, for her unborn children continued to be a heavy draw on her body despite Jeena's and Valann's attentions, and she often suffered nausea and, more alarming, occasional dull, tight cramps for which Jeena could find no cause.

Ordered to stay near Val and the Gifted ones, Chyrie quickly found a new way to put her beast-speaking gift to use. She found that when she reached out to the brighthawk to converse with Dusk, she could direct the keen-eyed hawk through the forest in search of rare herbs or fungi to be used in the potions and salves being made by every human or elf with the necessary skills. Jumping from the brighthawk to squirrels, brushleapers, or diggerfoots, the potent plants were easily harvested for the brighthawk to carry back to Chyrie. Even the rare starleaf plant, which could be magically distilled into an incredibly potent healing tincture, could not hide from the keen eyes of Chyrie's winged or four-footed envoys, and Jeena admitted that several mothers or infants might have been lost but for the powerful potions that Chyrie's rare ingredients made possible.

Sharl was delighted to see the eagerness with which the elvan Gifted Ones and human healers and midwives pooled their knowledge. The elvan healers had a marvelous knowledge of every growing thing in the forest or near it that could be used for an almost endless variety of potions or salves. Even the poisons of various plants, fungi, snakes, and insects proved invaluable, and Rivkah was astonished to learn that the same mold that grew on old bread, properly prepared, had almost miraculous curative powers. The human healers contributed new healing spells, surgical techniques, and the strong liquor distilled from grains, equally useful drunk, to ease pain, or applied to wounds to cleanse them. Human woven-fiber cloth, porous, absorbent, and easily produced in quantity, proved a superior replacement for the leather the elves had always used, and could be quickly boiled and reused. The humans also supplied healing potions and powders made from ingredients bought or traded from distant lands, although these were used most sparingly, as there would be no way of replenishing them during a war.

Human healers were astonished to learn that most elvan healers were practiced and confident in many kinds of surgery, from the technique of cutting a child from its mother's belly to removing malignant growths, and were eager to learn to apply this knowledge to their own patients, but Jeena and Lusea were reluctant; it had been quickly discovered that a potion's effects on an elf and a human often differed, including the sedative potions the elves used for such procedures, and the Gifted Ones feared that those differences might render such treatment dangerous. A request from the human healers induced Sharl to order the corpses of any humans who died brought to the elves for study, but this proved a mistake, as those humans who resented the elves' presence started a rumor that the elves would desecrate their dead and use the corpses for foul and evil rituals. The families of the dead joined the uproar, and Sharl had to rescind the order.

Five days after the garrison was established at the south edge of the forest, Sharl received a short note via messenger bird that the garrison was under attack. Several tense hours later, a second message followed: The attacking force had been clumsy but savage, and the troops had driven them off with great difficulty. The barbarians had retreated northward, however, and the commander had no doubt they were reporting to a much larger force. If the garrison was to be maintained, more troops would have to be dispatched speedily, as they had suffered heavy losses in the attack. A rider would arrive soon after the message with additional details. A guard indeed arrived shortly after nightfall, soaked, bloody, battered, and utterly exhausted, but he insisted on reporting to Sharl before he would allow the healers to tend him.

Nearly two hundred fur-clad humans, armed mostly with swords and spears and completely without armor, had attacked shortly before midday. They had attacked straight on, no strategy or subtlety, throwing themselves into combat with a strength and ferocity that amazed the soldiers. They apparently had a mage of some sort directing balls of flame at the soldiers, but the garrison's mage had easily deflected the rather primitive magic. The barbarians had fought with fanatic determination, fearless in the face of superior weaponry; only the fact that the bowmen and crossbowmen had shot down a goodly number as they approached had allowed the soldiers to gain enough advantage to turn the barbarians away after a bloody skirmish. Of the 250 men Sharl had stationed next to the forest, less than a hundred were still alive, and most of those were wounded to some degree.

Sharl heard the report impassively, then left the guard to the attentions of the healers. He met privately with Val, Chyrie, and Rivkah in preparation for a meeting with his generals, and tersely repeated the guard's report.

"The site by the forest is too exposed," Sharl said. "We can't maintain it without throwing our troops away needlessly. I'm going to order the troops back, and leave only a small camp— a handful of men to watch. It will give us a few hours warning, at least."

"But what of the border clans?" Valann demanded. "What will you give them?"

"I thought you were only concerned with the Wildings," Sharl said sarcastically. "I can scarcely get a company around the forest to them in time to do any good."

Val flushed darkly.

"It is your duty to aid the elves allied with Rowan," he said coldly. "You are bound to do so. Must I insist?"

Sharl ran a hand over his face exasperatedly.

"You don't understand," he said. "All you would be doing is forcing me to send out my troops to be needlessly slaughtered. Your people have the shelter of the forest and the skill to use that to their advantage. My people are completely exposed. The barbarians aren't going to attack the forest now, not when their forerunners get back and report that they met resistance on that strip of land. The road and the presence of that garrison will let them know, if they didn't already, that there's a city nearby. They won't stop now to bother with the forest; they'll go for the richer looting at the city. They'll be coming straight for Allanmere now."

"Then why did you station your troops there?" Chyrie asked curiously. "Why did you not keep your men in the city and hope that the army would pass by to the east?"

"There's still the road," Sharl reminded her. "It's heavily traveled enough to be easily discernible, and it leads around the forest to Allanmere. I hoped that the advance force would be small enough that my troops could kill them to the last man, and that if none of their scouts returned, the army might indeed pass us by in favor of easier looting elsewhere. That seemed like a better chance than simply hiding and hoping they'd miss the south pass entirely."

"Then what will you do?" Valann asked.

"Just what I said," Sharl said resignedly. "Pull my troops in and prepare for a war. There's no further point in dispatching any troops outside the city. A garrison would only be wiped out, and wouldn't gain us any noticeable amount of time. I can't send troops through the forest; even if we could get all the various clans to let them pass, my men aren't trained for fighting in the trees, and a company that size couldn't possibly reach any area where they're needed in time to do any good anyway. All I can do now is get the city ready, and keep the barbarians' attention on us instead of the forest. I'll continue sending weapons as long as I can, I'll shelter as many of your people as can get here before the army, and if our mages can do any good from here, we'll do it, but that's the best I can do. Can you understand that, Valann?"

Val glared at him for a moment longer, then sighed.

"Yes," he said at last. "I understand. And Wilding would not have your aid if you sent it, in any wise. At least the rain is continuing; that is helpful to our kin, to wet the wood well so it will not burn easily."

"That aid is not without price," Chyrie said wryly. "The brighthawk does not like to fly in the rain, and it is growing more difficult to gather healing herbs. Rowan says the forest is turning to mud."

"We can try to stop the storm," Rivkah said doubtfully. "I think it would be difficult now—it doesn't seem inclined to stop anytime soon—but if you want—"

"I think your magical storm only began our typical spring rains." Val chuckled. "Every year the Brightwater and its creeks swell and flood. Every year the swamp rises. This year is different only in that the water came earlier than usual."

"The city's turning to mud, too," Sharl said with a shrug. "The downpour isn't going to help our troops any once their forces reach the city, but I think it's going to hurt the attackers more; we have shelter, after all, and they won't likely have anything better than hide tents. At least we'll be less vulnerable to fire arrows and the like."

"What's the status of the wall?" Rivkah asked worriedly.

"There are only three sections that aren't finished," Sharl said. He produced a second map, this time a map of the city, and indicated three sections marked in red ink. "Two places on the east wall and one on the south. It'll take at least four more days to finish them, and that'll be a hurried job. The northernmost section on the east wall is the one that concerns me. My mages say there's a weakness in the stone under the wall that may not support the wall's weight. It may be one of those hot springs. I don't know why it wasn't discovered before. Now they're trying to decide whether to tear out that section of wall and rebuild around the weak spot, or whether there's some way to fill in under it. There are many more places where the battlements aren't completed or hoardings built. I had to pull men off that work to cut stone in the pits."

"I can send Riburn back to the walls if you need her," Rivkah said hesitantly. "She's not specialized in stonework, but she's a good levitator."

Sharl frowned.

"Why did you take her off in the first place?"

"She's got a talent none of the others have," Rivkah told him. "She can chant fish right into the nets. We've been pulling the nets in full almost as soon as they're thrown out."

"Then leave her there. We need the food as badly as we need the stone." Sharl turned to Chyrie. "Could you do that?"

Chyrie was shocked to horrified silence, but Val answered for her, his voice sharp.

"Certainly she could not." The elf's eyes were narrowed. "Beast-speakers are forbidden even to hunt, for the pain it causes them. To touch a beast's mind and then bring it to harm—none of us could bear to do such a thing if we would."

"No need to be so angry," Sharl said mildly. "I was only asking. In any event, from what I've seen, Chyrie can only contact one animal at a time, and there are better ways for Chyrie to use her talents than pulling in one fish at a time."

"Indeed there are," Val muttered, still angry.

"What about your other mages?" Sharl asked Rivkah. "What kind of help can we expect from them?"

"The stoneworking teams aren't good for much else," Rivkah said, shaking her head. "They'll be heading back west before any conflict, unless you want to pay them well to stay. They're just not battle mages."

"We'll keep them," Sharl said firmly. "If the wall should need work during battle, we don't have anyone else who can do it. Go on."

"The mercenary mages we brought in are split about evenly between offensive and defensive magicks," Rivkah said. "About a dozen good mages total, plus five or six amateurs. Four healers and as many apprentices, half a dozen miscellaneous specialists, and then Loren and myself. We're the only jack-of-all-trades, though."

"No seers?" Sharl asked worriedly.

"No foreseers." Rivkah nodded. "True foreseers are in demand everywhere. The few who came were clumsy fakers, and I sent them back. Loren's got a fair gift for farsight and sensing, and he can use a crystal over a short range, and I'm a pretty fair magic-spotter, but one or two of the defensive mages are really good. I've already assigned the mages to their stations, and with the mages who can use crystals, we should have a fair relay of information from all sides of the city. That's about all I can tell you."

"Then I think that's all," Sharl said wearily, rolling the map. "If you have nothing else to add, I'll meet with my generals and report. I've got to get them to persuade their troops to work with elvan bowmen—or bow-women—on the battlements."

"There is one thing I would ask," Valann said quietly. "If all goes as you expect, and this army should attack your city, with our people harrying them from behind, and if this army finds the shell of this city too hard to break, and they turn to seek the softer fruit at their backs, what will you do then?"

"Then our ballistas, catapults, and bowmen have a fair target at their backs," Sharl said, looking Valann directly in the eye, "and our mages will strike at them as fiercely as if they were attacking our gates. Only our short-range defenses will be useless, and in a pinch I'll send out troops on horseback, so that if they need to retreat back to the city, they can get back in in plenty of time for us to close the gates. There's not that much open land between the city and the forest's edge. I wish the Blue-eyes would have allowed us to station troops within the forest. If they had, we'd have stood a fair chance of crushing the invading troops between the two forces like a nut between two stones."

Valann nodded slowly.

"Then I am reassured," he said.

"This battle is only half the war," Sharl told him. "If this city is even to survive, we need the elves' tolerance. If it's to thrive, we need their friendship and their trade. If the barbarians burn the forest or strip it bare, I won't get either. It's as simple as that."

"Rowan may make what schemes she will," Valann said quietly. "We are no part of them, although I wish her success and prosperity. My kin have chosen to bear alone the weight of their own future. If my mate and her children are kept safe, I am satisfied."

"We hold our mates and children as dear as you do yours," Sharl said. "Anything we can do to protect them will be done, I promise you."

"If what you say is true," Val said, extending his hand, "my mate and I will be honored to fight at your side."

Sharl raised both eyebrows, then smiled his charming sideways smile as he clasped Valann's hand.

"A fair beginning," he said.

X

CHYRIE WAKENED TO a tug on her thoughts, wincing as dull cramps seized her belly. Remembering that she had left Jeena's potion on the table with the wine, she started to sit up, when the cramping became a sharp stabbing pain. Her gasp brought Val instantly awake, and before she could even speak Jeena was at her side.

"What is it, little one?" Jeena asked, already sorting through her bag of herbs. "Is it the old pain?"

"This is sharper," Chyrie gasped as she felt the stabbing again. "I feel as if I would tear open."

Jeena dropped the bag and laid both hands over Chyrie's belly, her face tight with concentration. At last she shook her head.

"My children?" Chyrie whispered, her eyes wide, dreading Jeena's answer.

"Nothing is awry with your younglings," Jeena said quickly. "It is what they are doing to you that is not well. The two of them together are growing too quickly for your body. One of them, the male, is already quite large."

"What can be done?" Valann felt the tautness of Chyrie's belly. "She is already swollen as big as most of the women who are ready to bear."

"There is nothing else for it," Jeena said, shaking her head again. "It will take clever healing to allow her womb to expand farther, and it may need to be done again before she bears."

180

"Is there nothing else to be done?" Valann protested. "That will doubtless speed her unborn children further each time it is done."

"I see no alternative," Jeena said, examining Chyrie again. "She is too far in her pregnancy to be potioned to lose the younglings, even if she would consent to such—"

"Which I would not," Chyrie said firmly, gritting her teeth as pain ripped through her again.

"—and not far enough in her pregnancy that the young ones would survive if cut from her body," Jeena continued, giving Chyrie an absent nod. "There is nothing else to be done."

Val glanced reluctantly at Chyrie, who nodded permission.

"Do what you must," Chyrie told Jeena. "But please do it quickly. Dusk is calling me, and for him to call at such an hour must mean dire tidings indeed."

"I will show you what to do," Jeena told Valann. "This is subtler work than you have done."

This time, despite Jeena's skill, Chyrie barely choked down a cry of pain. For a horrible moment she thought she would surely burst asunder, and her unborn children thrashed vigorously, worsening the pain, but at last they quieted and some of the terrible tightness in her womb eased.

"She could bear at any time now," Jeena said worriedly. "I like it not. The male is very large indeed now."

"Help me to the window," Chyrie murmured to Valann when she could trust her voice again. Valann quickly lifted her and carried her to the window, and Jeena spread a fur on the stone sill for her to sit on.

(There you are,) Dusk thought relievedly as soon as she touched the brighthawk. (I feared some harm had come to you. You must tell the human lord to stand in readiness. There is a force of humans passing the forest with great speed and determination. They have been passing for hours upon hours now, but at first they were far to the east and we did not see them. I myself was alerted by a beast-speaker in Fir Grove, and they are far to the south. A part of their number is attacking the north edge of the forest even as we speak, but others are passing by unheeding. They are numerous as the

stars in the sky. Why would they pass us by unless they are
bound for the city?)

(I will tell Lord Sharl,) Chyrie thought quickly. (But how
fare the elves to the north?)

(I will show you, if you can bear being bounced from beast
to beast as a stone skips across the water,) Dusk thought. (I
have worked with the other beast-speakers, and they will help
to move our thoughts from beast to beast across the forest.
Join your thoughts firmly to mine, and this time I will be your
wings.)

Chyrie nerved her resolution and obeyed, strengthening her
link to Dusk and simultaneously relinquishing her hold on
the brighthawk. Abruptly her awareness of the brighthawk
spun away; with a dizzying rush, it seemed she touched a
dozen minds, seeing briefly out of the eyes of Dusk's owl,
a night-hunting weasel, a ringtail, a night warbler—finally she
settled into yet another owl, this one soaring over a horrible
scene below.

It was difficult to sort out the rapidly moving bodies; it
seemed to Chyrie that a fleshy river of humanity flowed inexorably around the forest's edge, the pounding of their feet causing a rumbling that rivaled the thunder. They ran as silently as
an army of that size could, making no cry, speaking no word
to each other.

Chyrie had had but the briefest glimpses of her assailants
at the altars, and had had little enough inclination or opportunity to examine the corpses later; these barbarians, however,
shocked her to inner stillness.

Like the elves, these humans wore leather, not the woven-
fiber cloth the humans of Allanmere took such pride in. The
leather these humans wore, however, were crudely cured furs
clumsily stitched together to form garments of a sort. Many
of the barbarians wore grisly ornaments—strings of teeth and
bones, dried or fresh fingers or ears, and cords of strung human
scalps, some still relatively fresh. Both the humans themselves
and the clothes they wore were caked with filth and blood from
previous battles.

There was nothing primitive, however, about their weapons.
Flashes of lightning flickered on steel swords of amazing

length and breadth, steel-tipped spears, and huge broad-headed axes. Others carried huge studded clubs, maces, or mauls. A few carried heavy, stout bows that awed even Chyrie—who could possibly draw such a monster? None wore armor or carried shields such as Chyrie had seen on the guards and soldiers, but many wore helms of a sort, crowned with the skulls of hideous-looking beasts.

Some bore wounds from previous battles, untended and often festering, but if their wounds pained them they made no sign. As Chyrie watched, one of the barbarians, his arm nearly severed, faltered and finally fell; the others ran on, ignoring him as they ignored the owl circling above them.

The scene shifted again, and now Chyrie looked down through the sharp eyes of a pale gray treefox, and this scene was by far more appalling than the last.

Elvan warriors scrambled from one tree to the next to fire their arrows or hurl spears. Several, recognizable as predominantly Dawn's Edges and Silvertips, but also a few other clans, lay dead on the ground. In a few places the elves fought the barbarians hand to hand, but for the most part the elves kept their distance as best they could, relying on their quickness, superior night vision, and the shelter of the trees against the savage strength and fearless determination of their attackers. It was apparent, however, even for the short time Chyrie watched, that the barbarians were driving the elves inexorably backward into the forest.

Dusk and Chyrie jumped dizzily again, and this time, for the first time, Chyrie looked out through Dusk's own eyes. He was in Rowan's speaking hut, gazing down at a map similar to the one that had been sent to Sharl.

(These areas are presently under attack,) Dusk thought, indicating the Dawn's Edge, Silvertip, and Little Creek lands. (Already the Dawn's Edges are being driven back from their lands. Soon they will have no choice but to abandon them altogether.)

(What of Wilding?) Chyrie asked quickly. (They are only a little southeast of Dawn's Edge and Silvertip. How do they fare?)

(I cannot say,) Dusk told her soberly. (We have no beast-speaker in their lands, no contact with their Gifted One. Their refusal to accept our aid was final.)

(But only a portion of the army is attacking the forest,) Chyrie thought confusedly. (Why do they not all attack, or pass us by altogether?)

(My supposition is that they wish to pass through the forest, rather than around it,) Dusk thought, (but are not so determined that they will commit their forces, knowing that there is a clear path to the city around the forest's edge. They do not follow any logical pattern of attack that I can imagine. Occasionally they still try to burn the forest, which is foolish if they wish to pass through or either hunt or gather food. It is inevitable, however, that they will win through in time if the attacks continue. We can pick them off with spear or arrow from the trees, but they come faster than we can kill them, and unlike our arrows and spears, their numbers seem endless. Once they come near enough to use their swords, their strength makes them formidable opponents. We will attempt to take captives for questioning, but even if we can understand their language, their ferocity is such that taking any alive will be very difficult. We can only hope that the main force passes us by soon.)

(I will warn Sharl immediately,) Chyrie thought. (If they are as far south as Fir Grove, Sharl's watchers will soon see them, and there are not many hours to prepare. I will be waiting for further tidings from you.)

"What is it?" Val asked when Chyrie's eyes cleared, but the tautness of his expression showed that he already knew. The other elves in their room had gathered quietly around, waiting fearfully.

"The army is coming," Chyrie said. "The first forces of it, at least. They have already reached Fir Grove. Others are attacking the northeast clans. There are no tidings of Wilding. We must tell Sharl, that he may alert his soldiers and begin to prepare."

Val called the servants instead and let them summon the High Lord and High Lady, and Loren as well, to meet them in the great hall, and to have food brought for them all. When the servants had gone, Val and the other elves, silent and frightened, helped Chyrie dress—her belly had now grown to an unwieldy size and she had to borrow a tunic from one of the larger Brightwaters—and he and Jeena helped her down the long halls and stairways to the hall. Sharl and Rivkah were already there, still in their night robes, and a sleepy Loren soon stumbled in as well.

Sharl listened grimly to Chyrie's tale, then unfolded his map and had her show him the areas Dusk had indicated. Chyrie described the weapons she had seen the barbarians carrying, and their amazing numbers, and the swiftness of their pace. Sharl sent a messenger to fetch his commanders before he turned back to the map.

"They have no armor," Sharl said slowly. "No ballista, no trebuchet, not even a siege tower or a ram—or if they do, it's coming later with the main force. No crossbowmen. That's good news, I suppose. But just the fact they've made it this far means they've succeeded without those things—through sheer numbers, most likely, or perhaps their mages are more powerful than I'd thought. I've gotten no messages from the north for a long time now. Their close-range strength will be formidable, and a good part of our troops are only half-trained farmers or herders. If they breach the wall or the gates, we'll be in serious trouble."

"They've got the few bows, and anything as stout as what Chyrie described will have a good range," Rivkah mused. "But the battlements are complete in most places. Our first line of defense—bows, crossbows, your heavy machines, and my mages—will have to make a decisive strike, and we need to keep them at a distance as long as we can, at least long enough to take the measure of their mages and plan our defense."

"I've had the moat widened and deepened," Sharl said, "and we have a goodly number of barrels of that foul, sludgy stuff from the swamp that burns so well. We'll pour it into the moat as soon as we take up the bridge, but even so, there isn't enough to burn for very long. We'll hold off lighting it until some of them actually try to cross, for maximum effect. Past the moat are pits filled with wooden spikes, and we'll scatter caltrops there as well. Both the spikes and the caltrops have been coated with the poisons the elves have been sending. That should keep them back a little longer. But you're right,

Rivkah. Our strength is going to lie in our ranged attacks, and we've got to keep them off the wall as long as we can."

He turned to Rivkah.

"I want you and Loren on the watchtower," he said. "Valann and Chyrie with you."

"Jeena should be with us," Valann said quickly. "She should not be far from Chyrie."

"I'm sorry, but I need Jeena at the wall," Sharl said, indicating a spot on the city map. "She'll be supervising the elvan archers, and she's the only one who can understand and relay my commanders' orders. With the poisons the elvan archers and my own are going to be using, it's a good idea to have a healer there, too, especially among all those pregnant women. Jeena, make sure your people take plenty of food and water onto the wall with them, and I'll count on you to know when any of them need to be pulled off their stations and see them replaced."

"No," Jeena said.

Sharl stared at her blankly.

"What?"

"No," Jeena said simply. "I will not do as you say."

Sharl scowled darkly and opened his mouth, but Rivkah laid a hand gently on his arm.

"Wait," she said gently. "Jeena, why do you say no?"

"First, this man is not my Eldest," Jeena said quietly. "He does not order me. And second, Valann is right. I will not leave Chyrie and my son, and I can scarcely take an infant to the wall. In any wise, I must be here at the keep to help Crystal tend any of our people who need me. Lusea also knows the human language; Loren taught it to her as he did to me. I have no doubt she will go to the wall and do as Sharl has described, if he asks her courteously and does not presume to command her."

"There's no place for courtesy on the battlefield," Sharl snapped.

"Then there is no place for my people there," Jeena said simply. "We are your guests, not your soldiers. Once we cease to be your guests, we will become your enemies. Do you understand that?"

"Foolish clans squabble while the forest burns around them," Valann said quickly. "I will speak to Lusea on Sharl's behalf, and Jeena can stay near Chyrie. It is as well, in any event, since Jeena has shown she can add her power to Rivkah's and Loren's. Please, let us not spend the precious time in anger at each other, when every moment's preparation might spare lives."

"He's right," Rivkah said, kissing Sharl quickly on the cheek. "Go and speak to your commanders. I can deal with both the mages and the elves, and my crystal network will help organize."

Sharl sighed and gathered Rivkah to him, holding her for a moment.

"Thank the gods I have you at my side," he said. "This city is the stronger for your wisdom. Please keep yourself safe."

"I have your entire army, the walls of the city and of the keep, and the height of the watchtower between me and danger." Rivkah laughed. "I could hardly be safer."

She turned to Val, Chyrie, and Jeena.

"You may want your packs and some of the furs from your room," she suggested. "I've already had a shelter set up on the top of the watchtower, and the servants can bring food whenever we need it. The wounded will be brought to the keep. Those of your folk who can't leave the keep can stay with the healers, helping if they can, even if it's nothing more than tearing cloth for bandages."

Jeena, Val, and Chyrie hurried back to their quarters to collect their belongings and leave Jeena's baby, whom she had named Ruri, with one of the Black Feathers who had recently given birth. Lusea was only too glad to muster every available archer from the elves' quarters; they had all been chafing at the inactivity and confinement, and worry for their clans had made the waiting doubly hard to bear. All the elves fit to serve at the wall quickly donned leathers waterproofed with beeswax, seized their packs, and hurried out with Lusea to find the wall shelters where they would wait, and the other elves moved their belongings into one room, to make space for the wounded to be brought in.

As Rivkah had said, a comfortable enough shelter had been

set up atop the watchtower, with a large hide tent. There were several guards stationed there now, and Loren had set up his bowls and bottles in one corner of the hide tent. Two small, careful fires burned in covered braziers, one at the battlements and the other inside the tent.

Val and Chyrie picked a corner of the tent for their pallet and packs, and helped Loren and Rivkah to do the same, and then there was nothing more to do.

"It's the waiting that's hard," Rivkah said in a low voice, staring out over the battlements. The city was lit with fires and torches, and hurrying figures could be seen everywhere. "I've already checked the crystal network. There's still hours to wait. Why don't the two of you get some rest while you can?"

"That is wise," Valann agreed. "Come, love. If we draw the flaps of the tent and bring the brazier out, it will be quiet and dark inside."

Chyrie agreed, and despite her anxiety, she felt safe and content in Val's arms, snuggled in the warmth of their furs, listening to the rain tapping on the roof of the tent. When Val's hands slid smoothly over her skin, however, Chyrie chuckled.

"I thought we came here to rest," she whispered.

"I said nothing of rest," Val corrected. "I said only that it would be quiet and dark in the tent, and indeed it is. But if you feel disinclined—"

"No." Unspoken between them was the realization that in the danger of the coming battle, this might be their last night together. "Only be careful, love, for my time is near, and we must be quiet, or we will embarrass Loren and Rivkah."

But if Loren and Rivkah were embarrassed that night, they did not say so.

Chyrie stood beside Rivkah, staring at the grim scene below. The barbarian tents were so thick that the once-green plain had turned brown. Some of the barbarians merely slept where they came to rest on the ground, despite the rain. Most were awake now, despite the late hour, once more trying the strength of the walls as they had for the past day.

The first attack had been brief and easily repelled. The first barbarians attempting to cross the moats died horribly when a single fire arrow ignited the swamp sludge floating on the water. Others never made it as far as the moat, falling into the pit traps or treading on the caltrops and dying of the poison only moments later. The moat fire quickly extinguished in the continuing rain, however, and the barbarians soon learned the locations of the pits and the properties of the caltrops.

While the barbarians attempted to cross the moats, the archers and crossbowmen on the battlements were far from idle. Volley after volley of arrows and crossbow bolts thinned the ranks of the attackers. Sharl held back the trebuchets and ballista, there being no central target, but so far the invaders had produced no weaponry more sophisticated than the few stout bows Chyrie had seen. The battlements offered adequate protection against those, although one careless guardsman quickly proved that the heavy bows and proportionally thick arrows were more than a match for the troops' armor.

By midafternoon, however, the moat had become choked with corpses, and the attackers could cross easily. The archers were hard put to keep sappers from reaching the walls with their hammers, drills, and chisels, and it took several caldrons of boiling water and heated stones and sand poured from the hoardings before the next wave was driven back.

The invaders seemed inexhaustible. As the sun set, the attack continued undiminished—no subtlety, no strategy, only a continuous rain of bodies thrown at the city's defenses. The archers and wall guards wearied and were replaced, but there seemed an endless and eager supply of barbarians to test them. All through the night, the pattern seemed a stalemate—another wave of barbarians would fling themselves at the wall and the gates, only to be slaughtered. A short time later, another wave would follow.

Rivkah had kept her mages busy, but to little effect after a brief but successful initial strike. They had managed to get a few bolts of lightning through, and the barbarian mages had hurled a few balls of fire, but for the most part, they only countered each other harmlessly. This troubled Rivkah deeply; she had had no idea that the primitive mages could muster enough power to stalemate her own.

By night, more forces had arrived, and the narrow strip of land was crowded with as many invaders as it could hold, and now some of their heavy weapons began to appear. There was no siege tower, but Allanmere's farseers saw several wooden ladders, two catapults, and four ballista, plus carts loaded with heavy boulders. To Sharl's dismay, the barbarians did not wait for dawn to begin a distanced attack; worse, one of the catapults was stationed near the weak section of wall.

The machinery had likely been captured, but apparently the barbarians had been no slow learners of how to use it. A lucky strike from the northern catapult struck the uncertain section of wall squarely, and it groaned ominously but did not break; an answering strike from Sharl's trebuchet, with some helping guidance from one of the mages, struck that catapult a glancing blow, crippling it. Ballista and catapult attacks on the main gate and southeast section of the wall did minimal structural damage, although several of the wall guard were killed. Sharl tried to keep the enemy's catapults firing, hoping to exhaust their much more limited supply of boulders, but the barbarians opted for another try at the wall, this time under cover of their own archers and more flaming attacks from their mages. While the wall troops fought off this new incursion, Sharl rode back to the keep to meet with Rivkah on the tower.

"They rely heavily on fire," Sharl said, gesturing at a new rain of fire arrows from the invaders. "The arrows, pots of burning pitch catapulted or thrown over the wall, fiery missiles from their mages. If we had more wood in the city we'd be in serious trouble. Thank the gods for those tile roofs and the rain. We've been trying the same tactic, but their wet hide tents don't burn any more easily than our stone. Have you had any luck spotting the mages?"

Rivkah shook her head unhappily.

"They're protected from magic-spotting just as we are. I've been watching the magical attacks, though, and they seem to come from near some of the larger campfires. I think their magic itself is fire-based. It's all we can do to block the attacks and try a strike now and then, and of course keep the rain coming down. Wilar tells me he's been trying any number of offensive spells, but they're countered almost immediately.

Loren's getting some interference on his crystal, too. I think they're finding a way to block the seers."

"Suggestions?" Sharl asked.

"Concentrate your fire on their campfires," Rivkah said. "Especially the larger ones. Maybe you'll take out some of the mages. More poisoned caltrops thrown over the wall might take some of the pressure off the wall guards. It worked well enough the first time."

"What about you?" Sharl turned to Chyrie. "What if you flew a bird or two—messenger birds, maybe—out over the army and see if you can spot the mages and the commanders?"

"If a bird should fly low enough to see as you wish," Chyrie said patiently, "they would simply shoot it from the sky for meat. Nor would it be simple to coax the bird to fly so low, into such danger. You must understand that I do not have the strength to force, only to ask. And we have no birds here that are accustomed to fly at night, in any wise."

"Can you at least contact Dusk?" Jeena asked thoughtfully. "It has been a day and part of a night. Perhaps he has tidings for us."

"That would be wise," Chyrie agreed. She composed her mind and *reached* through the resting brighthawk. It was a long moment before Dusk responded, and the tone of his thoughts was very weary, heavy with despair.

(At least you are safe,) Dusk thought in answer to her alarm. (We cannot stand against these barbarians for another day. They fall in great numbers, but where one falls, ten come to take his place. They throw themselves upon us faster than our archers can reload their bows. Many of the border clans have been driven from their lands inward, and still the invaders press forward. We cannot hold against so many. In some places they have burned parts of the forest, despite the rain.)

(Have you learned anything that might be of use to us?) Chyrie begged. (Any small weakness, any vulnerability that we could use against them?)

(We took five captives,) Dusk thought wearily. (Fortunately I studied the magic Rivkah used to teach you her language,

and we were able, after many efforts, to use it to learn their
tongue. The truth spell in Rowan's speaking hut served us
well then, although our captives took much—persuasion—
before they would speak.)

(What did you learn?) Chyrie asked eagerly.

(Little that we did not know already,) Dusk told her. (They
are primitive folk who cannot count their own numbers. They
follow the directions of their commanders blindly. I did learn,
however, why they had come. It served little purpose, but I
will tell you.

(They come from far to the north, from beyond a range
of great mountains,) Dusk told her. (Their legends tell that
once they lived south of those mountains, but that the land
was cold and filled with ice. They worshipped a god called
Gax, the ice warrior, the sworn enemy of the fire god of the
southern peoples. In time, however, the fire god drove their
people north, melting the ice until the children of Gax were
forced to pass the great mountains to the cold steppes. There
Gax battled the fire god and defeated him, although Gax was
greatly weakened by the battle, and imprisoned the fire god
under the ground and bound him there as a slave to serve
Gax's people. Since that time fire has been their servant, to
stoke their forges and to be molded by their mages.

(At times, however,) Dusk continued, (the fire god fights to
break free, strengthened by the worship of its followers to the
south. At such times the ground shakes mightily, cracks open
in the earth, and some of the mountains spew flame and ash
into the air as the fire god thrashes under the ground. At such
times Gax's followers must flee their land lest the fire god
break free and destroy them, and they journey south to slay
the fire god's worshippers both to weaken the fire god and
as sacrifices to Gax. Their women and children follow some
distance behind, gleaning whatever loot is left in the plundered
towns. The warriors continue to do battle until the cold season
comes, a sign that Gax has once more gained control over the
fire god and they may return.)

Dusk was too weary for further conversation, and Chyrie
released her touch on the brighthawk to tell Sharl what the
Gifted One had said. Sharl shook his head disgustedly.

"Ice warriors and fire gods," he said. "There's no chance we can hold out until winter. Rivkah, is there any way you can turn this storm into something colder, an ice storm, snow?"

"Sharl, it's almost *summer*," Rivkah protested. "Snow? Not a chance." She paused thoughtfully. "But maybe hail. I don't know if that would be enough, but it's worth a try. Jeena, Loren, and I together might be able to manage something."

"You'll have to distract their mages," Loren told Sharl, shaking his head. "Anything as powerful as a weather change is certainly going to draw their attention to us, yes, indeed, and we can't cast the spell and defend ourselves at the same time."

"How long?" Sharl asked worriedly.

Rivkah frowned and thought.

"Nearly an hour," she said. "That's just casting the spell. Then it'll take a little time for the storm to change. Can you—"

A huge crash, like the loudest thunder, interrupted their words, followed by a horrible groaning rumble. Even before they reached the battlements, Val and Chyrie could see what had happened—the barbarian mages had changed tactics and were now hurling their flaming balls into the wall itself, to devastating effect. The weakened section of the northeast wall had fallen, and two other sections were cracking under the assault.

"I've got to get troops into that gap," Sharl said urgently, taking Rivkah's hands. "We need that hail. Can you do it?"

"We'll do it," Rivkah said firmly, kissing Sharl quickly. "Now go. As long as the mages are working on the walls and the catapults are south, we're safe enough. Just an hour, that's all I need."

Rivkah and Loren started the spell immediately, Jeena waiting quietly by until her strength could be of use. Val and Chyrie stayed at the battlements, watching fearfully as another section of wall fell under the onslaught of the redoubled magical attack. Wind gathered around the tower as the spell progressed, and Val and Chyrie fetched their furs to keep them warm as they continued their vigil.

(They are not in the city yet,) Val thought comfortingly. (The soldiers are holding them back, for the gaps are too narrow for a large force to pass through.)

(Is there nothing we can do?) Chyrie thought. (I feel useless here.)

(Nothing unless you can bring the cold season early,) Val thought quietly, (or summon up a fire god to defend us.)

Suddenly he went still.

(I must speak to Rivkah,) he thought quickly, his eyes widening. (I think there is a way—)

He turned and ran across the tower top toward the mages, leaving Chyrie staring behind him a moment before she hurriedly followed.

"Wait!" Val shouted to the mages, screaming over the howling wind. "I know a better way!"

Jeena turned, and her eyes grew wide as she stared at something beyond Val. Chyrie whirled even as a new whistling sound grew over the storm, turning just in time to see a flaming boulder plunging toward them.

There was not even time to scream. There was only time for one thought—(Mother Forest, please spare my children!)—as something slammed hard into Chyrie, throwing her backward, and the ball of fire hit and the world exploded.

Chyrie flew backward and struck the battlement hard, but did not entirely lose consciousness as fire washed briefly over her, singeing her hair, and the tower shook under her. The pain in her head and back as she struck the stone was nothing to the sudden, rending tear within her as a part of her soul was torn away. For a moment she was too dazed to understand; then mind and heart and voice screamed as one.

(*VALANN!*)

There was no answer.

Groaning with pain, Chyrie pushed herself to her hands and knees and crawled back through the smoking rubble, oblivious to the pain as the hot stones burned or cut her hands, shaking her head to clear it. She was only marginally aware and relieved that her unborn children still stirred vigorously in her belly. She used a huge chunk of the battlement to lever her to her feet and forced herself to look for what she dreaded to see.

Valann's face was very peaceful, what remained of it, his open eyes calm and clear. From the position of his charred body, Chyrie realized that the object that had struck her before the fireball hit had been Valann. He had shoved her out of the path of the flaming ball.

She touched his lips, feeling the fading of his life warmth, too stunned even to grieve. There was a huge empty place inside her, a place that had once held warmth and love.

Two hearts that beat as one—

"Chyrie—" It was Rivkah, dirty and battered, her cheek bleeding heavily down her chin, but alive. She was cradling a keening Weeka. "I saw what happened. Loren's dead, too, and Jeena's leg is broken. There was nothing I could do. There just wasn't time."

Two bodies, one spirit—

"No," Chyrie whispered, reaching out to close Valann's eyes. "No, no."

"We've got to get off this tower," Rivkah insisted. "The barbarians are in the city, those that didn't turn to attack the forest. We're too exposed up here."

We are the seedlings of the Mother Forest.

The seedlings—

Follow an oak back to its beginning and you find a seed, Riuma had said. *This is the door to the heart of the Mother Forest . . . the seed to which we return—*

"NO!" Chyrie screamed.

She dove deep into herself, down to that secret place Riuma had shown her, smaller and smaller, the tiny seed at her roots that was the door to the heart of the Mother Forest, and *REACHED* with all her self.

Life exploded into Chyrie: life pulsing, stretching up tendrils to the surface of the soil, pushing upward to the world with blind seeking power; green life, brown life, golden life, life with scales and fur and feathers, life that twined up the trees and stretched out branches, life that dug into the soil and fed from the earth, life that swam, that flew, that crawled, that ran, that burrowed—

She was at the heart of the Mother Forest, she *was* the Mother Forest, and these were Her leaves.

Behind the surge of life came agony as a flower was trampled under pounding human feet, as chickens burned in the city's pens, as a Blue-eyes fell beneath the stroke of a great axe, as a panicked bird flew into a tree and broke its neck, as a bolt of lightning from the human city struck among the barbarians, burning them and the grass beneath them. She seemed to be drowning in a river of blood that spilled onto the earth, soaking it to the very roots—

(No, love. Turn away.)

And there was awareness, and with that awareness came fear, the fear of a doe fleeing the battle behind her, the fear of a blackbird waiting helplessly on her nest as the tree burned, unwilling to leave her eggs, the fear of a spider as a heedless sword swept toward its web—

(Turn away.)

All around her a hundred lives flickered and went out, from worms and insects crushed beneath unheeding feet to elves cut down in battle or in flight as the humans' scythes cut down the grain, to guards falling from the battlements, arrows piercing their armor. Chyrie could not open her mouth, but she was screaming in agony, lost in the pulsing life, lost in the pain, lost in the minds of a thousand thousand lives—

(No, my she-fox. I will not let you go.)

A hand reached out to her in the maelstrom and she clasped it gratefully, felt warm arms close about her, pulling her away from the vortex that threatened to pull her down. The storm of life, of awareness, of death, raged in her mind, but she stood firm on a steady rock amid that storm.

(I knew it.) Valann chuckled, his beard rough against her cheek. (Did I not say you would pull me back from the Mother Forest Herself? But I was wrong. Instead you came after me. You must go, love. This is not for you now.)

(You cannot leave me,) Chyrie thought desperately. (I cannot live with half of myself gone.)

(You cannot stay here,) Valann thought gently. (You must return to yourself. You have our two children to bear. Listen, you must tell Rivkah the answer. Dusk told us that the barbarians fled from the shaking of the ground, remember? She and her mages must make the ground shake to frighten them back. You must tell her that.)

(I will not leave you,) Chyrie thought adamantly. (If you must stay, then so must I.)

(I am a part of the Mother Forest now,) Valann told her kindly, (and She of me. To hold me to you is to hold Her—) For a moment the maelstrom engulfed her again.

(Then so be it,) Chyrie thought, and holding Valann tight, she *reached*.

Chaos swallowed her, but safe in Valann's arms, she held firm to her purpose, pulling away from the swirling, expanding life, the thousand thousand awarenesses that flowed around and through her, the pain of a thousand thousand deaths and as many births, back through the door to herself, to the top of the watchtower where Rivkah was shaking her desperately. More painful was the horrible battering of the mage's thoughts against her mind—grief that Loren was dead, concern for Chyrie, regret that Valann was dead, worry that Sharl was still in danger—and Chyrie screamed, clasping her hands to her head to contain the thoughts that, it seemed, must burst forth.

Then Val was there, once more her anchor against the flood, and Chyrie clung to him gratefully.

(Tell her.)

The terrible spinning awareness made it difficult to speak, but Chyrie forced her eyes open, pulling on Rivkah's hands to stop her worried babbling. Weeka scrambled from Rivkah's lap to Chyrie's and huddled there.

"The—earth—" Chyrie said painfully, pulling each word from the swirling in her mind. "It—shakes."

Suddenly Jeena appeared in Chyrie's vision.

"What is it, Chyrie?" she said quietly. "What are you trying to say?"

"Shaking—" Chyrie tried again. "The earth—"

Jeena reached out to touch Chyrie's cheek, and Chyrie felt a brief wisp of thought touch her, only to be swept away by the whirling currents in her mind.

Jeena fell back as if pushed.

"She is with the Mother Forest," Jeena gasped, pressing her hands over her eyes as if to shut out what she had seen. She shook her head briskly and took her hands away from her eyes, turning back to Chyrie.

"The earth shakes," Jeena repeated. "Shaking the earth. What do you mean? Can you tell me anything more?"

Chyrie gritted her teeth and clutched hard at Rivkah's hands, drawing some solidity from their strength.

"Their god," she gasped out. "They flee—"

"What Dusk's prisoner said," Rivkah said swiftly. "They come south when the earth shakes under them, believing the fire god is near breaking free there. But what does it mean?"

Jeena was silent for a moment, then her eyes widened.

"The earth must shake!" Jeena exclaimed. "That is what she meant. If the earth shakes, they will believe the fire god will break free here, and they will flee from it. Is that what you meant, Chyrie?"

Chyrie nodded gratefully.

"Can you make a spell to shake the earth?" Jeena asked Rivkah anxiously. "My people's magic is ill suited for such a thing."

"There's a spell to move earth," Rivkah said slowly. "I suppose if it were done on a large enough scale—but it'll take some time to set up, and I'll have to find the other mages first."

(Let her go,) Valann said. (You and I will do something about the ones in the forest, and keep the army from fleeing in that direction.)

"Come on, let's get you down off this tower," Rivkah said, reaching for Chyrie.

"No." Chyrie pushed Rivkah violently away; for a moment her fear cleared the confusion in her mind, and she waved Jeena away as well. "Go!"

"I can't leave you here," Rivkah argued. "This tower could collapse at any time. I don't know how badly damaged it is."

"No." Jeena laid her hand on Rivkah's arm, never taking her eyes from Chyrie. "The Mother Forest watches over her. Leave her be. Come, I will help you find the others after I am sure my son is safe. Arguing only wastes time while elves die."

Troubled, Rivkah let Jeena pull her away. Once they were away from her, the barrage on Chyrie's mind slowed a little.

She slipped the trembling chirrit into the front of her tunic and painfully crawled through the broken stone to the battlements, pausing only for a moment to touch Loren's still body. Loren had long since fled his broken flesh, and Chyrie passed by.

From the top of the tower she could see all the way to the forest, the bobbing lights there the only sign of the battle being waged in the Heartwood. But those bobbing lights belonged to the humans, no elf ever being so foolish as to carry fire through the forest, and they penetrated far into the trees.

(Shall we show them how the Mother Forest protects Her own?) Val asked. (Can you be strong enough?)

(With you, I can be strong,) Chyrie thought. (The Mother Forest has given me much. Let me be Her weapon tonight.)

(We two are a sword none can break,) Valann agreed. (Come, then, and let us strike.)

This time Chyrie was more prepared when she and Valann passed through that inner door. Now, however, Chyrie made no attempt to avoid the swirling vortex at the heart of the Mother Forest; instead, letting Valann be her anchor, she *reached* directly into it—

—and soared up from the roots to the millions of leaves above.

Were it not for Val's comforting presence, Chyrie would have surely gone mad as she looked out through a million eyes, sank a million roots into the earth, felt the wind pass over her bark/skin/fur/feathers/leaves—her mind could never hold it all, all the many awarenesses around her, lives flaring and flickering out and beginning. Chyrie concentrated her attention on the western part of the forest, where the elves fought desperately against the invaders, but still the inexorable force pushed them back, little by little.

(They are the leaves of the Mother Forest,) Val said, his love steadying her. (But all life comes from the seed, and we are that seed. We are a part of each of these, as they are of us, as your fingers are a part of your body. Let us flex those fingers.)

Together, the power of the vortex flowing through them, Val and Chyrie *reached*.

Their fingers flexed.

Humans cried out and broke off their attack as vines reached up from the earth to twine about their feet, and branches reached down from the trees to switch at their faces. Squirrels leaped from the trees and foxes from the bushes to claw and bite. Stags lowered their heads and charged. Snakes abandoned their holes to slither up the humans' legs and bite. The elves stared unbelieving as birds plummeted from the sky and the trees to peck and claw at the invaders' eyes, as bears charged from the thickets roaring their anger.

The barbarians were strong and determined, but they had had no thought that the forest itself might rise up against them. Many fled; those who did not, fighting the vines that clung to them and the wild beasts that assaulted them, were easy targets for elvan arrows or swords, once the elves realized that the forest's attack was not turned against them. The barbarians were forced back far more quickly than they had advanced.

Chyrie divided herself yet again, *reached* back toward the city. There was far less to work with here; there were few growing things except in the grounds of the keep, and most of the city's animals were secure in pens or stables.

But that could be changed.

Wooden fences and stable doors shattered at the determined attack on them. Horses, cows, sheep, goats, and pigs trampled the invaders under their hooves, kicked or bit at them. Barbarians on stolen horses tumbled screaming to the mud as their mounts turned savagely on them. Even chickens and messenger birds fluttered from their coops to peck and tear as best they could.

Accompanying the success of the attack, however, was a backwash of incredible agony as vines and branches were slashed or trampled, attacking animals wounded or killed, elves and humans dying. It took all of Chyrie's resolve not to pull back from the terrible pain and the knowledge of what she was doing, forcing these creatures to their deaths as no beast-speaker would ever do. Their blood threatened to drown her. Only a little longer—

It came first as the faintest of rumblings, almost lost under the crash of the thunder and pounding rain. Slowly the rumbling grew, grew until soldiers froze in midmotion, until the animals shied, until the clash of battle tapered to a sudden breathless silence.

The rumble became a growl, and the growl became a roar, as the earth came alive.

The tower shook ominously under Chyrie, and she realized quickly that the structure was already of dubious solidity after the hit it had taken. Once she could have climbed down it, but not with the confusion in her head, not bruised and battered and belly-swollen as she was. Checking to make sure that the shivering Weeka was safe in her tunic, she snatched her pack and Valann's and paused for one last look at her mate's still face.

(There is no need to grieve over empty flesh,) Valann told her gently. (Hurry, love, and save the lives you carry.)

The tower trembled even more as Chyrie crawled down the ladder as quickly as she could, and she took the stairs at a pace rather faster than safety dictated. Not stopping at the halls of the keep, Chyrie continued downward, dragging the packs after her. She could see through the windows that the front grounds of the keep were choked with humans, some battling but most stunned to stillness, and she chose instead the back doors of the keep. There were a few humans on the back grounds— some city soldiers, some barbarians—but she easily crept past them, distracted as they were by the shaking ground and by each other, and made her way to the wall at the northeast edge of the keep's grounds.

The roar had grown louder, and Chyrie could now hear screams throughout the city. She wondered what was happening, but there was no way to see from where she stood. She received several confusing images of crushing pain and crumbling stone from animals in the city, but shielded herself from those images as best she could, as they distracted her almost too much to walk.

(We will have to go over the wall,) Val thought. (There will be too many humans near the gates. Can you make the climb?)

(I need not,) Chyrie replied.

Not far ahead of her she could see how the barbarians had gained access to the inside of the keep: a heavy rope, tied with knots, hung over the wall from large metal hooks anchored at the top. Several humans lay unconscious or dead at the bottom, but Chyrie had no time to spare for them, and hurried to the rope. The heavy cable was almost too thick for her hands, but she was too skilled a climber to be daunted by that. She tied her packs to her own rope, and hauled herself painfully up the knotted rope as quickly as her painful and ungainly body would allow, pulling the packs up after her with considerable difficulty.

At the top of the wall were more corpses—city soldiers, this time—and another rope, this one hanging on the far side of the wall. Chyrie paused, despite the shaking of the wall, to look out over the city, and gasped at what she saw there.

Many buildings had already collapsed, including two of the wall towers and several sections of wall in addition to the gaps the barbarians had caused. In other places in the city, the very ground seemed to have collapsed in great, gaping pits. Fires were burning in several places, and most of the few thatched buildings were aflame. From what Chyrie could see, there was very little fighting still going on, but only part of the barbarian force had actually left the city as of yet.

A horrible roaring groan was growing from the earth itself. Chyrie stared unbelievingly, for a moment stunned to utter stillness, as the center of Allanmere's market split slowly open like a huge, gaping maw. The wall quaked and jumped under her, but Chyrie was far too horrified to move, and even Valann did not prompt her.

The gigantic crack in the stone widened slowly, and Chyrie could hear the screams as the small, dark forms near it toppled in, silhouetted against an orange-red glow coming up from the pit. Citizens and invaders alike fled hastily from the marketplace, dropping their weapons in their terror.

But the greatest abomination had only begun. As Chyrie watched, a monstrously huge hand, sheathed in red-gold flames, slowly rose from the crack, flailing about as if groping blindly for something. It extended slowly upward.

The gargantuan hand was the final blow. Too terrified even to scream, the barbarians turned and ran, trampling soldiers, animals, and each other heedlessly in their haste. Most dropped their weapons in their flight; others tripped and fell upon them.

Many fled headlong into the cracks and pits that had opened in the streets. Those that made it to the walls were easy prey for the few soldiers with enough presence of mind to attack them.

For a moment Chyrie was unable to move, frozen in horror at the flaming hand reaching searchingly from the pit. In the end it was not her courage or even Valann who saved her; it was Weeka, chattering and scratching at Chyrie's taut belly, that made Chyrie once more aware of where she was and how utterly dangerous her position on the stone wall was while the ground still quaked beneath her. She hesitated only a moment, thinking of Sharl and Rivkah, but her unborn children kicked painfully, and she turned away.

A roar of anger gave Chyrie only just enough warning to throw herself painfully to one side, and a huge, double-bladed axe struck sparks from the stone where she had stood. Chyrie drew her sword even as she turned, realizing as she did so how puny a weapon it was against the great axe, realizing that her pregnancy had largely negated any advantage her speed might have given her. She turned to see the barbarian's axe upraised over her, his mouth wide with fury—then that fury changed to dull amazement, and blood dribbled from his open mouth. Then he toppled slowly, revealing the sword in his back and the figure behind him—Rom.

Rom dropped to his knees beside Chyrie, and Chyrie smelled the blood on him before she saw the wet stain covering his right side. He gazed at her a moment, then laughed hoarsely.

"So it's you," he gasped. "Where's your mate, little elf, the mate who thought your life was worth more than my Ria's?"

Chyrie struggled for words, but his pain, pain of body and soul, overwhelmed her. She turned and pointed mutely to the tower, where smoke still rose.

"So he's dead, too," Rom said, laughing bitterly again. "So you know how it feels, little elf, to lose everything that makes life worthwhile."

He coughed, and blood bubbled at his lips.

"Ria died so you could live," he gasped. "Now I think I'll join her. I'm the lucky one, little elf." He leaned back quietly against the wall, coughed again once, and was still. The pain from him ebbed away, slowly, gently, into peace, and for a moment Chyrie's mind cleared.

"Fair journey," she whispered.

Chyrie sat by his side until another tremor shook her from her stupor. She turned and searched for the hook of the rope hanging on the outside of the wall; to her relief, it was firmly anchored. Awkwardly she slid down the rope, groaning as her feet thumped jarringly to the earth on the other side.

Once out of the city, the swamp's odor was overwhelming, but its very malodorousness gave Chyrie an anchor against the confusion in her mind. There was still dying going on in the city and in the forest, and each life that flickered out wrenched through Chyrie like a spear through her vitals, but she stumbled onward, heading instinctively to the forest with no more thought or direction than a wounded beast seeks its den.

Crossing the moat was simply but horribly a matter of climbing over the charred and bloody corpses that filled it, but nothing could shock Chyrie now from the chaos in her mind. The ground between the walls and the forest was littered with corpses and soaked with blood, and the ground strewn with caltrops and riddled with pits; here Chyrie had to force some conscious thought and pick her way more carefully. It took hours for her to cross the short strip of land, creeping painfully along and dragging the heavy packs, but Chyrie heard the sounds of battle dying out, both because of distance and because the barbarians themselves were retreating farther south with every moment. The earth still shook occasionally, but slowly the tremors, too, were fading away. The rain also slowed and stopped, and Chyrie hoped that meant that Rivkah and the other mages in the city were alive and able to stop the rain.

At last Chyrie reached the forest, only to face an even more horrible sight. She had stumbled uncaring past the corpses of barbarians and citizens of the city, but now mingled with the human corpses were the bodies of elves, hewn and mutilated with savage ferocity. Here and there a few still moved feebly, elves and barbarians alike.

Chyrie saw movement from the corner of her eye and melted into the bushes, her Wilding instincts serving her where conscious thought failed. The figures she had seen, however, were

far too small to be barbarians—Blue-eyes, Chyrie realized.
They moved silently among the fallen, tending the elves or
giving grace to those without hope with a single dagger stroke.
Each thrust speared agonizingly through Chyrie, and she bit
back screams; she had not realized how much greater the pain
would be when she was close to them.

(It is not only their pain,) Valann thought, pulling her back
to her own awareness. (Your time is coming. It is a little early,
but no matter. Come, we must find a safer place.)

It took several attempts before Chyrie could gather enough
concentration to coax a deer into the carnage at the edge of the
wood. More difficult was sneaking past the Blue-eyes to meet
it, and clambering onto the shivering stag's back was the most
difficult of all. She clung there blindly, too distracted for a time
to even direct the creature, letting him go where he would as
long as it took her deeper into the Heartwood.

It seemed a miracle that no one stopped her, but Chyrie
had no thought for anything but the pains tearing through her.
There was no hope of reaching the altars, or even Inner Heart;
Chyrie had wished at least to reach the clan of one of Rowan's
allies, but she quickly realized that she would never be able to
ride long enough to pass through Blue-eyes lands. There was
nothing to do but to find shelter as quickly as she could.

Finding a hiding place, to Chyrie's surprise, was far easier
than her other endeavors; she simply focused her attention
on one of the many bears in the area and quested through
its thoughts for the location of its den. The stag, of course,
would not approach this area, but once Chyrie slid from the
deer's back, she coaxed the bear itself to guide her. The den
was in the hollow of a huge tree, and the bear settled itself
ponderously outside the entrance while Chyrie spread her furs
on the ground and made a small nest for Weeka. By the time
she had finished, she could barely snatch a breath between
the pains.

(At last we will give these little warriors the freedom to kick
as they will,) Valann thought joyously.

(Well for you to say so,) Chyrie thought sourly. (It is not
you they kick. Would that you were here to help me through
this.)

(But I am here,) Valann reminded her. (I can no longer direct the healing energies, but my knowledge and skills are with me. No, do not lie down. Drink a little water if you can and stand for as long as you are able. Walk, if there is room.)

There was no room, and the cramps in her belly would not have let her walk if she had had the whole of the forest to stroll in. Instead she crouched miserably near the entrance of the den, inhaling the welcome scent of the huge, dirty bear and the fresh, rain-wet smell of the forest, both equally sweet and familiar to her.

Rain fell again, then stopped. Chyrie grew unbearably hot and threw off her tunic and trousers, already wet with birth waters. The bear moved restlessly when Chyrie bit back moans, snuffling worriedly at the entrance to the den. Weeka chattered distractingly in the corner, ignoring Chyrie's silent order to hush and leave her be. At Valann's direction, she shuffled through his pack until she found the pouches he wanted, stirring some of their contents into a cup of wine. The bitter potion did not ease her pain, but it gave her renewed strength.

Over and over she squatted, sweat running in rivulets down her legs, straining to push the younglings from her with every bit of strength in her body and will. Then the wave would pass and she would sit back and rest for a few precious moments before the next wave came.

She had seen a few births in the Wilding village, and more in their quarters at Allanmere's keep, and as the time passed, her fear grew. What if Jeena had been wrong and her children were awry? What if she perished in childbirth and left her children alone to die without her? Who would cut them from her body if she could not bring them forth?

(If we must, you will find a bird and send it to the Blue-eyes' Gifted One,) Valann thought patiently. (Even if they have no beast-speaker, they can follow the bird. The Blue-eyes would never have harmed you, and surely will not now.)

(My heart is as pained as my body,) Chyrie thought, gasping through another wave. (How can I live without you, and yet what could be more selfish than to snatch you away from the Mother Forest and your rebirth?)

(You have not snatched me away,) Val thought warmly. (You brought part of the Mother Forest with me. Oh, love, what I see there is glorious, but the greater miracle is here, this moment, with you.)

(I should let you go,) Chyrie thought despairingly. (But how can I?)

(My own spirit,) Val thought, (I will never leave you.)

Chyrie closed her eyes and bit down hard on a leather scrap, screaming behind her teeth as she pushed, certain her body would surely split in two—

Then blessed relief as her daughter coughed on the furs.

Hesitantly, fearfully, Chyrie reached for an absorbent skin, dreading to look; finally, however, she turned to her daughter.

The infant was small and strong and perfect, from her tiny toes to the black hair that curled around the tips of her delicately pointed ears. Chyrie cleaned her lovingly, each flawless inch revealed a celebration.

(Oh, Valann, she is beautiful,) Chyrie thought joyfully.

(What color are her eyes?) Valann asked.

The baby's eyes were squeezed tightly shut as she wailed, but Chyrie tenderly pressed one open. To her amazement, the baby's eyes were neither brown-black like Valann's nor amber as her own; instead, they were a deep blue-green, as if leaves and sky had bled together and mixed.

Chyrie had little time to ponder her daughter's eyes, however, before the pains began anew. It was worse this time, for Chyrie was already tired and her son was much larger than her daughter, and twice more Chyrie mixed potions from Valann's bag before the infant slid free of her body. For a moment Chyrie simply rested on the furs, too utterly exhausted to move; then her son's choking cry roused her. She turned to her son—

—and froze, stunned at what she saw.

He was almost half again as large as his sister, and already howling and thrashing his arms and legs vigorously, as if outraged at the indignity of his birth, but those limbs had a thick sturdiness Chyrie had never seen in an infant. His hair was black and straight, like Valann's, and the set of his face mimicked Chyrie's, but his ears were perfectly round. Suddenly the baby paused, drawing in breath for a new scream, and his eyes opened slightly, showing the tawny amber of Chyrie's own eyes.

Chyrie was still a long moment. Then she gently finished cleaning her son and lifted her children to her breasts.

(They are beautiful, love,) Valann whispered softly in her thoughts. (Both of them.)

(Both of them,) Chyrie agreed.

(And it is a fit day to give new life to the forest, when so many have passed on,) Valann told her. (How our clan will rejoice.)

That thought roused Chyrie from her drowsy contentment.

(I would see how they have fared,) she thought eagerly. (I will need our friends to help me manage these two little ones. Surely there must be—ah, yes, my friend the spot-tailed hawk.)

There was no reaching now for the sharp-eyed bird; it was with her already, and Chyrie had only to sort through the many visions in her mind to look out through its eyes, to soar through the trees to the Wilding village.

A black and smoking ruin met her eyes.

The trees were gone. The hanging shelters were gone. Only the scattered stones of the Wildings' ovens and their equally scattered bodies marked that this had once been a living clan. Scavenger birds were there already, picking at the flesh of the dead. Most, horribly burned or mutilated, could not be recognized.

It could not be. Surely it could not be. Chyrie sent the spot-tail flashing through the forest, here and there, back and forth. Surely some few must have survived.

There were none alive on Wilding land. If any had survived, they had fled to another clan, and Chyrie knew deep in her heart that that they would never have done.

(I will never leave you,) Val thought again, his silent "voice" very small, very distant.

Chyrie had not screamed during her bearing, and she did not scream now. She held her children to her and wept quietly.

XI

SUNLIGHT ON WET leaves, now turning red and yellow with the decline of summer. The smell of warm damp earth. Tender new seedlings reaching up through blackened ground.

Two humans, a man and a woman heavily pregnant, rode into the Heartwood alone, unarmed, unarmored, following the elvan common road toward the heart of the Heartwood, but no Blue-eyes attacked them. They rode quietly, unhurriedly, seldom speaking to each other. They camped by the side of the trail, seeking clear spots where the vegetation had been burned. There were many such spots. No one came to their fire. The humans held each other in the night, silently.

After several days they reached Inner Heart, not long after sunset. They were met at its borders by a small hunting party of elves, who escorted them to the village. Most of the village's huts were empty now. The humans declined a hut, telling the elves they must begin their ride back that night. The man and woman were led not to the large speaking hut, which was now gone, but to a small fire at the edge of the village, where they waited patiently, not sitting.

Rowan came quietly, alone. She faced them across the fire.

"Share our food and fire, and be made welcome among us," she said.

"We are honored to share your food and fire," Sharl said quietly. "May joy and friendship be our contribution."

Rowan sat, and the humans did also.

"Those who returned from the city told me what passed there," Rowan said, opening a wineskin and pouring three cups. "I could scarce believe their tales of the ground opening and a monster reaching forth, but I felt the shaking with my own feet. Many trees fell, but the invaders on our land turned and fled."

"The shaking was real," Rivkah said. "The crack in the ground and the hand were illusion. I did it myself. We terrified our own people as much as our enemies, I'm afraid."

"And how do your people fare?" Rowan asked.

Sharl shook his head.

"When the wall was breached, we lost many people," he said. "More were killed when the ground shook. The largest part of the survivors are the mercenary troops I brought in, and they have left now. Most of the city's buildings have fallen, and large parts of the wall. Of what still stands, only a few buildings are truly safe. Several sections of the keep fell, and only a few parts are livable. There are huge holes in the ground where the rock collapsed into the springs under the city. It will take years of work before the city is rebuilt, and we have no money to hire the work done. I will have to go north again to my family and raise money to try again."

He accepted the cup Rowan passed to him and drank in silence for a long moment.

"And your people?" he asked. "I saw fires deep within the forest, although Rivkah and her mages kept the rain falling until we were sure the army was retreating."

Rowan lowered her eyes.

"Many clans were destroyed to the last child," she said softly. "The lands of other clans have been ruined beyond any hope of sustaining them for many years. When the border clans were first attacked and driven from their territories, they fled inward and drove other clans in turn from their lands. By the time the barbarians turned away, most of the border lands had been burned or trampled beyond habitation, and many of the inner lands had been badly damaged as well."

"What of the alliance?" Rivkah asked gently.

Rowan shook her head.

"There is no alliance," she said. "They fought well together—beyond anything I had hoped or dared to even dream. Our Gifted Ones achieved magic we would never have believed possible. But when all was finished, they fell to fighting for the good lands remaining, where there is still game to feed them through the winter. Now the clans raid each other as they did before." She sighed. "I could not hold them together, no matter how I tried."

"New ideas take time," Rivkah said comfortingly. "You might say this fruit didn't have time to ripen." She hesitated. "Is Dusk well?"

"Dusk is not well." Rowan's lips thinned. "A human spear, poisoned with their own feces, struck him while his mind flew with a bird. He will be long mending, body and mind, but he will mend." She was silent for a long moment. "I was told Valann has returned to the Mother Forest."

"He was killed at the same time as my teacher," Rivkah said sadly. "We buried them together. Have you heard anything of Chyrie? She disappeared right after Valann was killed, and nobody's seen her since. No one saw her leave the city, but we haven't found . . ." Her voice trailed off awkwardly.

"You have not found her body." Rowan sighed. "We have seen nothing of her. Jeena passed through Inner Heart, and she said—" Rowan stopped, shaking her head. "What she said is impossible. Chyrie is gone, I fear."

"No."

The voice that spoke was a harsh croak, rusty with disuse. Rowan, Sharl, and Rivkah stared into the darkness, and saw firelight reflect in tawny amber eyes.

The elf that came forward was almost unrecognizable as Chyrie. She was clothed in leather that looked tattered until the observer realized that the ragged pieces blended perfectly with the color-shifting leaves of late summer. The same vine designs curled over her skin where it was not covered, perhaps more thickly than before. She was still slender and wiry, her hair the same mess of golden-brown curls; but the soul that looked out through her amber eyes was wild and alien, giving her face a feral cast it had not worn before.

"Thank the gods you're safe," Rivkah said gratefully. "We searched the city for days, and as far into the forest as we dared to go. Every time we found a female elf's body I was afraid—" Her voice trailed off as Chyrie turned those unearthly eyes on her.

Rowan stood and slowly approached, reaching toward Chyrie. Chyrie danced back as an animal might shy from a hunter, and Rowan stopped.

"Then Jeena was right," Rowan whispered. "Oh, little one, have you gone so far away that you cannot come back to us?"

Chyrie gazed at her impassively for a moment; then unexpectedly she grinned, a fleeting ray of sunshine that passed across her face and was gone as suddenly as it had come. She turned back to the bush she had emerged from, then turned again, two bundles in her arms, and the chirrit, Weeka, perched on her shoulder. She placed one of the bundles in Rowan's arms and the other in Rivkah's, folding back the protective flap of leather to reveal the small, staring faces of her children.

"Oh, Chyrie, she's beautiful," Rivkah exclaimed, letting the baby clasp one sun-browned finger. "And so tiny. What lovely eyes she has."

Rowan stared at the infant on her lap, and slowly unwrapped the leather from around him, lifting the baby high. He crowed with delight, reaching for the shiny beads in Rowan's hair.

"I see," Rowan said slowly. She lowered the baby back to her lap, then shifted him in her arms so she could hold him close, rubbing her cheek on the thick black hair.

"I see," she said again. She looked up at Chyrie and smiled. "He is beautiful, Chyrie. And perfect. His eyes are much like yours, are they not?"

"But his ears," Sharl protested. "Aren't all elves—" He fell silent. "Oh," he said, at last. "I see."

Chyrie squatted beside Rivkah, lifting the chirrit from her shoulder and holding it out. Weeka chattered protestingly and ran back up Chyrie's arm to resume its place on the elf's shoulder.

"I think she should stay with you." Rivkah smiled. "Loren would have wanted you to take care of her, and she seems very happy." She held the baby out carefully. "Do you want her back now?"

Chyrie shook her head, and Rivkah was surprised to see that the amber eyes were very full. Chyrie reached out and touched her daughter's cheek gently, then backed away. She turned to Rowan, took the older elf's hand, and laid it on the baby boy, caressing the infant's face tenderly before she backed away.

"Valann," Chyrie said hoarsely.

Rowan gazed at the baby for a long moment, then nodded slowly and met Chyrie's eyes.

"Of course," she said. "He will be the son my womb never bore, to me and to my people."

"Oh, no," Rivkah protested. "Chyrie, you can't mean—I couldn't possibly—"

Chyrie touched Rivkah's lips gently, silencing her. Another quicksilver smile flitted over Chyrie's face, and she folded the baby's fist again around Rivkah's finger.

"All right," Rivkah said quietly, tears in her own eyes. "I'll love her as if she were my own daughter, Chyrie. I swear it."

"When Rivkah bears my heir, they'll be betrothed," Sharl promised. "If Rivkah and I aren't the ones to build this city in peace with the elves, your child and mine will be."

To Sharl's amazement, Chyrie chuckled, a hoarse little laugh, that said as plainly as words, "Any daughter of mine will have something of her own to say on that matter."

"Chyrie?" Rivkah said softly. "What's her name?"

Chyrie backed to the edge of the clearing, then gave Rivkah one last grin.

"Ria," she said. Then she was gone, as silently as she had come.

"Ria," Rivkah repeated, her lips trembling. She looked down and touched the tiny brown cheek as Chyrie had done. "Thank you, Chyrie. Doria would have been proud."

Rowan gazed for a long time into the darkness where Chyrie had disappeared, then turned back to Sharl.

"Did you return here because of the geas?" she asked.

Sharl grinned that engaging sideways grin.

"The geas would have made me come back," he said. "But this time I came because I wanted to."

Rowan nuzzled little Valann's dark hair.

"And you meant what you said?" she asked. "You still intend to build your city and to make peace with the forest?"

"I *will* do it," Sharl said firmly. "It will take time and money and a great deal of work, but it will be. And if I am not the one to do it"—he glanced at Rivkah, holding Ria a little awkwardly over the bulge of her own belly—"they will be."

"Then I will continue to try to bring the clans together," Rowan said softly. "If you will not surrender the dream, how can I?" She shook her head. "I release you from the geas I laid upon you."

Sharl raised both eyebrows.

"I could demand many things of you," Rowan said in answer to his unasked question. "But you give me hope, and your son and Chyrie's daughter to fulfill that hope. What more than that could I ask?" She patted the baby's back. "And when you send your children to the forest, Sharl of Allanmere, this child and others will be waiting to greet them in friendship. Go and build your dream, and we will mend, our lands and our spirits. One day it will be as we both wish."

"Thank you." Sharl stood, then helped Rivkah up from the log on which she was sitting. "I will wait for that day as eagerly as you do."

Chyrie watched the man and woman ride slowly back south, the woman cradling the baby as tenderly as if it were made of spun spider-silk. When they were out of sight, she mounted the doe waiting beside her and returned to the temporary den she had woven in the branches of a willow tree leaning over a small creek. Inside the nest, she pulled off her tunic and trousers and carefully fed the tiny fire in the small clay firepot until the shelter was warmly lit.

She reached into the pack beside her and pulled out several small clay pots, pulling out the stoppers to glance critically at the colors inside—bright shades for adding flowers, berries, butterflies. Then she shook her head, smiled, and reached for the green and brown pigments and the packet of needles, then contemplated the place on her hip where the two vines came closest together.

Working slowly but skillfully, she began to make the two vines one.

Captivating Fantasy by

ROBIN McKINLEY

Newbery Award-winning Author
"McKinley knows her geography of fantasy . . . the atmosphere of magic." —Washington Post

___ **THE OUTLAWS OF SHERWOOD** 0-441-64451-1/$3.95
"In the tradition of T.H. White's reincarnation of King Arthur, a novel that brings Robin Hood delightfully to life!" —Kirkus

___ **THE HERO AND THE CROWN** 0-441-32809-1/$4.99
"Transports the reader into the beguiling realm of pageantry and ritual where the supernatural is never far below the surface of the ordinary."
—New York Times Book Review

___ **THE BLUE SWORD** 0-441-06880-4/$4.99
The beginning of the story of the Kingdom of Damar which is continued in The Hero and the Crown, when the girl-warrior Aerin first learned the powers that would make her a legend for all time.

___ **THE DOOR IN THE HEDGE** 0-441-15315-1/$4.99
Walk through the door in the hedge and into the lands of faery—a world more beautiful, and far more dangerous, than the fairy tales of childhood.

For Visa, MasterCard and American Express orders ($15 minimum) call: 1-800-631-8571

FOR MAIL ORDERS: CHECK BOOK(S). FILL OUT COUPON. SEND TO:
BERKLEY PUBLISHING GROUP
390 Murray Hill Pkwy., Dept. B
East Rutherford, NJ 07073

NAME_____

ADDRESS_____

CITY_____

STATE_____ZIP_____

PLEASE ALLOW 6 WEEKS FOR DELIVERY.
PRICES ARE SUBJECT TO CHANGE WITHOUT NOTICE.

POSTAGE AND HANDLING:
$1.75 for one book, 75¢ for each additional. Do not exceed $5.50.

BOOK TOTAL $ _____

POSTAGE & HANDLING $ _____

APPLICABLE SALES TAX $ _____
(CA, NJ, NY, PA)

TOTAL AMOUNT DUE $ _____

PAYABLE IN US FUNDS.
(No cash orders accepted.)   258

NEW YORK TIMES BESTSELLING AUTHOR

ANNE McCAFFREY

THE ROWAN
"A reason for rejoicing!" —WASHINGTON TIMES

As a little girl, the Rowan was one of the strongest Talents ever born. When her family's home was suddenly destroyed she was completely alone without family, friends—or love. Her omnipotence could not bring her happiness...but things change when she hears strange telepathic messages from an unknown Talent named Jeff Raven.

_0-441-73576-2/$5.99

DAMIA

Damia is unquestionably the most brilliant of the Rowan's children, with power equaling—if not surpassing—her mother's. As she embarks on her quest, she's stung by a vision of an impending alien invasion—an invasion of such strength that even the Rowan can't prevent it. Now, Damia must somehow use her powers to save a planet under seige.

_0-441-13556-0/$5.99

For Visa, MasterCard and American Express orders ($15 minimum) call: 1-800-631-8571

FOR MAIL ORDERS: CHECK BOOK(S). FILL OUT COUPON. SEND TO:

BERKLEY PUBLISHING GROUP
390 Murray Hill Pkwy., Dept. B
East Rutherford, NJ 07073

NAME _____

ADDRESS _____

CITY _____

STATE _____ZIP _____

PLEASE ALLOW 6 WEEKS FOR DELIVERY.
PRICES ARE SUBJECT TO CHANGE WITHOUT NOTICE.

POSTAGE AND HANDLING:
$1.75 for one book, 75¢ for each additional. Do not exceed $5.50.

BOOK TOTAL	$ ____
POSTAGE & HANDLING	$ ____
APPLICABLE SALES TAX (CA, NJ, NY, PA)	$ ____
TOTAL AMOUNT DUE	$ ____

PAYABLE IN US FUNDS.
(No cash orders accepted.)

EXTRAORDINARY ADVENTURES
by New York Times bestselling author

PIERS ANTHONY

__Virtual Mode   0-441-86503-8/$5.99
Enter a realm where it is possible to travel between this world
and another world full of wonder. When Colene finds a
strange man lying on the side of the road, he speaks of this
magical place. Colene suspects Darius is crazy...but she's
prepared to follow him to an infinite world of dragons,
monsters and impossible dreams.

The Apprentice Adept Series—Welcome to the astonishing
parallel worlds of Phaze and Proton. Where magic and
science maintain an uneasy truce. And where Mach, a robot
from Proton, and his alternate self, magical Bane from
Phaze, hold the power to link the two worlds—or destroy them
completely.

__OUT OF PHAZE	__PHAZE DOUBT
0-441-64465-1/$4.99	0-441-66263-3/$5.50
__ROBOT ADEPT	__UNICORN POINT
0-441-73118-X/$5.50	0-441-84563-0/$5.50

Bio of an Ogre—Piers Anthony's remarkable
autobiography! A rich, compelling journey into the mind
of a brilliant storyteller. "Fascinating!"—Locus

__BIO OF AN OGRE   0-441-06225-3/$4.50

For Visa, MasterCard and American Express orders ($15 minimum) call: 1-800-631-8571

FOR MAIL ORDERS: CHECK BOOK(S). FILL
OUT COUPON. SEND TO:

BERKLEY PUBLISHING GROUP
390 Murray Hill Pkwy., Dept. B
East Rutherford, NJ 07073

NAME _____

ADDRESS _____

CITY _____

STATE _____ ZIP _____

PLEASE ALLOW 6 WEEKS FOR DELIVERY.
PRICES ARE SUBJECT TO CHANGE WITHOUT NOTICE.

POSTAGE AND HANDLING:
$1.75 for one book, 75¢ for each
additional. Do not exceed $5.50.

BOOK TOTAL	$ _____
POSTAGE & HANDLING	$ _____
APPLICABLE SALES TAX	$ _____
(CA, NJ, NY, PA)	
TOTAL AMOUNT DUE	$ _____

PAYABLE IN US FUNDS.
(No cash orders accepted.)

263